THE RELUCTANT SINNER

THE RELUCTANT SINNER

June Tate

This first world edition published 2009
in Great Britain and 2010 in the USA by
SEVERN HOUSE PUBLISHERS LTD of
9–15 High Street, Sutton, Surrey, England, SM1 1DF.
Trade paperback edition published
in Great Britain and the USA 2010 by
SEVERN HOUSE PUBLISHERS LTD

British Library Cataloguing in Publication Data

Tate, June.
  The Reluctant Sinner.
  1. Women dressmakers - England – Southampton – Fiction.
  2. Tuberculosis - Patients - Family relationships – Fiction.
  3. Medical care, Cost of – Fiction. 4. Brothels –
  England – Southampton – Fiction. 5. Southampton (England) –
  Fiction. 6. Great Britain – History – George V, 1910–1936 –
  Fiction.
  I. Title
  823.9'2–dc22

ISBN-13: 978-0-7278-6849-7   (cased)
ISBN-13: 978-1-84751-198-0   (trade paper)

All Severn House titles are printed on acid-free paper.

Severn House Publishers support The Forest Stewardship Council [FSC],
the leading international forest certification organisation. All our titles that
are printed on Greenpeace-approved FSC-certified paper carry the FSC logo.

Mixed Sources
Product group from well-managed
forests and other controlled sources
www.fsc.org Cert no. SA-COC-1565
© 1996 Forest Stewardship Council
FSC

Typeset by Palimpsest Book Production
Grangemouth, Stirlingshire, Scotland.
Printed and bound in Great Britain by
MPG Books Ltd., Bodmin, Cornwall

With love to my dear friend Maggie Dias. We met in Portugal, many moons ago and have shared the good and the bad times together. She is an amazing lady!

Acknowledgements

As always my love and admiration to my daughters, Beverley and Maxine. As a mother I am truly blessed.

One

Daisy Gilbert put away her needles and thread, rubbed her tired eyes and was thankful that her working day was over. She sat up straight and arched her back to try to alleviate the ache in her shoulders and neck, caused by bending over the material as she sewed. She was certain that all seamstresses must end up a hunch-back unless they took the greatest care. To this end, she walked upright as she left the workroom, anchoring her hat first with a hatpin.

Ever since Britain declared war on Germany the previous month, the country had seemed in turmoil, but to Daisy, at eighteen, the seriousness of the situation was beyond her comprehension. All she and her workmates were worried about was keeping their jobs. She worked for a small but prestigious gown shop in Southampton's London Road, whose clients were wealthy and, she hoped, would not be too affected by events. It was vital for her to be employed. Her father suffered with tuberculosis and was unable to work and her mother took in washing to earn extra money.

How Daisy hated going home on wet days when damp sheets hung in the scullery and the living room, near the fire in the black leaded stove, making the air damp and unpleasant for the family. She was certain it wasn't good for Fred, her father, but he told her not to fuss, they needed the money.

Sitting on the tram on the way home, Daisy felt her eyes closing. She wished she was on the tram that went round the city for two hours twice a week with a military band playing on the top deck in an effort to boost recruitment. At least that would keep her awake.

The prime minister, Herbert Asquith, had called for more recruits and all around the town were posters with the face of Lord Kitchener, pointing, with letters under saying, *wants YOU. JOIN YOUR COUNTRY'S ARMY!* She wondered if her boyfriend, Jack, would answer the call? She hoped not.

Jack Weston was nineteen and worked in the docks, learning to be a riveter. They had met at a fair on the Common one bank holiday when Daisy had walked around with her friends. She was trying, without success, to knock a coconut off a stand and voiced her disappointment. Jack had stepped up and said he would get her one, which he did with great force and dexterity. This had annoyed the stall holder, to their shared amusement. Handing his trophy to Daisy he had introduced himself, and they had been walking out ever since.

Daisy's skill at decorating the gowns with bugle beads, sequins and embroidery made her an asset to her employer – Mrs Evans, known as Madam to her staff and clients. Without her knowledge, Daisy already had a few private clients on whom she would call when they required alterations or further embellishments to older gowns. As the main wage earner in her household, the extra money from her private clients was vital towards the well-being of her family.

Her favourite was Mrs Flora Cummings, a flamboyant woman of doubtful reputation, who had come to the gown shop to purchase her garments and who had quietly asked Daisy to do extra work for her, outside of shop hours. She paid well, so Daisy was happy to oblige.

Flora ran two establishments in the dock area. One was a brothel run under the guise of a bed and breakfast, with rooms to rent for the night with a girl of your choice, from the four girls on offer with breakfast thrown in, if desired. This catered for the hoi polloi of the constantly changing seafaring population. Seamen who were far from home, looking for female company and sexual gratification. Soldiers, waiting to be shipped to France to face the enemy and wanting to hold a woman in their arms. The second establishment catered for the upper echelon of society, disguised as a club with a licence to serve alcohol. The Solent Club offered several rooms for their clients' use, and the hostesses at the club were always fully booked.

Flo, as Flora was known to her clients and friends, had her own private establishment in Bernard Street where she lived and enter-tained her lover, Jim Grant, the landlord of the White Swan in Oxford Street. And to her home address was where Daisy would go to work on Mrs Cummings' clothes.

Daisy also liked one of Madam's wealthy clients, a Mrs Grace

Portman, an army officer's wife who used to visit the shop on a regular basis. She lived in the Manor House in Brockenhurst and Daisy, scrimping and scraping for every penny, often wondered how it would be to live like Grace Portman.

Jack would listen to Daisy's tales after her visits. 'Well it's all right for them officers,' he remarked. 'They have a good life but the ordinary soldier has to rough it in comparison. Still, on the battlefield, a good officer is what a soldier prays for.'

'You're not going to join up are you, Jack?' she asked nervously.

'I have been thinking about it,' he confessed. 'Several of my pals are going to. The accommodation's supposed to be good and if you live at home during the training period, they pay you two shillings a day board and lodging over and above. That's good money.'

Daisy felt her heart sink at the thought.

'There's no need to rush into it, Jack,' she said. 'Why don't you wait a bit and see what happens, after all they say it'll be over by Christmas.' She caught hold of his hand. 'I don't want you to go away from me, not yet.' She gazed up at him, eyes filled with fear.

Putting an arm round her shoulders, he said, 'I'll wait for a while, there's no immediate rush so don't you fret none.'

She breathed a sigh of relief. She had read the account of the bloodbath at Mons, where the loss to the British troops had been so high. To think of her beloved Jack caught up in such fighting, filled her with horror.

The war was the main topic of conversation in the sewing room the following morning.

'I'm seriously thinking of changing my job,' declared Agnes, one of the seamstresses.

'Doing what?' asked Daisy, somewhat surprised as she and Agnes had joined the establishment together two years before.

'With all the men joining up, there are lots of jobs going. The munitions factory is looking for workers and they are taking on women to be conductresses on the trams. And the pay is better!'

One or two others confessed they too had been thinking on the same lines.

'What about you, Daisy, would you change jobs?' asked one of the women.

She shook her head. 'Not me, I'm sticking at what I do best.

I have plans of my own for the future and leaving here wouldn't suit at all.'

They all became very interested. 'What plans are you talking about?'

'Getting married to that handsome fellow, Jack, I expect,' called out one of the girls.

'Eventually, but I'm going to have my own business, that's my plan.'

A buzz went around the room as they all voiced their surprise. 'Bloody hell!' Agnes exclaimed. 'How on earth are you going to do that?'

'I'm trying to save enough money to rent a couple of rooms somewhere. I'll need good needlewomen so don't any of you forget how to hold a needle if you change jobs.'

'But you'd need sewing machines as well, then there would be wages . . . how on earth will you manage all that?'

'I don't know, but I will, I promise you all.' And she picked up her needle and started working. It was a dream she'd harboured for some time and truth to tell, she couldn't imagine how she would ever be able to accomplish it, but she clung to the hope. Everyone had to strive for something in life and this was her goal.

It had been a dry breezy day, and when Daisy arrived home, there was no washing hanging around indoors, but she found her mother, Vera, busy attending to Fred who was having a violent fit of coughing, holding a handkerchief to his mouth, gasping for breath as he eventually stopped the terrible hacking.

Daisy rushed to his side with a glass of water. Her blood froze as she saw the telltale red stains on the handkerchief. She gazed up at her mother who was fighting back the tears, trying not to show her distress.

'Go and make a cup of tea, Mum,' she suggested, giving Vera time to pull herself together. Putting an arm around her father she spoke softly to him with words of encouragement.

'There, Dad, you're all right now. You settle back in your chair and Mum will bring you a nice cup of tea.'

'Sorry to be such a nuisance,' Fred said weakly.

'Don't talk rubbish!' his daughter scolded, then walked into the scullery.

'You all right, Mum?' she asked.

Vera, too full to speak, just nodded. Then taking a deep breath she looked at Daisy, her face drawn. 'How much longer can he go on like this?'

'Now come along, Mum, don't think that way. We just have to take each day as it comes. Dad's all right now, so don't let him see you distressed, it won't help him.' She gave her mother a quick hug and returned to her father and told him about her day at work. At the same time she was wondering how she could earn enough money to send him to a nursing home for a break.

A few days later, she was sharing her concerns about her father's health with Flo Cummings as she sewed sequins on to a blouse.

'If I don't do something, he's going to die sooner than he should!' Tears filled her eyes.

Flo looked thoughtful. She was fond of this young girl who did such beautiful work and wondered how she could help. 'You could come and work for me in my club in the evenings,' she said.

Daisy looked confused. She knew of Flo's reputation and had heard about the Solent Club. 'Doing what?'

'You could serve behind the bar. I've got a good barman but he's knocking on a bit. What I really need is a good-looking young girl to help him. Add a bit of glamour to the place.'

'Glamour – me?'

Flo studied her from top to toe. 'You know, Daisy, with the right clothes, a new hairdo and a bit of make-up, you'd really be something.'

'Are you trying to turn me into a tart?' Daisy asked, outraged by the suggestion.

Flo burst out laughing. 'Good God, no! I've got enough of those. You would be there to serve the drinks and that's all.'

Daisy's eyes narrowed. 'You wouldn't expect me to entertain any of your clients would you?'

'Absolutely not! I'm not trying to ruin you, Daisy love; I'm just offering you a way to earn some extra money to send your dad to a place he'd be cared for. That's all. It's the only thing I can think of to meet your requirements. I'm fond of you, Daisy, and I want to help.'

'My Jack would have a fit if I told him I was going to work in the Solent Club!'

'Then don't tell him! Men don't have to know everything. Besides you're not engaged to him are you?'

'No, we're just walking out. That's all.'

'There you are then, you are a free woman to do what you like. It's up to you, Daisy.'

As she sewed, Daisy thought of Fred and how her mother was worried to death about his health, working her fingers to the bone to earn extra money. This would be a godsend to them all. What was more important, her dignity or her father's health?

'How much money will I earn, Mrs Cummings?'

'You work for me three nights a week, I'll pay you five bob a night and you get to keep your tips. If you smile at the men and spread a little cheer as you serve them, you should do very well.'

Daisy thought quickly. Fifteen shillings on top of her wages and the money from her private work which she could do on the nights she wasn't working for Flo – and tips, she could well afford to send her father away for a break.

'I'll do it!' she cried.

'Good girl. I'll tell the barman. Come along after work tomorrow for an hour before we open and he'll show you the ropes. Then you can start next week. I suggest you keep this to yourself, Daisy. I've always found it better that the fewer people who know your business, the better.'

'Thank you, Mrs Cummings. I won't forget your kindness.'

'Listen, love, you'll be good for business, so I'm doing us both a favour.'

As Daisy walked home, she was filled with trepidation. Yes, she would be able to help her father, but she was worried about working in the club and being associated with its reputation. But it was a means to an end and she was grateful. If she found it dangerous in any way, she could always leave after her father had had a break. But she would have to tell her mother, there was no way round that. Vera would want to know where the extra money was coming from.

Vera looked shocked as Daisy told her of her plans.

'The Solent Club! It's just a knocking shop.'

'I'm only going to work behind the bar, Mum.'

'Oh, Daisy, I don't think you should. You'll get a bad reputation working there.'

'What's my reputation compared with Dad's health? I know I'm not doing anything wrong. I'll be earning an honest living, bringing in enough money to send Dad to a place that will make him feel better. It won't cure him, we know that, but it will prolong his life and to me that's worth anything.'

Vera hugged her. 'You're a good girl, Daisy. The choice is yours. Whatever you decide, I'll go along with, but you mustn't tell your father. We'll say the doctor has managed to secure a bed for him.'

And so, Daisy Gilbert started her evening job as barmaid at the Solent Club the following week.

Two

Taking Flo Cummings' advice, Daisy told no one other than her mother about her evening job. As the end of her working day drew nearer on the Thursday she was due to start, her heart seemed to beat faster as an element of fear grew with every passing hour. It wasn't the serving of drinks that worried her, as Harry the barman had been most patient as he'd showed her the workings of the beer pumps and the bottles of spirit on optics. He had made a list of the prices of everything for her benefit. There had been no animosity about Daisy helping behind the bar from the man, which had been a great relief to her.

'It can be frantically busy here at weekends and I could do with the help and the company,' he told her.

'Company? How can you be lonely with a full bar?'

'Ah well, the customers only pass the time of day or order, then as far as they're concerned, you don't exist. Then it's nice to have someone to gossip to as you work. Besides, my old bones start to ache towards the end of the night; you'll be able to take a lot of the load off me.'

'What are the customers like?' she asked tentatively.

'A mixture, good and bad. You just smile and be polite, anyone steps out of line, you be firm with them. Then they'll respect you. Don't worry, Daisy, you'll be fine.'

After hurrying home to wash and change, Daisy ate a hasty meal before leaving for her first night at the Solent Club. She kissed her dad goodbye and walked towards the door.

'Where you off to then, my girl?'

Daisy looked past him at her mother, who frowned and shook her head.

'Just off to visit a client who wants some work done, Dad.' Well it wasn't entirely untrue.

'You work too hard, Daisy love, don't be too late home or you'll be fit for nothing in the morning.'

Outside she took a deep breath and stepped out towards the

Solent Club. But when she arrived, to her surprise, Flo was waiting for her and took her upstairs to one of the bedrooms.

'Right, Daisy, take off the drab coloured dress and put this one on. I need a bit of glamour in the bar as I told you.' As Daisy went to protest, Flo interrupted. 'Trust me, love, you'll look a real lady not a tart, but you must learn how to make the best of yourself. Now come on, don't be shy, get that dress off. You haven't got anything underneath that's different from me but yours will be in better shape!'

Flora was outrageous but Daisy had to laugh at her bluntness and she slipped out of the offending dress and hung it up.

Half an hour later Daisy stood in front of a long mirror and gasped at her own reflection. The dress in burgundy rayon was demure enough with its high neck, but the bodice fitted perfectly and showed off her slim waist and full bosom. The long skirt tapered out giving her freedom of movement. Her hair was brushed loose and dressed with tortoiseshell combs, then with an added touch of mascara and lipstick – Daisy Gilbert was a beauty!

Touching her hair Daisy stared at the figure before her. 'Is that really me?'

Flo beamed with delight. 'Didn't I tell you with a bit of help you would really be something?'

'Yes you did, but I didn't believe you, I can't get used to it. Cor! I wonder what my Jack would say if he could see me now?'

'He'd realize what a lucky bugger he is! Come along now, we open in fifteen minutes. Let's try out the new you on Harry.'

Harry was drying glasses when Flo and Daisy walked in. The man turned briefly, looked at the two women and said, 'Good evening, ladies,' and turned away. Suddenly he stopped and turned again. 'Blimey, Daisy! Is that you?'

'What do you think, Harry?' she asked nervously.

'I think I wish I was twenty years younger, that's what I think, girl. You'll bloody well knock 'em dead tonight. Go on, give us a twirl.'

Daisy obliged happily. She felt she had taken on a new persona which made it interesting. She would pretend to be someone else, after all she looked so different. It wouldn't be Daisy Gilbert working here it would be . . . Gloria, yes that was the name, after all didn't she look and feel glorious? She told Harry and Flo of her decision.

'After all, no one who knows me as Daisy could possibly recognize me in this get-up; I even feel different.'

'I think it's a splendid idea,' said Flo. 'Gloria it is.'

The door to the club was unlocked and opened for business. Daisy kept busy washing and wiping glasses, trying to stop her hands from shaking, waiting for the first customers to arrive and when the door opened and three men walked in, Harry came over to her.

'Right, girl, off you go, give them a smile and serve them.' Seeing her look of trepidation he said, 'Come on, Gloria, you can do it!'

Yes, she thought, Gloria can and she walked to the end of the bar, smiled at the men and said, 'Good evening, gentlemen, what can I get for you?'

They all looked at her with surprise and pleasure.

'Well, things are looking up,' said one. 'I won't have to look at Harry all night. Three scotch and sodas please, young lady. What's your name?'

'Gloria,' she said and went to the optics and put a measure of scotch in each of three glasses.

Harry sidled up to her. 'Take the soda siphon to them and let them help themselves,' he advised knowing that she would be unaware of the force the soda could be if the handle was pressed down too hard. He didn't want her to be embarrassed serving her first customers.

Daisy watched the men serve themselves and realized why she had been thus instructed. Looking over at Harry, she mouthed the word, *thanks*. He just winked at her, knowing in future she would be prepared.

The club started to fill up. It was then Daisy saw the girls starting to circulate among the men sitting at the tables and watched as they persuaded them to buy more drinks – how they got friendly with some, sitting close to them, fondling their faces, flirting with them until one by one, they walked up the stairs together and how a short time later, they came down and moved on to another punter. She thought of her mother's words. There was no doubt about it, this *was* a knocking shop! However the men, although they flirted outrageously with her when ordering their drinks, treated her with respect and tipped her as she served them. She smiled and thanked them and moved on to the next customer. She gazed at the glass jar at the back of the counter that Harry had given her, and watched it slowly begin to fill.

An hour before closing time, the door opened and a big man

entered alone. Harry quickly moved her away, saying, 'I'll look after him myself.' She noticed that not one of the girls approached him during the time he sat drinking. She was curious and watched him as she served and once or twice caught him looking back at her. She quickly turned away. There was something menacing about him that when she saw him glancing in her direction, she became nervous. Yet he hadn't spoken to her.

'Who is that man?' she asked Harry when they stood next to each other pouring drinks from the optics.

'You make sure you keep out of his way, love. He's a bad 'un.'

When the bar eventually closed, Daisy questioned him again about the stranger. 'Who is he?'

'That's Bert Croucher. He's the local butcher and has a very nasty temper.'

'None of the girls went up to him, I noticed,' she remarked, curiosity getting the better of her.

'They're too bloody scared of him. He roughed up one of the local brasses in Canal Walk one night and he was lucky to get away without a prison sentence. It's said he paid her not to report him.'

'Yet Flo lets him use the club. That surprises me.'

'Ah well, Flo doesn't scare easily and he spends money. She told him straight, "You can drink in my club and that's all. No women. Any trouble I'll call the police." Besides, she spends a lot of money in his shop and he wouldn't want to lose her custom. He doesn't come in every night, mainly at weekends.'

Before going home, Daisy changed back into her own clothes and removed her make-up, twisted her hair back into a bun and walked back to the bar to say goodnight to Harry.

'Here, don't forget your tips, girl. You earned them. The customers like you, you should do well.'

'Thanks, Harry, I enjoyed myself. It was certainly different. See you tomorrow night.'

As she walked home, she smiled to herself. She wouldn't tell her mother too much, she would only worry. She certainly wouldn't mention Bert Croucher. He scared her and she didn't need her mother to know that.

Vera was sitting, waiting, by the dying embers of the range when Daisy let herself in. Her mother took some warm milk from the top of the range and made her daughter some cocoa.

'How did it go?' she asked with a worried frown.

Kicking off her shoes and rubbing her sore feet, Daisy said, 'It was fine. The club was quite busy but what with Harry having shown me everything and written out the prices, I was fine. I suppose in time I'll know them by heart.'

'You're going to stay then?'

Daisy grinned broadly and took a bag of money out of her pocket and poured the contents on to the table. 'These are my tips for tonight, Mum, and I've two more nights to go. Of course I'm staying.' She counted out the coins on the table. 'Blimey! There's three pounds here. We'll soon be able to book a couple of weeks at the convalescent home for Dad.'

Tears welled in Vera's eyes. 'Oh, Daisy love, that would be wonderful!' Then she hesitated. 'You are quite safe working there aren't you?'

'Safe as houses,' she replied. But she didn't mention the butcher.

The following morning in the workshop, as she picked up a garment to be embroidered, Daisy felt weary. It was just as well that she was only going to work three nights a week she thought. With such intricate work, she needed her sleep to be able to see what she was doing. But if it meant her father would get a break and care, it would all be worth it.

'You're quiet this morning,' remarked her friend Agnes.

'I didn't sleep well last night,' was the excuse that she gave.

She said the same thing to Jack who was waiting outside when she finished for the day, when he told her she looked tired.

'I was going to suggest we go to the cinema,' he said.

'Not tonight, love,' she told him. 'I'm going home to get my head down; I've got a bit of a headache. I've had to do a lot of close work today.' Daisy hoped it sounded convincing as she had to hurry home, get something to eat and set off for the club. She'd been told to wear comfortable shoes as Friday and Saturday nights were usually busy. 'But you go,' she suggested.

'How about tomorrow then?' he persisted.

'Sorry, Jack, I've got a dress to finish for one of my clients, but we can go for a walk if you like on Sunday?'

'But we always go out on a Saturday!'

Oh dear, thought Daisy. She would be working every Saturday

in future. How was she going to get round this without telling him what she was doing? 'I am sorry, but I have a lot of private work on at the moment, all rushed jobs, but I'll be free on Sundays.'

He didn't look very pleased. 'Some bloody courtship this is turning out,' he complained.

'I'm really sorry, Jack, but I'm trying to make enough money to send Dad off to a nursing home for a short stay. He's been so poorly lately and it will do him good and give Mum a much-needed break.'

This he accepted, and with a smile he said, 'You're a good girl to your family. If only I was out of my apprenticeship I could help you.'

She tucked her arm through his. 'Oh that's really kind of you, but one day you will be and then we can start and plan our future.'

He kissed her goodnight outside her door. 'I'll call for you after lunch on Sunday then.'

As she let herself into the house, Daisy wondered just how long she could get away with this subterfuge. But nothing was going to stop her getting the money together that she needed and without this job it would be an impossibility.

Three

Flo wasn't at the club when Daisy arrived, but she'd asked one of the girls to help her change, do her hair and to show her how to apply the mascara.

Daisy was a little shy when Stella approached her and told her of Flo's instructions.

'Come on, love,' said Stella, 'you'll soon be able to do this for yourself. You're a really pretty girl,' and she giggled. 'If you had a mind to come my side of the bar you could make a packet!'

Daisy blushed at the thought. 'I couldn't!'

Stella grinned at her. 'I was only joking, love. It ain't so bad you know. It's usually all over in a few minutes. The punters are too horny to wait. Most of them don't really get their money's worth; they barely have time to take their trousers down before it's all over.'

Daisy's curiosity got the better of her. 'Do you enjoy it?'

'Sometimes. If you get a feller who's a good lover and can take his time. Yeah, sometimes I've been known to actually come, instead of pretending.' Seeing the look of puzzlement on Daisy's face Stella said, 'Oh bless my soul, you're a virgin. How lovely, I don't get to meet many of those. You don't know what I'm talking about do you?'

Daisy, more than a little embarrassed, shook her head.

'Well darlin' when you get married, if you're lucky enough to find a man who knows his way around a woman's body, you'll know what I mean and believe me when it happens – it's bloody marvellous!' She finished dressing Daisy's hair. 'There you are, now I'll show you how to use your mascara.'

Daisy walked downstairs to the bar to start her second night as Gloria, the new barmaid, wondering what the evening would bring and how much she would make in tips.

One of the ships had docked that afternoon, carrying injured soldiers back from the front. Many had been involved in the battles in Flanders – in particular at Ypres. It had been a harrowing ordeal for the crew and several of the officers had come to the club to drink away the misery they had encountered.

At first they discussed among themselves the appalling injuries they'd had to deal with. A few had been involved in the ship's hospital where the ship's surgeon had operated on some, whilst others were tended by nurses who travelled with the men, but helped by some of the ship's crew members with the lifting and moving of the many patients.

'Poor sods,' said one man. 'Some will never work again, if they survive at all, and I don't suppose the government will take care of them.'

'All right,' said another, 'let's drink to them. I need to get the smell of blood and the taste of ether out of my mouth and I need to feel the soft skin of an enthusiastic woman!' And the party began.

The girls were kept busy and as Stella walked towards the stairs with one of the men she looked over at Daisy and winked. Daisy wondered if the man would be a satisfactory lover or not and when Stella returned, she looked over at the girl with more than a little curiosity as they had been gone for some time. Stella glanced over and with a broad grin, unobtrusively gave Daisy the thumbs-up sign and patted her chest above her heart. It seemed as if the girl had been lucky and Daisy couldn't help but wonder just what it would be like to be bedded by a man.

One of the young officers came over to order some drinks. 'What's your name?' he asked.

'Gloria,' said Daisy, without hesitation.

'Well, Gloria, how would you like to come out to lunch with me tomorrow?'

She looked at him in surprise. She had noticed that he was one of the few who had not taken a girl upstairs and wondered why. He was tall and good looking and to her mind a good catch, but when the girls had approached him, he'd laughed and chatted with them, but that had been all.

'I'm sorry but I'm not free,' she said.

'And why's that?'

'I work during the day. I'm only here three nights a week and anyway, I'm spoken for, I have a young man.'

He paid for the drinks and said, 'Well I think he's a lucky devil! If ever you change your mind, you just tell me.'

As he walked away, Harry sidled up to her. 'They'll be queuing up for a date with you, before long.'

'Don't be so daft!' she exclaimed.

'What's daft about that? You're a good-looking girl. Not every man who comes in here is looking for a good lay.'

She flushed at his blatant description. 'Really!' she said.

Harry burst out laughing. 'You are such an innocent to be working in a place like this and believe me that has a certain charm about it,' and he walked away to serve a customer.

Towards the end of the evening, Flo walked into the club and was soon enjoying the company of the ship's officers. Daisy watched with interest as Flo fussed about her customers and entertained them. She was obviously a practised hostess and the drinks flowed even more. When closing time came, Daisy was very surprised to see Flo leave the premises with one of the officers.

Stella came over to say goodnight. 'You are causing more than a little interest with the men,' she told Daisy.

'Whatever do you mean?'

'One or two of the punters even asked me if you were free to spend time with them!'

Daisy's eyes widened. 'To go upstairs with them do you mean?'

Laughing, Stella said, 'That's exactly what I mean. A man would pay good money to take your cherry, darlin'. You should think about it, you could make a bloody bundle this side of the bar. Well, I'm off. Ta ra.'

As she walked home, Daisy couldn't help but ponder over Stella's remarks. She wondered just how much money the girls made. Not that she would even consider joining them, as she was earning enough for her needs.

Flo Cummings stretched languidly, turned back the covers of her bed and slipped her legs over the side. Looking at the clock she saw that it was noon. She got to her feet and rubbing her eyes walked over to the window and opened the curtains, blinking at the sudden light. What a bloody night that had been! As she sat brushing her hair she relived her night of passion with the first officer. What a man he was! He navigated her body as if he were docking his vessel into a very tight space. He manoeuvred her like an expert until she begged him to take her. He chuckled as he smothered her with kisses, then drove himself into her depths. As she thought about it now, she ached and lusted after him. But the bed was empty.

Flo didn't take many men to her bed these days; after all she had a lover. She'd been having an affair with Jim Grant, the manager of the White Swan, for a few years now. She didn't feel disloyal to her lover if she slept with another man; after all, Jim still shared a bed with his wife. Gone were the teenage years when Flo had sold her body rather than starve. Now she had money and she was particular, but last night there was something in the eyes of the young officer that drew her to him. It certainly had been worth it and she hoped he would come into the club again. Sooner rather than later, but now she must dress and get on with her day.

She walked to Three Field Lane to the bed and breakfast, to collect the takings from the previous night. The girls were up and about, cleaning the place after the influx of seamen. It had been a full house and therefore profitable.

Flo walked around the bedrooms to check for cleanliness which was essential she felt for a good business. Walking into one bedroom she saw one of the girls standing beside a workman who was repairing a bed. Flo called the girl outside.

'What the bloody hell is going on?' she enquired.

'Sorry, Flo, but I had a bleedin' big fireman in last night and he got a bit excited.'

'Did he jump on the bed?'

'No, he jumped on me . . . but I was on the bed.' She lifted her dress to show Flo her bruises. 'After, he was right sorry and gave me a big tip.' She giggled. 'That wasn't the only big thing about him. It gave me the fright of my life!'

'For goodness' sake, can't you control your men?' Flo remonstrated and she stalked off down the stairs.

At the Solent Club, Harry was cleaning and restocking the bar. 'Good night last night, Flo. My goodness, those men can drink! Mind you, the toilets were a bit of a mess this morning, I can tell you.'

With a grimace, she said, 'Just make sure they're cleaned thoroughly. I want them spotless for tonight. I've got a private birthday party booked in the back room and the caterers will be here later. Set a table against the wall. They'll be here around five thirty so open up and let them in.' And with a final glance, she left the building.

★   ★   ★

It was Saturday morning and Daisy was working away, embroidering a bodice of an evening dress, pleased that it was a half day only in the workroom as she was so tired. With a bit of luck she'd be able to get her head down for a couple of hours this afternoon in readiness for a busy night at the club. Tomorrow she'd promised to spend the afternoon with Jack, who was getting very niggled at not being able to see her as often as he would like, and she kept telling him when he met her from work that she was busy doing extra work for her father. This was true of course, but Jack believed she meant she was sewing and Daisy, not wanting to let him know the truth, didn't say anything.

With the little money she had saved and her tips, she'd managed to book a bed for her father in a private nursing home from the middle of next week and as far as she was concerned, that justified everything . . .

Vera was busy washing and ironing Fred's pyjamas, ready for his stay in the home. She had told him that the doctor had arranged it all.

'But he didn't come and see me,' he said, more than a little puzzled.

'He didn't need to, love. He knows how you are and he said that this would do you the world of good so don't you start and be difficult.'

'How long am I going to be there?'

'To be honest I don't know, Fred, we'll have to wait and see.'

'I'll miss being here with you and Daisy,' he said and Vera heard the uncertainty in his voice.

'I'll come and see you every day but they'll be able to give you the medicines and care you need. You won't have to sit with damp washing hanging around you.'

'I didn't mind. At least I was with you.'

'Well soon you'll be surrounded by lots of young nurses, fighting to look after you,' she teased.

He gave a wan smile. 'Lot of bloody good that'll be, me in this state. I can hardly chase them round the bed, can I?'

'No, Fred love, you'll be laying back in clean sheets with them fussing over you. Many a man would pay good money for that.'

He didn't answer and Vera could see he was tired. She tucked a blanket round him and made him comfortable on the settee.

Walking to the scullery she said, 'You have a nap and I'll make you some good beef broth.' But when she was alone, she leaned on the sink and cried as she remembered the virile young man who had won her heart so many years before. She quickly dried her tears as she heard the key in the door as Daisy returned home.

Seeing her father was asleep, Daisy walked into the kitchen. She saw her mother's red eyes but didn't comment. She emptied the basket she was carrying.

'Here're some vegetables and a piece of scrag end of lamb. I thought we could have a stew later, Dad would enjoy that. Has he eaten much today?'

'He had some porridge this morning and I beat up an egg in hot milk this afternoon. I'm going to make a broth for him; he can have some of that when he wakes.'

Daisy put her arms around her mother and hugged her. 'He'll be better when we get him into proper care. I'm sure he has doubts about going, but it will be good for him and give you a break.'

'Oh, Daisy,' her mother sobbed into her chest. 'I'm going to miss him so much.'

'Of course you are, so will I, but you'll see him every day. You don't need to take any washing in any more, after this week, so you won't be so tired.'

'Are you sure about that?' Vera asked.

'Yes, Mum. I'm earning good money now, so you just enjoy the perks. Good heavens, you've earned a break!' She released her mother. 'I need to try and get a bit of sleep before I go out tonight.'

'I'll call you in good time to eat before you leave. You need to keep your strength up too,' Vera told her, and she began to prepare the vegetables, pleased to be able to occupy her hands and mind with other things.

Four

When Daisy arrived at the club, Harry warned her they would be extra busy this Saturday evening as there was a private party as well as their usual customers.

'Although the party is in a private room, some of the men will wander out to pay for a girl,' he told her. 'I've brought in a couple of extra cases of beer and there,' he pointed to the shelf with the optics, 'you'll find extra bottles of spirits too.'

The bar started to fill quickly. Some of the men filtered off to the party, while the uninvited stayed in the bar. Flo had hired a couple of waiters to serve the partygoers and Daisy and Harry were run off their feet, keeping up with the orders from both places.

Midway through the evening, Daisy saw Bert Croucher enter the bar and walk through to the private room. Wandering over to Harry she asked whose party it was.

'One of the wholesalers in the town. Why?'

'I just saw the butcher go in there.'

'He's a friend of the birthday boy,' Harry told her. 'If you ask me, Ken Woods is as hard a case as Bert Croucher. They went to school together so I'm told. A right couple of tearaways they were too, by all accounts!'

For the next two hours, Daisy was so busy she didn't give the men another thought until she bent down to pick up a bottle top off the floor and when she stood up, Croucher and another man were standing at the bar, in front of her. She quickly looked for Harry, but he was busy serving.

'Good evening, gentlemen, what can I get for you?'

The stranger leered at her. 'Hello, darlin', I'd like two double scotches and ginger ale and one for yourself.'

'Thank you, sir, but I don't drink when I'm working.' She didn't want anything from this man, whom she disliked on sight.

'Well that's a first,' he said, grinning at the butcher. 'But it's my birthday, girlie, and I insist that you join me in a drink.' Although he was smiling at her, his eyes were steely cold and Daisy knew it wouldn't be wise to cross him.

'Very well, sir, if you insist. I'll have a tonic water.'

'Put a gin in it,' he ordered defiantly.

Daisy straightened her back and stared at him and said, firmly, 'You asked me to join you in a drink and I have, but now you must let me decide what it is that I want.' And she turned away before he could argue. She poured two large scotches into glasses and opened two bottles of ginger ale, then poured a tonic water into a glass. She put these on a tray and turned back to the counter. She handed the glasses and bottles to the men, lifted her glass to her mouth and drank.

'Happy birthday, sir,' she said, trembling inside.

Harry walked over at that moment and said, 'Gloria, will you serve the gentleman at the end of the bar?' As she walked away he looked at Ken and Bert and asked, 'Everything all right, gentlemen?'

'Sparky little girl, that Gloria,' said Woods.

'A nice girl too,' said Harry firmly. 'I wouldn't like to see her bothered.'

Woods laughed loudly. 'You her guardian angel, Harry?'

'Something like that,' he said and turned away.

The two men walked to a table and sat down and before long were in deep conversation, returning to the party after a while, to Daisy's great relief.

Towards the end of the night, several men came into the bar from the private gathering and took the woman of their choice upstairs in a steady stream. Having had a lot to drink, they were very loud and Daisy began to feel nervous, wondering if there was going to be any trouble. She was pleased when Flo entered the bar an hour before it closed accompanied by a tall man.

'That's Jim Grant, the landlord of the White Swan,' Harry told Daisy. 'He's Flo's boyfriend.' Having seen Flo leave with one of the ship's officers the previous night, Daisy was somewhat surprised.

Flo worked her way around the bar talking to everyone and managed to keep the noise down and those in their cups in order. Watching her go from one to another, Daisy realized what a clever woman her employer was. She also noticed Ken Woods head for the stairs with one of the girls. As he went to walk past Flo, she stopped the man and had a quick word with him. Daisy saw a flash of anger on his face and then he smiled at her, leaving Daisy wondering what Flo had said to him. And when half an hour later the girl came back downstairs, she saw Flo look at the girl with a watchful glance. The girl just nodded unobtrusively and Flo walked away and joined her escort.

It was late when the bar closed and both Harry and Daisy were exhausted. Flo came over and introduced Daisy to Jim Grant.

'You both worked well tonight,' said Flo with a smile. 'Let's have a quiet drink together.' As Daisy went to refuse, Flo said, 'Listen, love, it will do you good. Sit down and take the weight off your feet before you go home.'

As they all sat together, Harry asked, 'Did Woods behave himself?'

Flo laughed. 'Bloody right. I told him as he went upstairs, I didn't want any complaints from my girl after he'd done with her . . . or else! He didn't like it but I have to protect my girls from the likes of him.' Turning to Daisy she said, 'He likes to be a bit rough with his women, and that's fine with the girls on the street – but not mine.'

Daisy felt her blood run cold and she hoped that Woods wouldn't be a regular customer. Bert Croucher frightened her enough without his mate. The two together would be too much. She'd have a nervous breakdown.

As they finished their drink, Flo said, 'Jim will walk you home, Daisy. It's late and on a Saturday night around here I'll feel better knowing he was with you.'

'Come on, love,' said Jim, 'it won't take long.' Turning to Flo he said, 'I'll see you later. Don't start without me!'

She roared with laughter. 'You cheeky bugger.'

As Jim walked her from Oxford Street to French Street, Daisy had a strange feeling that they were being followed. She turned round once or twice but in the dimness of the street lights she didn't see anyone.

'You're a bit jumpy, girl,' Jim remarked. 'You are perfectly safe with me I can assure you.'

But she was more than pleased to get to her front door and to safety, and as she counted the large amount of the tips she'd made that night, she felt better.

After a long sleep-in and a good lunch, Daisy was looking forward to seeing Jack. She decided she'd like to walk through the park

and get some fresh air. Then perhaps stop for a cup of tea somewhere. This would give her and Jack time to catch up with each
other's news.

When he called for her and she suggested this, he agreed with
her plan.

It was a chilly afternoon and now, in October, the trees were
shedding their leaves as they walked through the park. Both of
them kicked away at the piles of them on the ground, like a couple
of children.

'This reminds me of splashing through puddles as a youngster,
filling your wellies through being over enthusiastic,' Jack remarked.
He caught hold of her hand and asked, 'What have you been up
to? I feel I haven't seen you in ages.'

'I've been busy doing extra work and I've got enough money
now to send Dad away for a bit.'

'Blimey! You must have been working your fingers to the bone
to do that.'

Daisy knew she had to be careful not to give the game away
as she spoke. 'Fortunately there has been plenty of extra work to
keep me going and I'm sorry, Jack, but I'll be tied up on Saturday
nights for quite a while.'

He did not look pleased at this. 'I look forward to our Saturday
nights,' he complained. 'Can't you do this work some other time?'

She shook her head. 'I can't, no. I have to take all the work I
can get, especially now I've got a bed for Dad. I want to let him
have as much care as he can, so I must make as much money as
possible as and when the work is there. And at the moment, I've
plenty to keep me going.'

Jack felt a bit guilty over his displeasure at this news, especially
as he knew just how poorly Fred Gilbert was and he did admire
Daisy's tenacity, but he felt neglected in the process.

'So when *can* I see you?'

'Only on Sundays for the next while, I'm afraid. But my time is
all yours then. It's just for a little while, Jack. It won't be for ever.'

He saw the concern in her eyes and capitulated with a smile.
'All right, Sundays it is. Come on, let's go and find a cafe and have
a hot cuppa. I'm getting cold out here.'

As they walked out of the park and down Above Bar, Daisy saw
the young officer from the club who had invited her out to lunch,
approaching. Before she could look away, he saw her.

'Good afternoon, Gloria,' he said as they passed each other.

Daisy gave a quick smile, lowered her gaze, and quickened her stride.

'Gloria!' Jack exclaimed. 'That man called you Gloria.'

'Well obviously he took me for someone else,' Daisy swiftly replied. 'Look, there's a cafe open, come on.' And she dragged Jack by the arm towards the place, thankful to find a refuge.

Jack ordered tea and toast for them and then sat back in his chair, staring thoughtfully at Daisy.

'What?' she asked.

'You don't look like a Gloria at all,' he mused. 'No, the name doesn't suit you one bit!'

If you only knew, she thought.

They decided to go to the cinema and Daisy insisted on paying for them to go to the upper circle. 'It's my treat,' she insisted, trying to make up to Jack for her absence. They settled in the back row, and as the film started, he put his arm around her.

'Now this is more like it!' he said.

The film, *The Kidnapped Bride*, was a comedy with young Oliver Hardy and soon had them chuckling loudly. The pianist playing in the pit was excellent; he matched the music to the movement in the silent film with flare which added greatly to their enjoyment, and as the credits rolled at the end of the programme, Jack kissed Daisy tenderly before the house lights came on.

As they walked home, Daisy felt guilty lying about working at the Solent Club, but she knew he would be furious if he knew the truth. But she did wonder how long she would be able to keep up this subterfuge.

Jack held her close to him as they arrived at her home. 'I'll see you next Sunday then,' he said and kissed her goodnight.

Vera, her mother, was tidying up when she walked in to the room.

'Dad in bed?' asked Daisy.

'Yes he went up early, but he's asleep now.' With a frown Vera said, 'He's worried about going away, but I've explained he'll get good treatment there and he does realize this, of course.'

Daisy knelt by her mother. 'We'll miss him too, but you'll be able to go every day and I'll pop in some evenings when I'm not working.'

'I worry about you working at that place,' said Vera. 'God knows what sort of men go there.'

'You'd be surprised, Mum. They are mostly decent chaps. We had several ships' officers there the other night. They are away from home and are lonely.'

'Are they married?'

Daisy laughed. 'I've no idea and I'm certainly not going to ask them!'

'I hope they don't think you're on the game too,' Vera stated, outraged at her own thoughts.

'Believe me they know I'm there to serve drinks only. I've not had any worries in that respect – and besides, Harry the barman looks after me like a father.'

Vera rose from her chair. 'Well come on, love, let's get to bed or we'll be too tired for anything in the morning.'

As she undressed in her own room, Daisy couldn't help but think about Bert Croucher and his mate. Now they were not nice men and she hoped they wouldn't be a problem if they used the club frequently. They made her nervous as soon as they walked in the bar. She climbed into bed knowing that she would be busy in the workroom in the morning but at least she had her evenings free until Thursday. Any private work she had could be done in the safety of her own home. But at least her father would be cared for. That was the most important thing right now.

Five

The workroom was very busy as Madam had received a large order. One of her clients was sailing to India to join her husband who was in the army and recently stationed there. The wife needed a complete new wardrobe, made up with cotton and linen materials, to meet the tropical weather – and everyone was working flat out.

A new girl, Jessie Brown, had been hired to join the workforce to help cope with the work in hand. She was a good needlewoman but was loud and chatty.

'If you could sew with your mouth, Jessie,' snapped Madam, 'our workload would increase a hundred per cent!'

The others sniggered. None of them liked the new girl and enjoyed seeing her put in her place.

'Go on, 'ave a good laugh, why don't you,' she cried after Madam had left the room. 'As if I give a shit what you lot think.'

'Don't you let Madam hear you swear,' warned one of the girls, 'she's very particular about such things. She says we are serving ladies of quality and must behave accordingly.'

'Ha! Ladies of quality? I saw Flo Cummings come out of here with a package and she certainly is no lady of quality!'

'That's not for you to say, Jessie!' Madam stood in the doorway, glowering.

'You know how she makes her money, don't you, Madam?'

Madam straightened her back and stared imperiously at the girl. 'I don't consider that any of my business – or yours. Every client who uses this emporium will be treated with respect and will not be discussed behind their backs. Now get on with your work!' She turned and left the room.

'Well like it or not, that Flo Cummings makes her money from prostitution. I bet Mrs Posh Frocks doesn't know that,' Jessie declared. 'And what the bloody 'ell is an emporium?' No one knew.

Daisy sat listening nervously to Jessie gossip, but stayed out of the conversation. This girl knew far too much. Imagine if she found out about her working as a barmaid at Flo's club, it would be all round the workshop and she might lose her job! Then where would she be?

Her spirits were lifted when she was called into the waiting room to measure Grace Portman for a new dress. Daisy liked Mrs Portman, she was a real lady, but this morning she was looking sad.

'Is something the matter?' asked Daisy as she wrote down the measurements.

'I had a letter from my husband this morning,' she said.

'Is he all right?'

'Yes, thank God! But he's not happy at all. Apparently the weather conditions at the Somme are bad. The trenches are filled with water and they are fighting to hold their positions. But apart from that, he's fine.'

'I'm sure the captain is well able to take care of himself.'

'He is a good soldier, but he's headstrong. I just hope he doesn't do anything stupid, that's all. And how are you, Daisy?'

Daisy found Mrs Portman easy to talk to and told her all about her father.

'I am sorry,' said Grace, 'but once he's settled in the home, he'll feel better and then he'll be a happier man.'

'I do hope so,' said Daisy.

Grace looked at Daisy and thought how brave she was under these circumstances. She assumed that the girl was the main wage earner in the family and the responsibility on her shoulders must be huge. How fortunate she was to live the life of privilege that she did, but that brought its own responsibilities, especially with her husband in France. It fell upon her shoulders to see to the estate and keep things running smoothly. Everyone had their problems it seemed.

When Daisy arrived home after her working day, she sat by the fire with her father, knowing he would be moving out in the morning. Her heart was heavy as she looked at the emaciated figure before her and she remembered the fit man who used to lift her over his shoulders when she was a child. To see him now was hard to take. She tried to assure him that the move would be beneficial.

'You'll be well taken care of, Dad. If you need medication the nurses will see you get it. The place is so very well equipped to cope with patients with your illness.' She took his hand. 'It will also stop Mum worrying about you.'

'Your mother is a good woman, Daisy love. I know she worries and for that reason, I'm willing to go. I know I'm living on borrowed time and this will make it easier on her. I'm so grateful to the doctor for fixing me up with a bed.'

Daisy was relieved that her father had accepted the lie they had told him. Had he known how and where Daisy was working, to pay for his stay, he would have been distraught!

The family sat down together to eat their supper, knowing it would be some time before they did so again. Daisy planned to pay for his care as long as she was able.

'I've made your favourite, Fred,' said Vera. 'Steak and kidney pudding with a nice creamy rice pudding to follow.' She smiled warmly as she gazed at him. 'You eat that, my lad, it'll grow hairs on your chest!'

'As long as it doesn't put lead in my pencil,' he laughed, 'only I don't think I'm up to that.'

'Fred Gilbert, what a thing to say, you cheeky devil.' But as she watched him pick at his food and leave more than he ate, she hoped that once in the nursing home, his appetite would increase. At least that would give him some strength to fight back.

Daisy was pleased that her father could find something to laugh about because she knew that deep down he wanted to stay with his family. She admired his bravery. It took a strong man to accept that his days were numbered and she wondered how they would cope when he was no longer with them. The doctor had been frank with her and her mother as Fred's illness grew worse and they had been grateful for his honesty.

'Not that this knowledge will soften the blow when the time comes,' he had said, 'but at least there will be no surprises.'

The following morning, Daisy kissed her father goodbye. She'd arranged for an ambulance to collect him and her mother would go with him and see him settled.

'I'll come and see you this evening,' she said, trying to smile.

'No, love, leave it until tomorrow. By then I'll be able to tell you what it's like. Your Mum will be with me today. I'll see you tomorrow. Take care of your mother,' he added. 'She'll be a bit lost without me.'

Daisy walked down the road with tear-filled eyes. She loved her father deeply and it broke her heart to see his weakened state. She could do no more for him, but she would work hard to give him the care he needed and deserved for as long as she was able.

The next few days flew by it seemed to Daisy. Her father had settled well and she was working at home in the evenings on garments for her private clients and tonight she was back working at the Solent Club again.

Flo had laid out a black silk blouse for her to wear with a long black skirt. Stella was once again there to help her get ready for the evening rush.

The transformation complete, Daisy walked down the stairs as Gloria, her new persona. 'Hello, Harry.' She smiled as she greeted the barman.

'Hello, love. My, you look good enough to eat,' he chuckled as he looked at her. 'The girls will start to be jealous of you, you look better than they do.'

'Behave yourself!' she chided. 'I'm not dressed like them at all,' which was true. The ladies of the club wore clothes that were tight-fitting and low-cut to show off their décolletage, tantalizing the clients.

'That's what makes you so attractive. A man likes to guess what's beneath the clothes. It's more of a mystery.'

'Harry! You are outrageous.'

'No, love, I'm a man and I understand how a man thinks.'

As the evening wore on, Daisy began to believe he spoke the truth as the men she served looked at her with admiration and some . . . with unadulterated lust. In fact one or two had propositioned her.

'Gloria,' pleaded one, 'I can't take my eyes off you. I'll pay double if you let me take you upstairs.'

'Now, sir,' she said politely, 'you know I'm here to serve drinks and that's all. Now you behave or I'll be cross with you.'

'I love a woman with spirit,' he said. 'They are so much fun in bed.'

'I really wouldn't know,' she said tartly.

'Oh my God, are you a virgin? How marvellous! Name your price.'

Her curiosity was roused. 'How much would you be prepared to pay?' she asked.

'Twenty pounds!'

Daisy was amazed. That was a fortune. With a smile she said, 'Your money is safe. I'm not for sale at any price,' and she walked away to serve another customer.

Later on during the evening, Bert Croucher and his mate, Ken Woods, came in the bar together. After Harry served them they sat at a table, deep in conversation.

'If you come to the warehouse early tomorrow morning,' said Woods, 'I'll have three sides of beef for you and two lambs. They are fresh, killed yesterday.'

'Any trouble attached to them?' asked Croucher.

'No, they are part of a large consignment and I can assure you the paperwork won't show the missing items. I've covered that,' Woods said with a sly grin. 'Usual price, so we should both make a bit on the side.' He sat back in his chair and looked around. 'I really fancy that Gloria,' he said. 'I'd like to see what's under those clothes.'

'You've got no chance!' snapped Croucher who also lusted after her.

'We'll see about that,' said Woods and, rising to his feet, he walked over to the bar. 'Two large scotches and ginger ale,' he told Gloria, 'and of course one for yourself.'

'No thank you, sir, it's too early in the evening for me,' and she turned away to fulfil his order.

When she returned he smiled and said, 'I would very much like to take you out to dinner one evening, you know, somewhere special. I'll treat you well I can promise you.'

Daisy felt her legs start to tremble as the man peered at her with a steely gaze. 'Thank you but I'm spoken for and my young man wouldn't like it if I went out with anybody else.'

'I can well understand that,' he said, 'but he doesn't have to know does he?'

'I'm not in the habit of lying, sir, and anyway I wouldn't go even if I wasn't courting.'

His eyes narrowed. 'I'm not good enough, is that what you're saying?' There was a menacing tone to his voice and Daisy knew she would have to step carefully.

'Not at all, but I don't have any spare time, I'm far too busy,' and she walked away to attend to another customer.

Woods walked back to the table where his mate was laughing quietly.

'She blew you out, didn't she? Well, Kenny boy, you must face the fact you ain't the answer to every girl's prayer.'

The other man was fuming inside but just grunted in reply.

When, at the end of her shift, Daisy told Harry about Ken Woods' invitation, he looked perturbed. 'Don't you go near that bloke, he's bad news. He's a very dodgy character and is known to have a nasty vicious streak. I'll keep my eye open and if he comes in I'll try to be free to serve him in future.'

'Thanks, Harry,' she said, but the man had scared her. She thought to be on the wrong side of him would be dangerous and she prayed that in future he would leave her alone.

During the following week, when Daisy visited her father, she walked down the corridor towards his room, breathing in the faint smell of ether and disinfectant, and she was pleased to see a slight improvement in him. He didn't look so drawn and he was a better colour.

'They do look after you well here, love. The food is good, but not as good as your mother's of course. And would you believe it, see these French doors; well they open them to let the fresh air in.'

Daisy looked perturbed. 'Don't you feel the cold?'

'No, love. They give me a hot water bottle and wrap me up in a blanket. It's really nice, I like it and of course I can watch the birds in the garden. You'd be surprised how quickly the day passes and of course your Mum comes and sits with me in the afternoons.'

She was delighted that her beloved father seemed so happy; it took a load off her mind and the fact that Vera was now free of the loads of washing she'd once had to do made it all worthwhile. Daisy was tired of course, working during the day and doing her private work in the evenings, then the club three nights at the week's end, but looking at the smiling face of her father, she knew it was worth every working hour and her aching back.

On occasion, during the week, Jack would call on Daisy and sit with her as she worked. He *said* he didn't mind but seeing her on Sundays only wasn't enough. Daisy was pleased with his company, although when she had very close work to do and needed to concentrate, his cheerful chatter was distracting. But she couldn't complain as he was so good-natured about it all.

But on the following Sunday when they were out walking together and Daisy passed not one but two of the customers from the Solent Club and they greeted her as Gloria, Jack demanded an explanation.

'What the bloody hell is going on, Daisy? There was that man the other week who called you Gloria and now today two more men. Three people can't mistake you for someone else!'

She knew she had no choice but to tell him the truth. They sat on a park bench as she tried to explain.

'The Solent Club! You're working in that knocking shop! I don't believe it.'

'Flo Cummings offered me the job so I could afford to pay for Dad to be looked after. The extra money I make there pays for the fees.'

He was appalled. 'And what else do you do for the money? Do you earn it on your back?'

She slapped his face hard. 'How dare you! Don't you know me at all?'

He glared at her, his face flushed with anger. 'It seems that I don't. My Daisy would never contemplate walking into such a place, let alone working there. No, I don't know you.'

She desperately tried to make him understand her need for the money.

'What do you think your father would say if he knew how his bed is being paid for? He would be ashamed.'

'What's there to be ashamed of? I'm only working behind the bar serving drinks and don't you ever think of telling him, Jack Weston! I would never be able to forgive you if you did.'

'And who does he think got him his bed?'

'I told him it was the doctor and he believes me.'

The anger blazed in his eyes as he looked at her. 'More lies! How can I believe anything you say to me now?'

Daisy glared at him. 'I've told you the truth; it's up to you to believe it or not.' She stood up. 'I think you'd better take me home.'

They walked in silence to her door. Daisy turned to kiss him goodbye, but Jack stood back. 'What you've told me today has shaken me to the core, Daisy. I'll have to try and get my head round it.' And he walked away.

Daisy watched him for a while but he didn't look back and eventually she put the key in the door and went inside too weary and upset to think.

Six

On Friday evening the bar was busy as usual when four young men came in together. They were celebrating the birthday of one and as a special present, the lads had brought him here to be with a woman. There was a lot of joshing going on between them, much of it to cover their embarrassment. It was obvious from their raucous behaviour they had never visited such a place before.

Stella strolled over to them, ignoring the lewd remarks as she approached. Then she spoke. 'Good evening, now may I suggest that if you wish to behave like schoolboys, you leave now and wait for school to start in the morning?'

'Ooh,' sneered one, 'listen to that!'

'However,' continued Stella, 'if you are here for pleasure and enjoyment and wish to stay, I would strongly advise you to act like men.'

Three of them looked sheepish as her remarks hit home but the fourth gave Stella an arrogant stare. 'And who might you be to tell us how to behave?'

'That's none of your business but believe me when I say I'll have you thrown out unless you change your manner.' As the mouthy lad went to argue, Stella looked at his feet. 'What size shoes do you wear?' she asked.

Thrown by this the lad answered, 'Six, why?'

Stella grinned and crooked her little finger. 'It never fails, small dick, big mouth!'

The others roared with laughter at their friend's discomfort as she walked away. The birthday boy spoke up. 'This is my treat so you lot, shut up! Especially you, Stan,' he said to the loudmouth. He looked around the bar, his gaze resting on an olive-skinned girl sitting there. 'That's the one I want,' and he walked over to her and after a short conversation, she led him to the stairs. He turned to his mates and, grinning broadly, he gave a thumbs-up sign.

The others declined the services of any other girls and Stan went up to the counter and ordered another round of drinks. Daisy felt him staring at her and when he'd paid, he stared even harder.

'Don't I know you?' he asked.

'I don't think so. Your face isn't familiar.'

He walked away shaking his head and as he sat drinking with his friends he watched Daisy with a puzzled expression until the birthday boy came back down the stairs, smiling all over his face.

'Thank you, lads, that was the best birthday present I've ever had!'

The others crowded around. 'What was it like? What did she do to you? What did you do to her?' All were filled with vicarious curiosity.

The young man chuckled. 'Oh, no, I'm saying nothing. You want to know what happens behind closed doors, you pay to find out!'

There were groans of disappointment all round, but none of them had the courage to find out for themselves. They eventually finished their drinks and left the club.

Stella wandered over to the bar and ordered a gin and tonic.

'You handled that lot well,' Daisy remarked as she served Stella.

'We girls are not here to be sneered at by them or anyone,' she declared. 'We are here to do business just like any shopkeeper with goods to sell, but that doesn't mean we have to be denigrated by the likes of them, or anyone for that matter.'

'Denigrated! That's a big word,' teased Daisy.

'I had a good teacher,' said Stella. 'It's only circumstances that have brought me here. This is a means to an end and when I've saved enough money, I'm off.'

As she walked away, Daisy wondered what was Stella's story? She looked at each girl in turn. They were all different one from another and she supposed behind each and every one, they had a story to tell. She'd never thought about that before. After all, she was here to earn enough money for her dad otherwise she would never have considered working in a place like this. Then she thought of the young man who thought he knew her, but as she wracked her brains, she couldn't recall ever having seen him before.

The following morning in the workroom, the mystery was solved when Jessie shared her latest piece of gossip.

'Hey! What do you think, girls? My brother and his friends went to the Solent Club last night.'

There was a gasp from the others. 'Whatever was he doing there?' one asked.

'One of his mates had a birthday and they took him there to pay for a woman!'

Daisy's heart sank. Jessie's brother sometimes came to meet her after work and that, she realized, was the young man in the club last night. No wonder he stared at her. Dressed differently and with her hair down and make-up on, he wouldn't have recognized her immediately . . . but how long would it be before he put two and two together? She would have to watch out for him and keep out of his way. She doubted that he would visit the club again, so with a bit of luck, she wouldn't be found out. But it was a worry.

Sunday arrived and no Jack! Daisy was upset that she'd not heard from him after she'd had to confess about her evening job. She had hoped he would have realized the importance of having to earn the extra money for her father's welfare and though she was sure he was sympathetic to her needs, he obviously couldn't accept her methods. Surely he knew her well enough to know she wasn't selling her body? She decided to use the extra time on her private work in hand, so she pulled out her workbox and settled down.

An hour later there was a knock on the front door and putting down her work, she went to answer it. There standing before her was, Jack.

'Hello, Daisy, can I come in?'

She stepped back. 'Of course.' She followed him into the living room. 'Would you like a cup of tea?' she asked.

'Thanks, that would be nice.' He didn't say anything while she made it, but once she sat down and poured the tea, he spoke.

'I've been doing a lot of thinking,' he started, 'and I'm sorry I flew off the handle the other day, but I was so shocked by what you told me.'

Daisy gazed at him, irritated by the pompous tone in his voice.

'And I do understand the need for the extra money, but I'm sure your father wouldn't want you to earn it in such a place.'

She felt the anger flare within her. 'How dare you decide what my father thinks? What right have you to sit there and say such a thing?'

'Because I think you are in moral danger working there with those women.'

'What do you mean, *those* women?'

'Well I mean to say, they are *without* morals, earning their money the way that they do. No decent woman would sell her body.'

'You don't know what you're talking about, Jack Weston! All the girls working in the Solent Club are very nice; they all have their reasons to be there. They're not sluts you know.'

He laughed derisively. 'Of course they are.'

'I won't have you say such a thing; they're working girls, making a living like anyone else.'

'Oh, come on, Daisy, they're prostitutes!'

'And what would you call the men who come in and pay for their services then? Because without them and their demands, there would be no need for the girls to work.'

'Men will be men, Daisy.'

'So it's all right for them, but not the women? That really is *so* hypocritical. Double standards I think they call it. Anyway have you ever been to such a place?'

'Good God, no!'

'Then you are not in any position to judge. You're like all the rest; you make judgements of things you know nothing about.'

'Maybe you're right, but I don't want you working there any longer.'

She was absolutely livid. 'You can't tell me what to do!'

He glared at her. 'If we are to continue courting, you'll have to leave. Imagine what my family and friends would say if they found out about you.'

Daisy placed a hand on her heart and with a feigned outraged air said, 'Oh the scandal of it all!'

'It's not funny, Daisy!'

'No it definitely is not! My father needs that bed and you are asking me to choose between the two of you.' She glowered at him. 'Well you lose, Jack. My father comes first and if you can't live with that, you'd better leave now.'

'Are you sure about this?' he asked as he rose to his feet.

'Get on, get out – and don't bloody well come back!'

He took one look at her and seeing the anger in her eyes, let himself out of the house.

Daisy sat, fuming. She just could not understand his attitude. How could anyone who loved her ask her to give up her work? Not at a time like this. Not knowing the situation. How could he put what others would think first, before her dying father?

At that moment Vera arrived home from the hospital. Taking off her coat she said, 'Not out with Jack today then?'

'He just called round, Mum, but I want to finish my work. How was Dad?'

'Much the same, but he has a better colour in his cheeks and he seems to be eating a little more.'

'Sit down, Mum. I'll make you a cup of tea. You look frozen.'

'There's a bitter wind out today,' her mother said, and she warmed her hands by the fire.

There was a bitter wind in here too, thought Daisy, but she kept her thoughts to herself.

There was another stormy atmosphere in the living room of the White Swan as Bertha, Jim Grant's wife, let off steam as she waved a bill at him.

'What are you doing paying for a dress to be made for bloody Flo Cummings?' she demanded.

'What are you talking about?' he asked, playing for time.

'It says here. Madam Evans, one dress for Mrs Florence Cummings. Fifteen guineas!'

'It was a birthday present,' he said.

'Fifteen bloody guineas! That's more than you ever paid for any birthday present for me.'

'Now come on, Bertha, let's not pretend. You've known about me and Flo for years. We have an understanding you and I, so why the sudden aggro?'

'Fifteen guineas is why!'

'I'd have done the same for you if you had the same interest in your appearance as Flo has.'

This silenced Bertha Grant for the moment. It was true, she'd let herself go over the years. She worked hard in the bar and looking after Jim and the household too, but this stuck in her craw. Well she would take herself off to Madam Evans and order some new clothes too. Let her old man pay for that bill and see how he liked it. She stomped out of the room.

Grant scratched his head. Bloody women! He was lucky he supposed. His wife wasn't that interested in sex and she'd been relieved when he took a mistress because that meant he turned to her for sexual satisfaction less and less. He had made it plain that he was happy to stay married to Bertha as long as she understood that he needed Flo.

Bertha liked being the landlady of the White Swan and the security of a husband so she'd turned a blind eye as long as Flo didn't come into the pub. That was her territory and she wouldn't have Flo Cummings walk on her home ground. But today, faced with the bill for so much money, she suddenly became possessive . . . and jealous. Well, Jim would have to pay dearly for his peccadillo.

Later that day, the door of the dress shop in London Road opened and Madam greeted her new client. 'Good afternoon, Madam, can I be of service?'

Bertha Grant smiled with satisfaction and said, 'Yes. I need several new garments and I would like to look at some patterns and material.'

Some time later, Daisy was called to the front of the shop to measure a new client. 'A Mrs Grant. Landlady of the White Swan in Oxford Street,' she was told.

This intrigued Daisy, knowing that Flo was the mistress of this woman's husband. Picking up her tape measure, pad and pencil she walked into the reception area.

As she took the measurements, she wondered why the woman seemed so hostile. She was very abrupt when she spoke, not that she was rude to Daisy, she wasn't, but something had obviously upset her. It wasn't long before Daisy understood.

'I believe you make garments for a Mrs Florence Cummings.'

Daisy knew she would have to be diplomatic. 'Yes, Madam, I believe we do.'

'Does she have many made?'

Taking a deep breath, Daisy said, 'I couldn't really say. In any case we are not allowed to discuss our clients, Madam forbids it. All transactions are absolutely confidential.'

'Quite right too!' the woman snapped.

Daisy thought that wasn't really what she meant, but at least she was spared any cross-questioning as she carried out her work. The order when she'd finished was for two day dresses, an evening blouse and skirt and a short jacket. The bill was hefty as she'd chosen expensive material.

When the total was told to Bertha, she gave a smile of satisfaction. 'That's excellent. When the garments are finished, send the bill to my husband. When shall I come back for my fittings?'

Madam made several appointments, wrote them on a card and handed it to her.

'Thank you,' said Bertha. 'I'm going to get a lot of enjoyment out of wearing these garments.'

After Bertha had gone, Daisy returned to Madam and said, 'We must make sure that Mrs Grant isn't booked in at the same time as Mrs Cummings or they'll be trouble.'

'I know, I've just realized that. Oh dear why do men have to be so dreadful. I know all about Mrs Cummings but at least she doesn't bring any of her business here and she spends a lot of money, but in all honesty I wish she'd go elsewhere. I don't want to lose any of my better clients because of her reputation. It is a worry.'

Daisy made no comment and with a sinking feeling, hurried back to her workbench.

Seven

The girls in the workshop were kept very busy during the following week. There was so much work in hand and Daisy was pleased to be called out to do a fitting for Mrs Grace Portman.

'How's your father?' Grace asked and listened as Daisy told her.

'And the Captain?' asked Daisy. 'Have you heard from him since I last saw you?'

Grace Portman shook her head. 'He did warn me that mail would be difficult. Getting letters mailed from the front line isn't easy, but I tell myself that no news is good news. I just wish there was something I could do to fill my time. I am involved with the nearby hospital, helping them where I'm able and of course the women in the village are knitting scarves and socks for the troops, but it doesn't seem enough somehow.'

Daisy just listened. She'd seen the troops marching to the docks of course. Southampton was an important military port, shipping troops out to France. From what she'd read in the papers, many thousands would never return, but she kept these thoughts to herself as she made alterations to the dress Grace was trying on.

'I write to Hugh of course,' Grace said. 'He told me how much it means to the men to receive mail from home. It takes time for it to be delivered and sometimes several letters arrive all together.'

'At least when they do arrive, that will give your husband and his men something to cling to,' Daisy said, not knowing what to say to comfort her client.

Grace had a similar conversation that evening when Giles Bentley, a neighbouring farmer, called on her. He had been friends of the family since childhood. He and Hugh had played together and Giles, like Hugh, had taken over the running of the farm and the land that went with it, allowing their fathers to retire.

Grace and he sat by the fire with after-dinner drinks, talking about the war. Giles had escaped the call-up as he suffered with a loss of hearing in one ear, sustained in childhood.

'I must say, Grace my dear, I admire the way you've buckled down and run the estate in the absence of your old man.'

'I didn't have any choice if I didn't want the old battleaxe moving back in,' she laughed.

'The indomitable Clara,' he said. 'You deserve a medal just for standing up to her.'

The evening lifted Grace's spirits. Giles was such a lovely man she couldn't understand how he remained single. They compared notes about the running of their property, and the prices of feed for the animals. It was good for Grace to have someone other than her estate manager to refer to, and she was grateful.

That evening when Daisy went to visit her father, she thought he had deteriorated somewhat and spoke to the matron about his condition before she left.

'It's to be expected,' the matron said. 'There are more drugs we can use to keep him comfortable but of course they come at a cost.'

'Please,' said Daisy, 'give him whatever he needs, and give me the bill for it. I want his last days spent in as much comfort as is possible.'

As she walked home she was thankful that she was in a position to be able to help him. But the following morning, her position changed.

As Daisy took her coat off in the staffroom at her place of employment Madam Evans came out of her office and said she wanted to talk to her. The coldness in her manner made Daisy nervous as she followed her employer.

'Sit down,' she was told. 'Miss Gilbert, I have something to ask you and I want an honest answer.'

'Of course, whatever is it?'

'It has come to my attention that you are working in the evenings at the Solent Club as a barmaid. Is this correct?'

Daisy's heart sank. Jessie's brother must have eventually recognized her. 'Yes, Madam. I work there three nights a week.'

The woman looked coldly at her. 'Surely you are aware of the kind of establishment it is?'

Daisy sat upright and staring the other woman in the eye said, 'Oh yes, of course, but I need the extra money. My father has tuberculosis and is in a private nursing home.'

The stern expression showed no sympathy. 'Very commendable of you, I'm sure, but couldn't you have found another situation?'

'I confess I didn't try. Mrs Cummings kindly offered me the job and quite frankly, Madam, I jumped at the chance!'

'I see, and do you intend to continue working there?'

'As long as Dad needs attention, yes.'

'Then I'm afraid I will have to dispense with your services.' Seeing the stricken look on Daisy's face she added, 'I'm sorry to have to do this as you are such a good seamstress, but I have my reputation to consider and if it became known that one of my girls was working in a brothel . . . well, it could lose me some of my clients.'

'I see,' murmured Daisy, who was panicking as to how she could now afford her father's care.

'I will give you an excellent reference. I think you deserve that at least.'

'Thank you, Madam. When do you want me to leave?'

'Now. Go and get your stuff from the workroom and come back and wait outside my office for your reference. Of course I won't comment on the reason for you leaving. I'll write it now and make up your wages.'

Daisy rose from the chair in a daze. Outside the workroom, she took a deep breath, then opened the door. The chattering stopped and there was silence as Daisy went to her table and started to collect her things.

Jessie was the first one to break the silence. 'My brother couldn't believe it was you in that place when he eventually realized who you were.' She grinned slyly. 'What's it like there?'

'Why don't you ask your brother?'

The other girls giggled. Agnes said, 'I'm so sorry that Madam has done this to you, Daisy. I'll really miss you.' There was a muttering of agreement from the others.

One angry voice called, 'You rotten bitch, Jessie. Couldn't keep your bloody mouth shut could you?'

'Well you know how stuck-up Madam is. If it got out about Daisy, trade could drop and we'd all be out of a job.'

'Don't give me that,' said the other seamstress, 'you're just a spiteful bitch. You couldn't wait to tell her − nearly broke your neck doing it I shouldn't reckon!' The others murmured their agreement.

Having gathered all her bits and pieces, Daisy looked up. 'Goodbye, everyone,' she said, fighting back the tears. And hurried to the door. Once she'd collected her reference, she walked outside the shop and leaned against the wall to recover from the shock. What on earth was she to do now? She had to find another job quickly to keep up the payments at the nursing home. As she walked down London Road she racked her brains trying to think of a solution. Perhaps Flo would let her work more evenings, perhaps a full week instead of three nights. The tips were good and with the extra wages she would still manage the bills. She would go and ask her.

Daisy took a tram to Bernard Street and knocked on Flo's door. It seemed an age that she stood waiting for an answer. She was just about to walk away when the front door opened. Flo stood there with tussled hair and her dressing gown wrapped around her.

'I'm sorry if I woke you,' Daisy said, 'but could I have a word?'

'Come in, Daisy. I'll make a cup of tea for us both and then we can talk.'

Flo made a pot of tea and as she poured it said, 'Right, now what's this all about?'

Daisy told her of her predicament. About the boys coming into the club and how one, the brother of a colleague, had recognized her and the subsequent result.

'Oh, love, I am sorry. That stuffy woman. She acts as if she never has to use the lavatory! I know she would rather do without my custom but she can't afford to. Bitch!'

'Could I come and work full-time behind the bar with Harry?'

With a frown Flo said, 'I'll have to give this some thought. The weekends are when we are really busy you see. I don't know if the earlier part would warrant me having extra help behind the bar.'

'Apart from the weekly bill, Dad needs extra medication now and I *must* find that extra money!'

Flo looked at the worried face of the young girl and said, 'Look, I'll think about it and try and come up with an answer. Come to the club tomorrow evening and we'll discuss it then. Now finish your tea, you look as if you need it.'

Vera Gilbert looked up in surprise as Daisy walked into the house. 'Whatever are you doing home at this time?'

Daisy told her what had happened.

Her mother gathered her into her arms and hugged her. 'I am sorry, love. That spiteful Jessie. So what are you going to do?'

'I'm seeing Flo tomorrow night to see if I can work a full week. If not I'll have to look elsewhere. I still have one or two private clients but at the moment I have only one who needs some work done. It's not enough, Mum.'

'Now you listen to me, Daisy love. You've been a good daughter to your dad, he's had a break and if the worst comes to the worst, we'll bring him home.'

'But I don't want to do that!'

'I know, but we have to cut our cloth according to the width. If you can't afford it you can't!'

'Well let's wait and see what Flo has to say.'

Flo Cummings was giving Daisy's predicament a great deal of thought. The young girl had caused quite a stir among the male members and many of them desired her. Knowing of her innocence Flo was aware of the money that could pass hands if she could persuade her to work the other side of the bar. Although Flo was not without sympathy for Daisy's predicament, she was a businesswoman who had come up the hard way. She knew, however, that Daisy would be horrified at the prospect, but this was too good an opportunity to miss. There was a lot of money to be made here. She would have a quiet word with Stella, her head girl, and get her to help persuade the girl.

Flo arrived at the Solent Club early that evening and drew Stella aside. 'I need to talk to you,' she said, and walked to a table and sat down.

'What is it?' Stella asked.

'It's young Daisy. Her employer has heard she's been working here and fired her. Now the girl has been paying fees at a private nursing home for her father who hasn't long for this world and now she's up the creek without a paddle.'

'Oh dear,' said Stella, 'but what do you want me to do about it?'

'She's coming in a bit later. I want you to talk to her, and get her to work with you and the other girls.'

Stella was shocked. 'You want her to become a brass?'

'I want her to earn the money she needs!'

Stella gave Flo a knowing look. 'Don't give me that, you know how much she'd earn for you. Well I'm not sure I want to help you. She's a lovely girl, innocent as the day is long and you want to destroy her!'

Flo gave a disdainful laugh. 'It hasn't ruined you has it?'

'No, but I made my own decision to make money lying on my back. Daisy isn't that kind of girl.'

'Listen to me, Stella; we are all that kind of girl if we have nowhere else to turn.'

'I'll certainly talk to her because I like her and see what she says but I won't push her into working for her money like I do. That will have to be her decision.'

'Fair enough! If she's desperate enough she'll do it. What with the war, there are not many establishments around wanting her skills. She'll come round to it in time. All her money will have gone on her father's bills. She'll need more money and soon. I can wait.'

Stella watched Flo walk away and thought what a hard bitch she was and with a heavy heart wondered what she would say to Daisy when she came in later. The last thing she wanted was for Daisy to become one of the girls and honestly she couldn't imagine her contemplating such a thing, no matter what her situation was. She walked over to the bar and ordered a drink, pondering over the problem she'd been handed. You had to be hard to be a brass, to let men paw you and use you. However hard she tried, she couldn't envisage Daisy in that situation. The girl was a virgin for Christ's sake! Her mind was as pure as her body. To set her down this road was a sin, but she had no choice but to do Flo's bidding. She hoped that Daisy would send her packing with a flea in her ear.

Eight

When Daisy arrived at the club a little later, Harry greeted her warmly. 'Hello, love, can't you keep away then?'

'I've come to see Flo; do you know where she is?'

'She was here a while ago. Hey, Stella, seen Flo?'

Stella walked over and said, 'She had to go out, Daisy, but she asked me to talk to you. Come on up to my room, I've got a bottle up there.'

Daisy followed Stella up the stairs and into a larger room than she'd imagined. It was tastefully furnished, if not simply. There was a small washbasin in the corner, a dressing table, side tables with lamps and the bed had a brightly coloured cover with several small cushions on it, giving it a mildly exotic look.

Stella poured them both a gin and tonic and sat beside Daisy on the bed. 'Flo told me about your problem. I'm really sorry you lost your job, love.'

'I was so shocked when Madam fired me,' Daisy told her, 'for a minute I couldn't speak. I'm hoping that Flo will let me work behind the bar, full-time.'

'That's what she wanted me to talk to you about.'

Daisy felt her stomach tighten and her heart beat faster. She had the feeling that Stella was going to give her bad news.

'Flo is unable to take you on behind the bar for the week. She said it wouldn't pay her to, I'm afraid.'

Daisy's shoulders slumped.

'However she did suggest another way for you to earn the money you need.'

'Did she? That's wonderful; I knew she wouldn't let me down.'

Stella wondered how the girl would feel when she realized that Flo wasn't quite the friend she thought. How could she put this so as to soften the blow?

'As you know and as I've told you often, the effect you have on our clients since you've been working here is really something.'

The eager expression on Daisy's face changed to one of suspicion. 'Go on.'

God, this is going to be hard, thought Stella, and she hated to be the one to put this proposition to this lovely girl of whom she'd grown really fond. 'Flo suggests that if you were to work the other side of the bar, you could make a great deal of money.' There, she'd said it!

Daisy looked at Stella in disbelief. 'Flo knows I'm not into all that. I made that clear to her when she took me on!' she cried.

'I know, love, and I told her I knew you wouldn't be interested and in my opinion she's out of line to even suggest such a thing. If I were you I would go and look for another job in the meantime. You'll still be behind the bar at the weekends, getting paid and collecting tips. If you get another job real soon, you'll be fine.'

'I don't have much time,' Daisy told her. 'Nearly all the money I have will be spent this week and I have to pay the rent and buy food for Mum.'

'You could bring your dad home,' Stella suggested.

Daisy shook her head. 'He doesn't have much time left, he's deteriorating each day. If he was at home, he wouldn't get the right care. Mum and I can only do so much, but where he is, they have everything to hand and trained nurses which he really needs at this moment. I've got to keep him there, Stella, I've got to!'

'Well, darling, you must go out tomorrow morning and try and get another job. I'll keep my fingers crossed for you. Now drink up, I've got to get to work.'

As Daisy walked home she was more than a little confused. How could Flo even consider asking her to become a whore? She didn't think any the less of the girls who worked the tables in the club. She'd taken their profession for granted, after all it was their choice and she'd got to know them and they were nice to talk to. But to become one of them – to have men touching her – and to have sex with a stranger. She remembered the young man who said he would pay twenty pounds to take her to bed. That was a great deal of money. But she just couldn't do it!

The following morning, she was up early and out of the house. She called in at all the places she thought might need a good needlewoman. Stores that sold garments and who did alterations, but without success. Tailors, who told her that they had their own staff, even dry-cleaners who might take in alterations, but to no avail. There was one vacancy in a gown shop but not for a month hence when one of their seamstresses retired. A month was far too long to wait and she had to refuse.

She even went along to the tram depot to see if there was a vacancy as a conductress, but there were no jobs on offer. Eventually she tried one of the factories, but they too were full. The manager explained his position.

'We've been inundated with women wanting to earn while their husbands are at the front,' he said. 'I've never known anything like it. It's like the emancipation of women! They've never been so free to earn, apart from going into service.'

That gave Daisy another idea and she went to an agency for domestics, but again was met with a refusal. With the men of the households away at the war, domestic service had been cut back, except in the big houses of the rich who were well served already.

By Thursday evening as she walked towards the Solent Club, Daisy was beside herself with worry. She'd spent every moment out looking for work, but the war had taken its toll. Jobs that men had vacated and could be done by women had been filled, but businesses were suffering with the shortages that war brings to a country and that meant cutting back on staff. Daisy couldn't have picked a worse time to be unemployed.

As she walked upstairs to get changed for the evening, Stella came up to her and asked, 'Any luck with a job, Daisy?'

'I can't find anything, anywhere. It's like someone has shut every door in my face. What am I to do, Stella?'

'Bring your dad home, love. You don't have any choice do you?'

'I do have a choice, but I honestly don't know if I could do it.' She looked at her friend with such anguish that Stella wanted to cry.

'Then don't. For God's sake, don't go down that road, you'll never forgive yourself.'

'Is it really so bad?'

Stella was at a loss. For her it wasn't a bad life because she had a goal. When she'd saved enough money she had plans and she knew that in the future she could look on the days spent in the club just as a means to an end. It would not fill her with a life of regret. But what of Daisy? Could she be that strong? She doubted it. Daisy should be married, surrounded by children and with a loving husband. Not working for Flo, catering for men's sexual favours. But she had to help this girl.

'It all depends how you look at it,' she said. 'When a man comes into my room, I look on it as being a job for which I'm paid. No more, no less.'

Daisy closed her eyes in despair. 'But you have to get undressed and have sex with a stranger. How on earth do you do that?'

'I just get on with it and think of the money.'

'Oh, Stella, I don't think I could be that brave.'

With a laugh, Stella said, 'Look, love, bravery has nothing to do with it. You'd be surprised how quickly it's all over.'

Quietly Daisy said, 'But I've seen some of the men you've had to take to your room. They don't all look particularly nice.'

Stella was highly amused. 'I don't always take that much notice, but then I've been at it a long time. Mind you I make it a rule not to kiss them!'

Daisy's eyes widened. 'Why ever not?'

'Nah. Don't fancy that. Look, Daisy, they may pay for my services, but they don't pay for my soul. Kissing to me is for someone special that *I* fancy – not for my punters.' She gazed at the girl and said, 'You would be such a catch that if you did decide to become one of us, you could lay down a few rules to Flo.'

'What do you mean?'

'Flo gets a cut of all our takings which pays for the use of the room. She gets four shillings out of every pound and of course the profit on the drinks they buy. You being an innocent could make bigger money to start with. Especially the first man who took you.'

'One young man told me he'd be willing to pay twenty pounds to take me to bed when he knew I was a virgin,' Daisy told her.

'There you are, what did I say and you could demand that she chooses carefully the punters she sends you. Not every Tom, Dick or Harry.'

'Oh, Stella, you make it sound all so easy. I'd be terrified.'

'Come on, it's time to go downstairs. You don't have to make a decision now.'

Daisy was getting desperate, especially when she went to visit her father the next afternoon and was handed another bill for medication, morphine for the pain and extra nursing. After paying that, she had very little money left until her stint in the bar at the weekend. But she wouldn't have enough to cover the bill the following week with all the extra charges. She didn't have a choice; she would have to bring him home. But when she spoke to her father, she was in a bigger dilemma than ever.

Fred took Daisy's hand as she sat beside his bed. It broke her heart to feel the bones in his hands where he'd lost so much weight.

'You know, Daisy,' he said, 'I'm so grateful to the doctor for sending me here. The nurses really know what they're doing and take such care of me. Your mother could never manage me now, it would be far too much for her, but at least I don't have that to worry about.' He gave a wan smile. 'This is not a bad place to finish my days you know.'

She knew then she would have to let him stay in the nursing home and would have to find the money to pay the bills. There was no other option open to her. She would have to accept Flo's offer. Her heart sank at the very idea, but now she really had no choice.

The following day she went to pay Flo a visit at her private address and stood waiting for the door to open, her heart pounding, her hands trembling.

'Come in, love,' said Flo when she saw who was waiting. So, as she thought, young Daisy needed money real bad. 'Sit down,' she said as they walked into the living room.

'So, Daisy, I assume that you have come about my offer?'

'I need the money,' Daisy said. 'But I want to know just how much I'll earn. I'm not selling myself to anyone unless I know it'll be worth every penny!'

There was a definite tone of defiance in her voice and Flo knew that her proposition would have to be a good one. 'Well, Daisy, in as much as you are a virgin, I want to get the best price from my punters.'

'You're not putting me up for a bloody auction I hope!' Daisy was appalled.

'Not exactly. But I'll make it known among a selected few and we'll see what transpires. Believe me, there'll be no shortage of punters.'

'But that'll take time and I want the money now. I *can't* afford to wait.'

'I'll give you some money up front.' She took a ten-pound note out of her wallet and held it out.

Daisy was not a fool. She'd given the matter a great deal of thought once she'd decided to go down this road and she was going to get as much money as she could. Once her father had ended his days, she was not going to work for Flo a minute longer than was necessary. She intended to make enough money so that eventually she would be able to open her own business. Stella was saving for a future and so would she. After all, she was making the supreme sacrifice in her eyes, so it had better be worthwhile!

She looked straight at Flo and said, 'Oh, no. That's not nearly enough!'

Flo Cummings was taken aback. She thought she was on to a good thing. Young Daisy, sweet and innocent, she'd make a packet from her while she could. After all, once her virginity was sold, being new to the business only held a certain cache for a while. After that she would be a whore just like all the others.

'What do you mean, it's not enough?'

'One of those young officers once told me he would be willing to pay twenty pounds to sleep with me when he realized I was a virgin and I'm sure you could find a man who would pay more. No, ten pounds is not nearly enough.'

'Considering you're new to the business, you've got some nerve, laying down the law to me.'

Daisy wasn't at all thrown. 'I may not know about being a whore, but I've learned enough being behind the bar to know what goes on and what men want. I've been propositioned enough times. And the moment I step from behind the bar and sit with the others, I know I'll be in demand. And you know it too!'

Flo started to laugh. 'Well, I never did! Daisy Gilbert, I didn't know you had it in you.' There was a look of admiration in the older woman's eyes as she asked, 'Is there anything else?'

'Yes,' said Daisy. 'I don't want the butcher as a client. I refuse to let him touch me.'

With raised eyebrows Flo said, 'He's never allowed near my girls. Don't you worry, girl, I'll be very particular as to who I'll choose as your punters.' She looked knowingly at the girl and said, 'Of course you know that I take a cut from your earnings?'

'How much?' demanded Daisy.

'You don't beat about the bush do you?' said Flo with a chuckle.

'How much?' Daisy repeated.

'Four shillings in the pound. After all, I supply the room and the bar, and make sure before you take them to your room that they spend a lot on drinks. You ask for a gin and tonic and—'

'I know, I'll be served straight tonic water with a slice of lemon. Don't you think I've served up enough drinks to know that?'

'Of course you have, I'd forgotten. Now what I want you to do is continue to work behind the bar all this week while I sort you out a rich punter.'

'All right but I want some money up front to pay my dad's bills.'

'How much?' asked Flo.

'I want twenty pounds and not a penny less.'

Flo took another ten-pound note from her wallet and handed them both to Daisy. 'Now you are committed. There's no backing out, I hope you realize that?'

'Yes, I know that,' and she put the money away, stood up and said, 'I'll be on duty in the bar as usual on Thursday evening.'

Flo rose to her feet and walked her to the door. 'No, you start on Tuesday. You won't regret this,' she said. 'I've been down this road and it's not all that bad, honestly.'

Daisy didn't answer. But as she walked down the street, she felt sick. What had she let herself in for? And having done so, how could she find the courage to keep her bargain? She knew that she was now committed to becoming one of Flo Cummings' girls. She had no other choice.

Nine

As Daisy walked away, she felt as if a wet blanket of despair had enveloped her. She had now made the choice to walk down a road full of unknown dangers. Whatever Stella had told her about being a whore and had implied it wasn't as bad as she imagined, Daisy's mind was full of pictures of the men she would have to take to her bed in a strange room at the club. She was terrified. What did she know about sex? Absolutely nothing! Yet here she was waiting for Flo to find a man who would pay the highest price to take her virginity! How strange, she thought. Her purity had never meant anything of great importance before. She'd never even thought about it, yet it was obviously something of great value . . . but for all the wrong reasons.

It would destroy her mother if she ever discovered that her daughter was to become one of Flo's girls. Tears welled in her eyes as she imagined her mother's shame if she ever found out. But taking a deep breath she told herself that it didn't matter, as it was for her father and the end justified the means. But it didn't really make her feel any better.

As she put the key into her front door she hesitated. She now had to lie to her mother, and the fact that it would be the first of many upset her greatly.

'How did you get on, love?' asked Vera. 'Did Flo give you extra hours in the club?'

'Yes, she did, starting next week.' Daisy forced a smile. 'And she was good enough to give me an advance on my wages so I could cover the nursing home bills.'

'She's got a heart of gold, that woman,' said Vera. 'Sit down, I'll make us a cup of cocoa and a sandwich,' and she pottered about, humming softly to herself.

Daisy listened to her mother's chatter as they ate but made an excuse soon afterwards that she was tired and went to bed. If she could only sleep, she could forget what was before her. But she tossed and turned all night long.

★   ★   ★

At the gown shop the following morning, Grace Portman stood while she tried on her new dress. It required a slight alteration and when Agnes came to see to it, Grace was surprised.

'Where's Daisy?' she asked. 'Only she usually sees to all my alterations.'

Agnes looked uncomfortable as she said, 'I'm afraid that Daisy has left, Mrs Portman.'

'What do you mean, left?'

'She gave in her notice,' lied Agnes.

'Where is she working now?'

Taking a pin out of her mouth, the girl mumbled, 'I really don't know,' and got to her feet. 'You can take that off now, Mrs Portman. If you care to wait, I can take that little bit in on the waist now.'

'Yes thank you, I will wait. I was hoping to wear the dress this evening.' When she was ready, Grace made her way to the reception and sat down. As Madam came through from the workroom, Grace voiced her concerns.

'I am so sorry that you have lost young Daisy. She was an excellent seamstress and a really nice young lady. I was very fond of her.'

Madam's face flushed crimson and she fluttered about. 'Yes, I was sorry to lose her, but you know these young girls, they go from one job to another.'

With a frown, Grace stared at the owner. 'I wouldn't have thought that was in Daisy's character at all. She always seemed to me to be very dedicated to her work.'

Madam Evans sniffed and in withering tones declared, 'Well, Mrs Portman, you think you know a person but then they turn round and surprise you. I am very disappointed in Daisy Gilbert, I can tell you! I'll just go and see if Agnes has finished that slight alteration.' And she left Grace alone.

Puzzling over the owner's remarks about her former employee, Grace sensed there was more to it than she'd been told and promised herself that she would eventually get to the bottom of Daisy's departure, but not today. The next time she came in she would ask a few discreet questions of whoever came to measure her. Madam Evans, she was sure, would not tell her any more.

On Tuesday evening, Daisy walked into the Solent Club, then upstairs and changed into the clothes that Flo had laid out for her before going to the bar to be greeted by Harry.

'Flo told me you'd be working all week,' he said. 'Mind you I'm not sure we'll be that busy, but it's nice to see you, love.' And he moved away to stack the bottles of beer.

As the club began to fill, Flo arrived and started walking round, talking to some of the customers. Before long, Daisy saw some of the men looking at her speculatively and with a certain smile. She felt herself colour with embarrassment as she realized that Flo was marketing her to the punters. As the bar got busier there was a certain buzz among the customers, a lot of chatter between the men, a lot of joshing, and the odd argument. It was a strange atmosphere which didn't escape Harry's notice.

'What's going on here tonight?' he asked Daisy quietly as he wiped glasses.

'I've no idea,' she lied.

'Well something has got their tails up but for the life of me I can't put my finger on it.'

Daisy tried to behave normally but when the men came up to the bar to order their drinks, their attitude towards her changed. Whereas before this evening they would flirt with her, knowing she was unavailable, now they were less respectful and louche in their comments. Overhearing one or two, Harry chastised the men. 'A little more respect for the young lady, *if* you please, gentlemen!' As they walked away he muttered, 'Don't know what's got into everybody tonight, I really don't.'

Daisy wanted the ground to swallow her. She was really fond of Harry and when he did eventually find out she was to become one of the girls, what would he think of her then?

The following evening, the young officer who'd invited Daisy out to lunch walked in the club and over to the bar. 'Hello, Gloria, how are you? I missed you, you know.'

She smiled at him. 'I bet you say that to all the girls,' she teased.

'As a matter of fact, I don't,' he said. 'When are you going to let me take you out to lunch?'

'I don't know you,' she said. 'I don't even know your name.'

'Steven. Steven Noaks. There, now you have no excuse.'

Daisy would have liked to have accepted the young man's invitation under normal circumstances, but now she felt she couldn't. This young man came into the club just for a drink and the company of his associates, he never took a girl upstairs, and soon she would be joining those ranks and she felt he would then feel differently about wanting her company, so she politely refused. Later that evening she saw Flo approach him and her heart sank. She saw too how he listened to Flo and saw the shocked expression on his face before he looked over at her. She turned away.

Later that evening as closing time came, Steven walked over to the bar and said, 'I'll walk you home, Gloria.'

She was completely flummoxed by this and hastened to refuse. He wouldn't listen. 'I'm taking you home, I want to talk to you,' he said firmly. 'I'll wait outside.'

Once she'd changed into her own clothes, Daisy left the club, her heart racing.

Outside Steven took her by the arm. 'Which way?' he asked.

She pointed in the right direction and felt his hold tighten until they'd cleared the street, when he stopped suddenly and turned her to face him. 'What the bloody hell do you think you're doing? Selling yourself to the highest bidder.'

Under the street light she saw the anger in his eyes. 'Well?' he demanded.

She glared at him. All night long as she'd watched Flo canvass the punters, she'd felt like a piece of meat in a cattle market and was overcome with shame, but she'd taken Flo's money to pay the nursing home bills and there was no escape from the inevitable. But now, to be faced and questioned by this young man whom she liked but after all was a stranger, her pent up feelings surfaced and she raged at him.

'How dare you! What I do is my business and certainly none of yours.' She snatched her arm from his hold. 'Now leave me alone!' And she strode away.

Steven caught up with her and matched her pace. 'But Gloria, you're not like the others, you're different. You don't belong among Flo's girls.'

She kept walking. 'You know nothing about me and please, what gives you the right to badger me this way?'

'I don't have the right, but I can't stand by and let you do this.'

She stopped walking. 'Will you stop pestering me! Just mind your own business.' She pushed him and cried out in anger. 'Bugger off and leave me alone!' And she set off once again. This time the young man let her go.

As she walked on, Daisy felt tears of anger trickle down her cheeks.

Steven stood watching her . . . totally confused. He had no right to interfere but when Flo had approached him tonight, taking bids for Gloria's virginity, he couldn't believe what he was hearing. From what little he'd seen of the young barmaid, he'd assumed she was as innocent as she appeared. He'd been attracted by her naivety but to discover now that she was about to lose all that, and to the highest bidder, and become one of Flo's girls, had appalled him. He turned on his heel and walked away.

Back in the Solent Club, Harry at last discovered what had disturbed the atmosphere in the club as he had a nightcap with Stella.

'Flo's what?'

'Taking bids for Daisy's virginity.'

Harry looked askance. 'I don't believe you!'

'For Christ's sake, Harry, do you think I'd joke about a thing like that? The kid needs the money to pay the medical bills for her dad. The poor bugger's dying and she's got him in a private nursing home. She lost her day job because they discovered that she worked here and that might sully the reputation of the business if it ever came to light.'

'Well now I've heard everything,' he said. 'She obviously has her reasons, but honestly, Stella, she won't be able to stick it out, I'd put money on it.'

Stella drew on her cigarette in quiet contemplation. 'I wouldn't bank on it if I were you, Harry. We might all be surprised. She has a purpose and is determined to give her father a good death – and nothing will stop her from doing that. I admire her for it.'

'Her loyalty is misplaced!' Harry argued. 'What father would want his daughter to put herself in that position for him?'

'But he doesn't know and she'll never tell him. For my part I think she's a heroine.' She got off the stool. 'He must be a special man for her to love him so much that she'll do this. How many of us can truly say we deserve such devotion?'

Harry had no answer.

Ten

Ken Woods walked into the butcher's shop and beckoned to Bert Croucher. When the butcher finished serving his customer he walked over to his mate.

'What are you doing here, do you want some meat?'

Woods shook his head. 'Haven't you heard?' he asked.

'Heard, heard what?'

The other man grinned broadly. 'You know that tasty barmaid at the Solent Club? Well she's on the bloody market, mate!'

'Market! What on earth are you talking about?'

'Someone I know who uses the club was approached by Flo the other night. It seems that Gloria is joining the girls and Flo is looking for bids. The highest bidder takes the girl's cherry. By Christ, I tell you, that lucky bugger is going to be me . . . no matter what it costs!'

Bert looked livid. He had lusted after Gloria from the first moment he saw her and now when she was available, he was out of the running as Flo had barred him from hiring any one of her girls. He could have swiped the grin off Woods' face.

'What makes you think Flo will give you the chance? After all, you are not exactly one of her favourite clients are you? She watches you like a bloody hawk.'

This observation removed the satisfied grin from the man. What Croucher said was true. Woods knew that he was only a client on sufferance. If one of the girls ever complained about him to Flo, he would be unable to hire another again. He'd been very careful not to give any of the girls reason to do so, but now he wondered if his reputation would keep him off the list of bidders.

'Well, there's only one way to find out!' he snapped. 'I'll go to the club tonight and offer her a price she won't want to refuse . . . after all, my friend, everyone can be bought, we all know that.' Turning on his heel, he walked out of the shop.

Croucher returned to his butcher's block, taking out his frustration by chopping up a side of lamb into small cuts of meat.

★　　★　　★

Daisy and her mother were at the hospital, visiting Fred. Daisy had taken him a small basket of fruit in the hope of tempting her father's appetite. It seemed every time she saw him he had shrunk a little more, but Fred tried to keep cheerful when he saw his family.

'Do you think, Vera love, you could make me a small bread and butter pudding? The food here is fine but I don't have a great appetite. I do, however, have a longing for one of your puddings. I could really enjoy that.'

'Of course, dear,' she said. 'I'll make one when I get home and bring it tomorrow.'

'How's work going, Daisy? Is that woman still working you to the bone?'

Knowing he meant Madam Evans, Daisy quickly replied, 'Yes, thank goodness, we have plenty of work to keep us going, Dad.'

'And how's young Jack? I've not heard you mention him lately.'

'He's fine,' she lied. 'I've been so busy lately what with my private work at home, that we haven't been able to see so much of each other.'

'Never mind, Daisy, you have to make the money when you can what with the war and all. Everyone who can make an extra copper has to be grateful for the opportunity.'

Seeing how tired her father was, Daisy thought it time to leave and let him rest. As she and her mother made their way home, Vera said, 'You were quick off the mark about working at the shop.'

'Well I didn't want to give Dad anything to worry about. What he doesn't know can't hurt him.'

Vera caught hold of Daisy's hand. 'It breaks my heart to see him so frail, but thank God he's in that place because I don't think I could take care of him properly if he was at home.'

'Well you don't have that worry,' Daisy reassured her. 'Come on, let's go and have a cup of tea and a scone to cheer us up.' Knowing how each day after seeing Fred, her mother was in despair, she thought it would lift her spirits and her own and hopefully stop the thoughts of what was before her at the club, invading her every waking moment.

That evening, Harry and Daisy had only just finished setting up the bar for the night when the doors were unlocked for business. They stood chatting as their first customer walked in.

Daisy's heart beat a little faster when she saw it was Ken Woods.
'I'll serve him,' said Harry.

Daisy walked to the other end of the bar, but she could hear
Ken's voice clearly.

'What time will Flo be in?' he demanded.

'No idea, Mr Woods, as you know Flo is a rule unto herself;
she comes and goes as she pleases.'

The man sipped his drink and looked over at Daisy. 'I want to
see her, so I'll wait.'

Daisy glanced up and met his gaze. The corners of his mouth
widened and he leered in her direction, raising his glass at her, but
not saying a word.

She froze. No matter what Flo said, she would *never* have this
man as a client, she'd rather die! Was that the reason he wanted
to see Flo, to stake his claim? Remembering the predatory look
in his eyes, she was certain that it was.

Harry too had come to the same conclusion. He looked across
the bar at Daisy. How could she put herself in such a position?
He couldn't help it, he had to say something. He walked over to
her and in a quiet voice asked, 'Why, for God's sake, why are you
going through with this? Look at that bastard, how can you even
contemplate having him, and others like him, touching you?'

She looked stricken. 'I don't have a choice.'

Now he was angry. 'Of course you have a choice! Life is full
of choices, but please don't throw your life away like this. You will
always regret it!'

She started to explain about her father, but he interrupted her.

'Your father would rather die tomorrow than let you go through
with this. I know because I'm a father! I want to shake you until
your teeth rattle and make you see some sense.'

This was too much for Daisy and she burst into tears and ran
from the bar and up the stairs.

Ken Woods looked over at Harry and said, 'Now don't you go
upsetting the little darling; we don't want her damaged in any way
if you know what I mean.'

'Shut your filthy mouth!' Harry said. 'Or so help me I'll come
across this bar and shut it for you!'

Stella found Daisy sobbing in one of the unoccupied rooms.
'Whatever is the matter?' she asked.

'Harry doesn't want me to go through with it and made me

feel awful, and that Ken Woods is in the bar and I'm sure he's come in about me. Well I don't care what Flo says, I'll never let him touch me!'

'Now you listen to me, Daisy. You've decided to go down this path so you are going to toughen up! And let me tell you that the other girls aren't too happy about you coming to work on the other side of the bar.'

'Why ever not?'

Stella sat on the bed and glared at her, shaking her head. 'You have no idea have you? For a while, until the novelty wears off, you will be taking their clients away from them. Men like a fresh piece of meat, you know.' Stella didn't enjoy talking to Daisy this way but she had to make the girl realize exactly what was at stake and what it was really like to be one of Flo's girls.

Stella's directness had the desired effect. 'How long before the novelty *will* wear off do you think?'

'Until you become as hard as us. At the moment all this innocence is very attractive to the men. You are unsullied goods and, even after you've lost your virginity, many men will want to be the one to instruct you in the art of lovemaking, wanting to feel they were the one to teach you to be a real woman – the others just want a change.' She lit a cigarette.

'Give me one of those will you?' Daisy asked.

'But you don't smoke!'

'There're a lot of things I haven't done until now!' She lit the cigarette and choked on the first puff for a moment, then she seemed lost in thought.

Stella said nothing more, wondering what she was thinking.

'Right!' said Daisy eventually. 'You're quite right, I have to toughen up. I'm here to earn money, firstly to pay for Dad.'

'What do you mean, firstly?'

'Well it seems to me that I am worth a small fortune if I play my cards right. You once told me you had a plan and when you had enough cash you would leave, so that's my plan too. I want to open my own gown shop. There is no way I can afford to do so, or there wasn't until now.'

Stella looked amazed. 'You are full of surprises, Daisy Gilbert!'

'Let's face it, Stella, my reputation will be in shreds the moment I take my first client so I may as well get something out of it for myself. My lovely dad isn't long for this world and although I will have helped him spend the last of his days in the right hands, it would be foolish to lose everything just for that. I have to think of the future. I don't intend to end up being one of Flo's girls until I'm past it. There's no future in that.'

'I have to say, Daisy, I didn't think you had the balls for this. Now I think you just might have.'

'However,' Daisy said, 'in the beginning when I am such valuable property to Flo, who let's face it will make a packet, I will pick and choose my clients.'

'You what?'

'Oh yes, I will be exclusive, men will have to pay extra for me, while I have that power. After . . . God willing, I'll be on my way!'

Stella started to laugh. 'I am looking forward to Flo's face when you lay down the law. She really won't like that.'

'She can put up with it! After all, she will want her cut won't she? And I'll fix my own price.'

'Bloody hell, you'll cause mayhem here. It's such a good idea; I wonder how the others will take it?'

'Maybe they will come up with a plan of their own. I best get back to the bar.'

It was a very different girl who lifted the end of the bar and returned to work than the one who had left in tears. Harry felt a new sense of purpose as Daisy set about serving the customers and made no further comment to his associate. But at the end of the evening when Flo arrived, he was surprised to hear Daisy say she wanted a word with her employer after they closed.

He had no idea what was being discussed between them in the small room at the back which served as Flo's office, but he and the girls soon heard Flo's raised voice.

'You what?'

Stella sat listening with a satisfied smile. The outcome was going to be very interesting.

It was quite some time before Daisy walked out of the office, changed into her own clothes, put on her coat and walked towards the door. As she passed Stella, she smiled and winked.

Flo followed soon after and walking over to Stella demanded, 'Have you been scheming with young Daisy?'

Feigning surprise, Stella said, 'Scheming, me? I don't know what you mean.'

With a look of suspicion, Flo just grumbled to herself and walked away.

Several of the girls watched Daisy leave. 'There goes Miss Bloody Innocent!' one exclaimed.

'And our bloody money!' said another. She looked angry and said, 'Well she had me fooled. As a barmaid I thought she was rather sweet, a bit naive, but a nice kid . . . how very wrong I was. She's just a scheming little hussy.'

A brunette was equally scornful. 'I don't know what you're worried about; she has no idea what she's in for. You wait until she gets her first punter, that'll shake her to the roots I bet. She'll wish she was back serving drinks instead of serving men *on* her back.'

'Or any other position,' laughed another. 'It'll be interesting to watch.'

Listening to their tittle-tattle, Stella agreed. It would be interesting and she wondered if Daisy's determination would hold up? Time alone would tell.

Eleven

While Daisy was coming to terms with her new life, her skills were sorely missed at the workshop in London Road. Not one of the seamstresses had the talent to match her embroidery and flare and some of the clients were complaining.

'This beadwork on the bodice of my evening dress is not up to the standard I've been used to,' one lady complained. 'Ever since young Daisy Gilbert left, the workmanship has deteriorated. Unless it improves, I'll have to take my custom elsewhere!'

Madam Evans was in a panic and fussed about the woman promising to put matters right and when she marched back into the workroom with the garment she went berserk. Storming and raging at the girls.

Agnes spoke up. 'Sorry, Madam, but we do the best we can, but not one of us is as good as Daisy, she had a special talent. If certain people had minded their own business, you wouldn't be in this position.' And she glared angrily across the room at Jessie.

Following her gaze, Madam muttered angrily to herself. 'You are probably right.' Then she stomped away.

Jessie flushed with anger. 'It's no good blaming me. Madam wouldn't want her reputation ruined.'

'Your bloody jealousy will probably lose all of us our jobs if this goes on much longer. People will go elsewhere and all because of your big mouth.'

The girl began to argue but the rest of the girls spoke in unison. 'Shut up, Jessie,' they cried.

'Do you think the old girl will ask Daisy to come back?' whispered one of the girls to Agnes.

'Doubt it. She would be admitting she was wrong, wouldn't she, and she wouldn't like that. She's too bloody stuck-up.'

In her office, Madam Evans was mulling over such thoughts. Daisy was worth her weight in gold and now she certainly did regret asking her to leave, but there was no way she would ask her to return. If she did, it would be a sign of weakness and she'd lose all respect from the workroom and with that − her control.

No, there was no way she'd do that. She'd just have to try and find another girl with the same gift.

The following day, Grace Portman visited the shop to order an evening blouse and as Agnes checked her measurements, Grace questioned her about Daisy.

'For goodness' sake, Agnes, no one will give me a reason for Daisy leaving, now what on earth made her go?'

Agnes pulled the curtain of the cubicle closed after checking that her employer was not around. 'Well, Mrs Portman, you see Daisy got an evening job to make extra money and when Madam discovered this she fired her!'

'What, for having a second job?'

'No, Mrs Portman, for having the job as a barmaid in a brothel!'

'A brothel? Good heavens, where on earth is the place?'

Agnes told her. 'It's not as if Daisy was selling herself, she was only serving drinks, but Madam Evans said if word got out she'd lose her reputation.'

Grace was furious. 'Instead of which, she lost the best seamstress she had. How ridiculous!'

'Please don't let on I told you or I'll be for the chop too,' Agnes pleaded.

'No, of course I won't breathe a word.'

As she walked along London Road afterwards, Grace pondered over this information. Poor Daisy. She must be worried to death, thought Grace, knowing why she needed the money. But she couldn't think of a way to change the situation. A great pity as she liked the girl and really appreciated the fine work Daisy had done on several of her gowns. She hoped Daisy was still able to make the money she so badly needed.

The time had almost come for Daisy Gilbert to be deflowered! After much argument, Flo had been forced to accept Daisy's terms. The girl was worth too much money to her to refuse. Now in Flo's office the two of them went over the list of Flo's chosen men with the price they offered in a margin beside the name. To Daisy's great surprise, she saw the name of Steven Noaks at the top and queried it.

'Oh yes, this young man was very insistent. He said he'd better the highest price offered, and he's coming in this evening to speak to you about it. Tomorrow evening has been booked for you and all the men listed can't wait for your decision.' She grimaced. 'I can see there is going to be a lot of bad feeling in the bar among those who lose.'

Daisy looked down the list of monies offered. She was astounded at what was on offer. The bid had risen to fifty pounds! An astonishing amount of money. Was she really worth that much? How on earth could Steven afford to better that offer? As she thought about it, she was undecided. Was it better to take to bed a complete stranger or would she feel better if it was Steven who was so against her selling herself? She really didn't know.

When he walked into the bar later that evening, Daisy felt her cheeks redden as she went to serve him. He smiled at her and ordered a drink. When she put it down on the counter, he drew her to the far end of the bar away from other customers.

Taking her hand he said softly, 'Are you going to accept my offer?'

'But why did you add your name to the list after what you said to me the other night?'

'Because you are determined to go through with this ridiculous idea no matter what, so I want to be the first man to make love to you, to treat you tenderly, not frighten you. I couldn't bear the thought of some stranger just using you.'

She felt the tears prick and blinked them away. 'You won't hate me after?'

'I couldn't do that, Gloria, how could you think such a thing? Will you accept my offer?'

'But, Steven, it is so much money, how can you . . .'

He interrupted her. 'Shh, just say yes.'

Her voice caught in her throat and she just nodded.

'Then please tell Flo. I don't want someone else coming in and taking my place.'

'Wise choice,' said Flo. 'I'll inform the other men on the list. I don't want a bloody riot tomorrow evening.'

As she walked back to the bar, Daisy passed the other girls making their way to the bar ready for work. She smiled at them as she passed, but tonight there was no friendly repartee, just a feeling of hostility.

'So little Miss Innocence,' said one of them. 'You think this is a piece of cake don't you? Well, dearie, make as much money as you can; frankly I don't think you'll last until Sunday night!'

'So far you can pick the cream of the bunch. You'll look and think, yes he looks a decent man, but you wait until your bedroom door closes. They're usually the worst, but you'll learn as we all had to.'

Daisy felt sick in the pit of her stomach. Ever since it became known she was to work on their side of the bar, the once-friendly girls had slowly turned against her and as Stella had said, she would be taking some of their clients no doubt. But then Stella had told her to toughen up! So she just walked away.

It was a very long evening. Several men that had been on the list of bidders came into the bar only to be told by Flo that their bids had been bettered. When one or two started to argue, Flo was adamant. 'Sorry, but the bidding is now closed.'

One or two, after much mutterings, tried to book Daisy for another night only to be told that Daisy – or Gloria as she was known – would choose her punter and the price! This made them furious.

'What game are you playing here, Flo?' one man asked angrily.

She shrugged. 'I know and I'm not happy about it, but it's the only way the girl will work. Take it or leave it!'

The man glanced over towards the bar and stared at the subject of his desire, then at the other girls. No, he'd had them all, some several times; he was looking for someone fresh. He may not have been the first but young Gloria had this look of innocence about her that was very beguiling.

'Put me down on the list then.' He leaned closer. 'There's a couple of quid in it for you, Flo, if you can get me in.'

She grinned and said, 'I'll see what I can do. I'll put you down for nine o'clock on Friday and keep my fingers crossed, but be prepared to pay extra.' As she walked away she chuckled to herself. This girl was going to make her a bundle. How many men a night could she persuade Daisy to take, she wondered? It would all depend on how she felt after the first time she supposed. Then an awful thought came to her. What if Daisy didn't have the balls to go through with it after tomorrow? No, she couldn't have that, the girl had made a deal with her and by God, she'd make sure she kept her part of it.

When it was time for Daisy to leave the club that night, Harry insisted she stopped and had a drink with him. 'I'm going to miss you working with me behind the bar, love. I suppose nothing I can say will make you change your mind?'

She shook her head. 'Will you still be my friend, Harry?'

'My dear Lord of course, why ever not?'

'I would be really upset if you thought less of me. After all, I'll be one of Flo's girls after tomorrow night.'

He took her hand. 'Listen to me, love, you will never be one of Flo's girls, ever. You are different. It's what's inside a person that counts and inside, you are a good woman. I hope you are successful, because I know this isn't an easy decision.'

Flo walked over and said, 'Come in a bit early tomorrow, Daisy. I've got a lovely dress for you to wear. I want you looking your best; after all it's an important night for all of us.'

Harry gave her a withering look, drank up and said goodnight.

'I'll have Stella dress you; she'll be able to give you a few tips before you start.'

The matter-of-fact tone in Flo's voice brought home to Daisy that Flo Cummings looked on her as a piece of merchandise. Something to be sold for the most money possible and she wondered just how she could ever have felt she was a friend. Well that was fine. She now knew exactly where she stood. Flo would have to treat her well from now on if either of them were to be successful. She rose from the stool and left the club.

The following day, Daisy tried to keep busy. She helped her mother clean the house and prepared the vegetables for the evening meal while Vera went to visit Fred. Daisy made an excuse for not going with her. She couldn't face her father knowing what the evening held for her. She would feel too ashamed to sit talking to her father. Instead she went for a walk and spent her time window shopping. To her surprise, Agnes walked out of the door of a haberdasher's just as Daisy was passing. The two greeted each other warmly and decided to go for a quick cup of coffee and a chat.

'Tell me all the news,' urged Daisy.

'Well,' said Agnes, thrilled to see her friend, 'since you left Madam has lost a few of her valuable customers.'

'Really?'

'I'm afraid that none of us are the seamstress that you are, Daisy love. Your fancy work was exceptional and none of us can match it, so some ladies have gone elsewhere. Pity you don't have your own place; you'd do just fine I'm sure with your skills.'

This was just what Daisy needed to hear. If she could save enough money to start her own business, then selling herself wouldn't be so bad.

'If by some miracle this ever happened, would you come and work for me, Agnes?'

'In a second! And so would a few of the others, I'm sure. Madam is becoming impossible. I don't suppose she ever approached you about coming back did she?'

'No, sadly not. I would have been only too happy to have done so had she asked, believe me. I miss you all . . . except for Jessie of course.' And she laughed.

'That rotten bitch. She won't be there much longer I wouldn't think. She messed up a collar the other day on a piece of very expensive lace. Madam was not pleased. Then the cheeky girl argued that it was the material that was poor, not her sewing. I ask you! How's the bar work going?'

'Oh you know, it's a job and I'm earning money. I'm not doing it by choice.'

'Oh I must tell you,' said Agnes with a chuckle. 'Remember that Mrs Grant, the landlady from the White Swan you measured? You know, whose husband is the lover of Mrs Cummings?'

'Oh yes, I remember her well.'

'When her husband got the bill for the stuff she ordered, he came into the shop and created merry hell!'

'Why?'

'Because she spent so much money there.'

'What happened?'

'You have to hand it to Madam Evans, she handled him beautifully. She said that she could not interfere with the clothes his wife ordered – or Mrs Cummings, and as both the bills were sent to him for payment what did he suggest she do? There was no answer to that so he paid up! What a hoot.'

As they parted company, Daisy walked home, chuckling over their conversation. She was indeed sorry to hear that the gown shop was losing business, but it wasn't her fault. Her boss had a choice, and she chose the wrong way when she fired her. If only things had been different. But life is full of what ifs.

★   ★   ★

Daisy tried to eat her meal listening to the account of her mother's visit to her father, but she pushed her food around her plate until it was time to leave for work.

'You take care,' said Vera. 'You work so hard, standing all them hours.'

'See you later,' said Daisy and thought *well I won't be standing so much tonight that's for sure*. She wondered what creation Flo had for her to wear? This time would it be a dress that was less demure, one which showed her attributes like the other girls? Well she certainly wouldn't dress like a tart, not for anyone!

Stella was waiting at the bar for her. She ordered a couple of gin and tonics for them and then took Daisy upstairs. Handing a drink to her she said, 'Here, get that down your throat, it'll relax you.'

Daisy's hands were trembling and she had to hold the glass with both hands.

Stella tried to make light of her nerves. 'No one is going to kill you, love, it's not that bad. As for the lucky young man, I couldn't have chosen better myself. He looks kind, but better still, he looks experienced. The room is booked for the whole evening, so enjoy yourself.'

'The whole evening, not just for the hour?' Daisy asked wide-eyed with terror.

'Yes, the evening. Listen, the poor bugger has spent enough money for you, it's worth more than a short time.'

Daisy looked up at Stella. 'What do I have to do? You have to help me here. I know nothing about sex.'

Seeing the fear mirrored in Daisy's eyes, Stella took pity on her and sat on the bed, instructing the young girl in the world of sex as only a prostitute could. But she was gentle in her way, trying to lead Daisy carefully into the act of seduction.

At the end of it all, Daisy said, 'I think I need another drink!'

'One more and no more,' said Stella. 'A punter and certainly your first won't want a drunk in his arms, especially after paying out so much. Just lay back and enjoy it is my advice to you above all else. Now let's get you dressed.'

Flo had laid out a simple white lace blouse with a high neck and a plain black silk skirt for Daisy to wear. The simplicity of it only enhanced her innocence and Stella thought how very clever of her employer. There wouldn't be one man in the bar that night who wouldn't want to have been the lucky punter and they would be queuing up to book her in the future. Her long luscious hair was brushed and gleaming, tied back with a satin black bow.

Stella took her into the room that was hers for the evening. It was softly lit. Fresh soap was ready in the washbasin, and a clean towel, and on the bedside table was a packet of contraceptives. Stella told Daisy to make sure every punter wore one.

'If they refuse, then you refuse to be with them. Don't forget, it's of the utmost importance. Shall we go?' asked Stella as there was a quiet knock on the door. 'The young man has arrived.'

As Daisy walked down the staircase with Stella, a hush descended over the bar as everyone watched her. Stella gave her hand a squeeze and led her over to Steven, who was waiting.

Twelve

Daisy sat at a table with Steven, her hands trembling so much she gripped them together in her lap. 'Everyone is staring at us,' she said.

'Don't take any notice. Would you like a drink?'

Shaking her head she said, 'No, thanks, let's just get on with it, shall we?' She wanted to escape the stares from the men sitting in the bar, many of whom had been on the list of bidders, hoping to be the chosen one. There was a feeling of resentment from some and an angry buzz from the girls as they watched the couple.

'As you wish,' said Steven who then rose from his seat and holding out his hand to Daisy, led her up the stairs to their designated room.

Once there, Daisy looked uncertain. 'Shall I get undressed?' she asked quietly.

Steven took her into his arms. 'There's absolutely no hurry,' he said. He tipped up her chin and kissed her softly on the cheek. 'I want you to enjoy this moment,' he told her and kissed her gently on the lips.

Daisy found herself slowly responding to his gentle persuasion and began to relax as Steven caressed her. As he continued his slow seduction, she felt him undoing the buttons at the back of her blouse, slipping it off her shoulders, then he kissed her bare neck, cupping her breast as he did so.

She caught her breath and stiffened at such intimacy.

'Relax,' he murmured, 'I'm not going to hurt you. I would never do that.'

Eventually they lay together on the bed. Daisy could hardly believe what was happening to her. Here she was in the arms of a man who was not her husband, devoid of most of her clothing, being made love to. But strangely, because it was Steven and not a complete stranger, she wasn't overcome with shame. Beneath his practised fingers, she was beginning to enjoy this strange intimacy.

He was talking softly to her, leading her in her first sexual encounter with delicacy and affection. He slowly explored her body with soft kisses and caresses. Making her feel special, with his words. What was it that Stella had said, 'Lay back and enjoy it?' And after a while, that's precisely what she was able to do, surprised by her own abandonment, as her body responded to unfamiliar feelings of passion.

Later, as she nestled within his arms, Daisy found herself puzzling over just exactly why her virginity had been worth so much money! Steven could have laid with any of the other girls and made love to them for very much less. As he took her maidenhead, she'd cried out, but was that worth *so* much? Surely not? Would she look any different, she wondered, when she was dressed and looked in the mirror, would people be able to tell she was no longer a virgin? She could hardly wait to see.

Steven draped a towel around his bare midriff and lit a cigarette for both of them. Daisy averted her eyes for a moment and then thought how ridiculous that was. This man had been naked as he had climbed on top of her before thrusting himself into her depths, so why now was she suddenly so shy? Nevertheless, she covered her bare breasts with the sheet.

Taking the offered cigarette she drew on it and spluttered.

Laughing, Steven said, 'I forgot you don't usually smoke, at least I've never seen you do so.'

She laughed and tried again, with greater success. 'I know, but I wanted it.' She lay back against the pillows. 'Will you be in the bar tomorrow?'

The smile faded. 'No, Gloria, I sail in the morning.'

She was shocked. 'When will I see you again?' she asked.

'I don't know, but if I was not sailing I doubt I would come here again.'

'Why ever not?'

He stared intently at her and said, 'Because I couldn't bear to see you take another man to a room for sex.'

She was devastated. In those few words he'd forced her to face the future. She'd been able to put such thoughts to the back of her mind as he had treated her like a lover and not a prostitute, carried away as she had been with the passion of the moment. She blinked back the tears which threatened.

'I see, well I can understand that. I just hope you feel that you got your money's worth tonight, that's all.'

He looked angry. 'Don't talk like that, it makes you sound hard and I know you're not.'

But he'd hurt her and she was on the defensive. 'Don't be silly, after all this was a business arrangement and nothing more. I would hate to think you felt short-changed in any way!'

'It was far more than that,' he cried. 'I wanted you to know what it's like to be made love to by someone who cares about you instead of some man who will come to you for their own pleasure with scant thought to you as a person. And believe me, Gloria, in this business there are too many of them.'

'I'm sure you're right, Steven, and believe me I am grateful to you, but it was unkind of you to point that out to me. You've ruined it all!'

He looked crestfallen. 'I'm sorry, I meant tonight to be something special.'

She was immediately contrite and caught him by the hand. 'It was special, Steven, and I am grateful to you, honestly I am. I'll never forget you, really I won't.'

He took her into his arms. 'Then let's not argue about it and enjoy the time left to us.'

Before the evening was over, they made love again but this time there was a certain urgency about it, as both knew it was goodbye.

Towards the end of the evening, they dressed. Steven drew her into his arms and kissed her. 'I hope you get what you want out of life, Gloria,' he said. 'I'll think of you often.' He walked over to the door, glanced back at her, then left.

Daisy walked over to the mirror and stared at her reflection. She didn't look any different! But she was different. She had taken her first punter. Now she was definitely one of Flo's girls.

The following night, Daisy took another man to her bed. She'd chosen him as he looked a gentleman and was well dressed. He'd not argued over the price he had to pay for her favours and had been one of the unlucky bidders for her first night.

There was no preamble with him. As soon as they got to the room he told her to get undressed. She lay, waiting, her hands shaking with nerves.

'For goodness' sake!' he exclaimed. 'Stop looking so scared. I'm not going to kill you, I'm going to fuck you!'

She recoiled at his vulgarity. There was no tenderness with him. He was there to get his money's worth and satisfy himself. Which he did – without tenderness, like a pig at a trough. When it was over, he got dressed and looked at her, without feeling. 'I'd have liked to have taken your cherry, darling, but that was almost as good. You were lovely and tight, not like some of the girls.'

Daisy flew to the toilet and was violently sick.

During the next few weeks, Daisy, as Gloria, was kept busy. Men queued for her favours, much to the displeasure of the other girls and she discovered how Steven's remarks as to how men would just use her were sadly true. She learned to shut out what was happening to her, while keeping control of what she would allow her punters to do. Stella had told her not to allow anything she didn't want.

'These bastards will try and get away with all kinds of sexual deviations. Things they would never ever ask of their wives, only of a whore. You decide what's acceptable to you.'

Daisy became hardened to this and more so towards her punters. She made the rules. No kissing, straight sex, any deviation, then book someone else . . . and she fixed the price. And still they came.

She followed Stella's example and looked on every man as money in the pot. Money for her father – and the rest for her business. She closed her eyes and ears to anything else. She changed. Her mother noticed and was saddened. Vera put it down to the extra hours she worked and the worry of her father's health, which now had run its course.

Daisy and her mother sat either side of Fred's bed, each holding a hand, waiting as death approached. Both silently praying for it to be over, to release the man, now skeletal with no quality of life – and when Fred eventually took his last breath, they were relieved, but shed tears for the man he had been. After, they clung together at the bedside, taking a last look at the man whom they both loved so deeply.

The funeral was a quiet affair. A few of their neighbours came. Agnes, from the gown shop and Stella, who was there to support her friend. As Daisy threw the handful of earth on to her father's coffin she at least felt that her sacrifice had not been in vain. During his final weeks, he'd been cared for in a way that would not have been possible had he been at home. It had also relieved the burden that would have been placed upon her mother. So now every penny she earned, apart from living expenses, would be put aside towards opening her own business. No one would stop her from achieving that.

The few mourners came back to Vera's house for sandwiches, tea or sherry. Daisy poured a stiff drink for herself and Stella. As she took a mouthful, Daisy said, 'Well that's that. Now I can move on. I have a future to build for Mum and me.'

Stella quaffed her drink and said, 'Well, Daisy, you have really surprised me.'

'What ever do you mean?'

'The way you have changed. I honestly didn't think you'd last as one of Flo's girls, not for a minute. I gave you two days at the most!'

Daisy gave a harsh laugh. 'Like you, Stella, it is a means to an end. If I had to lose my reputation for my father I decided that I might as well put it to good use and feather my own nest . . . or believe me, I would have fled before now. This is the only chance I have to build a future and I might as well take it.'

'Good for you. I've almost got enough money to build my own now and believe me I don't regret a minute and neither must you.'

'Oh, believe me, I regret every moment. When a stranger paws me and utters obscenities, I want to kill him. I hate what I've become with every fibre of my body, but I will make every man who wants me pay dearly for the privilege and when I eventually walk away, I'll remember how I had to work to make it. I know no man will want to marry me, knowing my background, and I'll never lie about it because if I do someone will remember and talk, but that's fine because I'll make another name for myself as a top-class couturier.'

Stella smiled and said, 'Good for you. I really admire your spirit and you will need it because your reputation will follow you for a while until you become established, then no one will give a damn. All they'll want is to be dressed by you, but before that, you'll have a battle on your hands.'

'Listen!' Daisy exclaimed. 'If I can put up with being one of Flo's girls, I can put up with anything if I have to.'

★ ★ ★

The following evening, Daisy was sitting at the bar talking to Harry, sipping her usual tonic water, when Ken Woods walked in and sat on a stool beside her.

Daisy didn't acknowledge his presence and continued to chatter to Harry.

'I want to book an hour with you,' said Woods. 'It's about time you made room for me on your list of punters.'

She looked at him coldly. 'I'm sorry, Mr Woods, but there never will be room for you among my clients,' and she started to get off the stool when he grabbed her by the arm.

'You are such a stuck-up little bitch!' he snapped. 'You think you are so special. Well let me tell you, girlie, flat on your back you ain't no different from any woman.'

'If that's the case, Mr Woods, why are you getting all fired up? Book one of the other girls, they don't cost as much anyway, you'll get more for your money!' And snatching her arm away, she walked to the back of the room and sat down with Stella.

'You keep away from that bugger,' warned Stella. 'He's been panting after you ever since you came here to work behind the bar.'

'I know,' said Daisy, 'he and his friend the butcher give me the creeps. No one could pay me enough money to take him on as a client.'

Flo entered the bar as they chatted and Daisy saw Woods waylay her and talk earnestly to her. Flo nodded and walked over to Daisy.

'Mr Woods . . .' she began.

'Don't bother, Flo,' interrupted Daisy. 'I'm not interested in him.'

'He's prepared to pay handsomely,' Flo argued.

'Not interested,' snapped Daisy.

'Well I bloody well am.' Flo's cheeks flushed with anger. 'You're losing me money!'

'Well, Flo, if you're so worried, you take him on.' Daisy glared at her employer daring her to argue further.

'You, my dear, are beginning to really piss me off with your attitude.'

'Am I? That works both ways. You agreed to the way I work and let's be honest I'm a bloody gold mine to you at the moment so don't kill the goose who lays your golden eggs!'

Flo stalked off towards her office.

'You take it easy with her,' said Stella. 'Flo can be a bad enemy, don't push her too far.'

'Listen, Stella, I know that my nights are numbered. The novelty of having me will wear off all too soon. Until then I'm going to make as much money as I can but I will pick the men and no matter how much that man Woods offered, it would never be enough!'

Daisy's next appointment arrived and she greeted him warmly as he ordered a drink. All the time she could feel the gaze of Ken Woods, following her every move.

Thirteen

There was a bad start to 1915. The upper Thames valley became flooded and Windsor Castle became an island in a lake. In January, the threat of Zeppelins became a reality as they crossed the Norfolk coast and bombed unsuspecting British towns, and, abroad, British troops defended the Suez Canal from Turkish troops. In March, the battle for supremacy launched the spring offensive in Ypres.

Captain Portman, with his company, was in the thick of the fighting, trying to capture a small hill. After detonating several mines, the hill had been secured. Hugh sat on a broken chunk of tree and lit a cigarette, sweat beading his forehead – thankful to still be alive. After taking his short break, he walked along the line of men, sheltering in dugouts, praising them for a job well done – proud of his men as he chatted to them, yet saddened when he was given the numbers of those who'd perished. But being a professional soldier, he knew that this was inevitable.

Later, he took the opportunity to write a few words to his wife, though God only knew when he'd be able to mail it. He pictured his home in Brockenhurst. The daffodils, in their hundreds, would soon be in bloom, the buds on the trees forming. He looked around at the devastation surrounding him, the mud, the barbed wire, the rotting bodies . . . yet this was his life and he revelled in it. His wife Grace could never even begin to understand.

Grace was sitting on a train heading for Southampton, gazing out at a very different scene. The verdant countryside, so fresh, watching the newborn lambs gambolling in the fields alongside their mothers and she thought how wonderful nature was. She'd kept busy helping rally her neighbours into knitting for the troops, helping out at the local hospital where she could and holding bazaars trying to collect money for parcels to send to the troops at the front. But today she was off to meet a friend for lunch and to shop.

After leaving the restaurant and bidding her friend goodbye, she walked along Above Bar, stopping to look in the window of one of the stores just as Daisy passed by.

'Daisy!' Grace called.

Turning round, Daisy was surprised to see Mrs Portman walking towards her.

'Daisy, how lovely to see you.'

Smiling, she greeted the woman warmly. 'How are you?' she asked.

'Oh, Daisy my dear, I have missed you so much. Madam Evans made a grave mistake in losing you.'

Daisy flushed with embarrassment. 'It's nice of you to say so.'

'Look, please come and have a cup of coffee with me,' urged Grace. 'I want to know how you are getting on.' She would brook no argument and Daisy found herself seated in a nearby coffee house, hoping that the woman wouldn't question her too closely.

Once she'd ordered, Grace said, 'Agnes told me why you were asked to leave, how ridiculous! I know you were working as a barmaid to earn extra money for your poor father, how is he?'

'Sadly he died at the end of last year,' Daisy told her.

'I am so sorry, my dear. So what are you doing now?'

'I'm still working at the club, but I'm saving my money. I want to open my own business.'

Grace clapped her hands with glee. 'What a perfectly splendid idea. You have a certain talent, Daisy, that shouldn't be wasted. I will certainly come to you when you do and I'll tell my friends. I would be able to bring you quite a bit of business.'

'That would be wonderful.'

With a thoughtful look Grace asked, 'Will you need a great deal of money to start?'

'I'm afraid so. Apart from renting premises, I need sewing machines, staff, materials, patterns and I would probably have to decorate whatever premises I get to make it attractive to my clients.' She sighed. 'I have some way to go yet.'

'Maybe not,' said Grace. 'Have you thought of taking on a partner? Someone who could help with the finances.'

Daisy shook her head. 'No I've not thought of that and I'm not at all sure it would work.'

'Why ever not?'

'Well, Mrs Portman, I have very definite ideas about the sort of clothes I want to make. I wouldn't like anyone to interfere on that side of the business and a partner might. I wouldn't put up with it.'

'And why should you! That is your line of expertise. I was thinking of a partner who would put up the rest of the money required, who perhaps looked after the books, sorted out the finance, you know, budgets, cost control, but leaving the artistic side to you.'

Daisy laughed. 'That sounds too good to be true!'

'I would be interested in such a deal, Daisy.'

'You?' She looked at the other woman in amazement. 'Why ever would you be interested?'

'I am going slowly crazy with Hugh away. I need an interest and I love fashion and the work that you do and I'm very good at figures; keeping the books would be right up my street, and that would keep me busy. I can't see why it wouldn't be a great success. What do you say?'

Daisy was completely flummoxed. 'I would need time to think about it.'

'Of course you would. I know this has come as a surprise . . . to me too!' And she laughed. 'But just think how exciting it would be?'

But Daisy was now worried. It all sounded wonderful, but she couldn't possibly accept. Grace had no idea how she was now earning her money; she probably thought that she was still just serving behind the bar. She couldn't possibly drag a lady like Grace Portman into business with a whore, not with her reputation. She couldn't, but how could she tell her?

'Come out to Brockenhurst on Sunday. Come for lunch; look I'll write down the time of the train and I'll have the groom meet you in the pony and trap.'

The curiosity of visiting Grace in her grand house overcame any other drawbacks and Daisy agreed. She would have to decline the offer but at least it would be nice to get out of the town and do so in pleasant surroundings, so she agreed.

At the Solent Club that evening as she sat waiting for her first client, Daisy chatted to Harry, who had steadfastly remained her friend.

'How much longer are you going to put yourself through this?' he asked as he polished some glasses.

'Until I have enough money for my own business. It's the only way I can save the money to do so.' But she knew that it would be some time until that had been achieved and as the weeks passed, the novelty of her being new to the string of girls was beginning to wear off; fewer men were now so anxious to pay her prices. Flo had already had a go at her about the situation.

'Well, I'm sorry,' she said, 'but you'll have to widen your choice of punters if this goes on.'

'What do you mean?' asked Daisy.

'Your chosen men are now moving back to the other girls. They're cheaper and they've had you, so why not save money!'

Daisy cringed at the basic description.

'Of course, there are those you've turned down who are still willing to cough up the dosh . . . like Ken Woods. His tongue's still hanging out for you.'

With flashing eyes Daisy said, 'Forget it! You know how I feel about the man.'

'That's all very well, but you are beginning to cost me money. If things don't improve, I'm afraid I'll have to book you anyone who asks. I can't afford your high-flying ideas. Those days are all but over my girl. Think about it,' and she stormed off.

Daisy was thinking about this as she talked to Harry. She loathed what she was doing with every passing day. As every man took his pleasure with her, she felt a little more of her self-respect being chipped away. And for every man who treated her well, there were those who made her feel like dirt beneath them. But she stuck it out and took their money. It would be wonderful to turn her back on it all and return to her sewing, and now the opportunity to do so was there, but she just couldn't take it. How very sad that made her feel.

On the Sunday, Daisy caught the train to Brockenhurst as directed by Grace Portman. On arrival a man wearing jodhpurs approached her.

'Miss Gilbert?'

'Yes, that's right.'

'Mrs Portman sent me to meet you. The trap's outside so if you'll follow me please?'

The man settled her and gave her a blanket to place over her knees, then with a click of his tongue and a sharp sting of his whip on the horse's flanks, they moved off.

How tranquil and beautiful this is, thought Daisy as they moved through the country lanes, passing several riders and walkers on what was a bright cool morning. When the trap turned into a wide drive and she saw the imposing Manor House before them, Daisy caught her breath. How magnificent it must be to live in such a place, surrounded by such lovely gardens. She realized that Grace Portman came from a wealthy background, but now seeing it for herself, she was overawed by it. There was no way she could expect a lady from such a background to become a partner. Her reputation would be in ruins if it ever got out that she was in business with a common prostitute.

Grace walked out of the heavy front door and met Daisy. 'I'm so pleased you came. Come inside; it's still quite chilly, so we'll have a drink to warm you.' And she ushered her into a spacious front hallway and then into a large sitting room, where a log fire was burning brightly. The aroma of the burning wood filled the air and was immediately comforting. Grace took Daisy over to a comfortable armchair by the fire and took her coat. She then walked over to a table filled with bottles and decanters of wine and poured out two glasses of sherry. Passing a glass to Daisy, Grace settled in a chair opposite.

'Cheers!' she said, and sipped the drink.

'Cheers!' said Daisy and did the same. The warmth of the alcohol slid down her throat and she savoured the taste. 'This is a splendid house, Mrs Portman.'

'Yes, I'm very lucky. It's been in Hugh's family for several generations. But it seems a bit like a mausoleum with him away. There's only me and the staff here. The house should be filled with children running around.'

'You don't have any?'

Grace looked sad as she said, 'No, unfortunately. My husband wanted us to wait until the war was over before we started a family. I didn't, but once he makes up his mind about anything, no one can make him change it, I'm afraid.'

'Never mind,' said Daisy, 'when he comes home, he'll be only too happy to do so. This war seems never-ending, especially as everyone seemed to think it would be over by Christmas.'

'Let's forget about the war, it's too nice a day to think about it. Come over to the window and look at the garden.'

They walked to the large bay window where expensive drapes were smartly held back by heavy cords ending in large tassels. This Daisy admired as she touched them.

'I thought you'd like them, with your artistic bent,' laughed Grace.

But the view from the window made Daisy gasp. There was a wide terrace outside with steps leading down to expansive lawns and flower beds. In the distance huge cedar trees stood out against the horizon.

'How beautiful,' said Daisy as she drank in the scene before her. 'You must have an army of gardeners to keep it so perfectly.'

'No such luck. They are all in the army, but I do have two older men who work very hard.'

A maid appeared and announced that lunch was served.

'I thought we'd have it through here instead of the large dining room; it's so much lighter and it catches the sun so well,' said Grace as she led Daisy to a conservatory filled with exotic plants. In the middle was a circular table set out for two. The aroma from the plants filled the air. The smell of hyacinths, in particular, filled Daisy's nostrils as she sat down and she felt as if she was in a different world.

The maid served them with a gently pungent leek and potato soup, with freshly made bread rolls, followed by roast beef and Yorkshire pudding with a selection of fresh vegetables. The lemon meringue pie which finished the meal was delicious.

When Daisy remarked on how succulent the beef was, Grace smiled at her appreciation.

'I'm lucky to have a cook who has been with the family for years and of course we get the beef from one of our farms nearby. We supply the army with it as well.'

The more she learned about Grace Portman the more Daisy realized how improbable it would be to be in partnership with her.

They returned to the fireside to drink their coffee and the moment Daisy had been dreading arrived.

Grace spoke. 'Now that you've had time to think over my proposition, what have you decided?' she asked.

Taking a deep breath Daisy said, 'Mrs Portman, I'm very grateful for the offer but I'm afraid I have to decline.'

There was a look of disappointment on the other woman's face. 'I would dearly like to know why, Daisy. You must have a good reason.'

Having spent time with Grace, a woman she both liked and admired, and seen the way she lived, Daisy made a brave decision.

'I couldn't possibly have you as my partner because your reputation would be in ruins. You see for the past few months, I've not
been working as a barmaid. To make the extra money I needed
for the care of my father I became one of Flo Cummings' girls. I
became a prostitute.'

Grace was stunned. She sat and looked at Daisy . . . and was
speechless.

'So you see, Mrs Portman, it would be impossible to accept your
offer. Had my circumstances been different . . .'

'Oh, Daisy! I am so very sorry that you were put in such a
dire position. Why ever didn't you come to me? I would have
helped you.'

The unexpected sympathy and kindness from such a cultured
lady overwhelmed Daisy and she fought the tears that threatened.
'It never ever occurred to me to come to you. You were one of
my clients.'

'But to have to do what you did, my God that was brave. Does
your mother know what sacrifice you made?'

'Good Lord no! She must never find out, she'd be so ashamed.'

'But, Daisy, if you accept my offer, you could walk away from
this life and start again!'

'How could I possibly involve you? My past is bound to come
out and you would be tainted by it if you were involved.'

'But don't you see, Daisy, once you are established the work
that you do is so exquisite that it would be a seven-day wonder
and would soon be replaced by your reputation as a designer?'

'And knowing now as you do all about me, you would still be
prepared to become my partner?'

'Absolutely!'

'No, you haven't thought this through,' Daisy insisted. 'Now it's
you who must take the time to think. You have a family name to
protect. Think of what your husband would say, your family – his
family. When you have, I think you'll realize it isn't viable.'

She rose to her feet. 'I think I should go now. I'll always remember
your kindness, this lovely house and spending today with you, but
I really think it must end here.'

'Very well, Daisy, but I will think about it. Give me your address
before you go. Here is a pen and paper. I'll have the groom take
you to the station.'

At the front door, Grace hugged Daisy and said, 'I'll be in touch.'

Daisy climbed into the trap and waved goodbye as they trotted down the drive. It had been such a memorable day, one that she would remember for a long time, but she'd been glad that she had told Grace Portman the truth, she owed her that much.

Fourteen

Vera Gilbert was grieving for her husband. She cleaned the house from top to bottom and then started all over again. The place seemed so empty. Although Fred had spent his final weeks in the nursing home, Vera had visited him every day, taking his washing home with her and washed and ironed it to take back the following day, but now she was at a loss to know how to fill her time . . . apart from this incessant cleaning and she knew that wasn't healthy.

Daisy was aware of this too and on Monday morning she told her mother to get dressed, as they were off for the day. 'Come on, Mum, we both need a change of scene – and wrap up warm. It's a bit sharp outside, certainly not at all like spring.'

They caught the train to Bournemouth. There was a sharp breeze coming off the Channel and they both pulled up the collars of their coats as they walked briskly along the promenade.

'Cor! This'll blow the cobwebs away,' Daisy remarked.

'It's just what I need,' grinned Vera. She felt renewed as she walked as if all the floss in her brain was being blown away. She needed to get on with life; Fred would have wanted it that way.

After a bit of window shopping, they went into a cafe and ordered fish and chips.

'Locally caught, it says on the menu,' Vera said, 'so it should be good.'

'Well you look better than I've seen you look in a while,' observed Daisy.

'I miss your dad.'

'I know and I miss him too and I'd give anything if he were here with us now, but I wouldn't want to see him here as sick as he was.'

'Me neither. It just takes time to adjust I suppose. The house is empty and I don't know what to do with myself,' Vera admitted.

Daisy peered across the table at her. 'You need to stop cleaning, Mum. It's becoming an obsession.'

'I know, I do know, honestly. I thought I might get my old hand sewing machine out. I used to be a good seamstress.'

'I remember; it was you that started me with a love for sewing.' Daisy sighed. 'I do miss it.'

'What happened to your private clients?' asked Vera. 'I haven't seen you sewing for some time'

This was true. Daisy hadn't pressed any of her old clients for further work in case they found out about her new role at the Solent Club. It seemed only right, but her fingers itched to get back to the work she loved.

'No one needs anything done at the moment,' she said hastily. 'Come on, let's go and do a bit of shopping.'

As they sat on the train on the way home, Daisy thought about Grace Portman's offer and wished with all her heart she could have accepted. How wonderful it would have been to open her own business and get back to being creative once again.

At the Manor House in Brockenhurst, Grace was having similar thoughts. Had it been just her, she wouldn't have hesitated in carrying out the new partnership, but Daisy had made a valid point. Her husband's family name. Hugh was very proud of his background. His family had all been army men and with great distinction. No way would he countenance any such liaison. He'd have blown a gasket at the very idea of a scandal and Grace, therefore, had to take that into consideration. Much to her chagrin.

Monday nights at the club were quiet and Flo's girls were sitting around, gossiping. As she had no bookings, Daisy decided to go home early. She was restless. All she could think about was opening her business – and looking around the establishment where she was forced to sell herself was beginning to pall more each night. How much longer could she put up with this sordid means to an end? It hadn't helped when Stella told her she would be leaving at the end of the week.

'At last I've got enough money to make a new start,' she gleefully told Daisy.

'What are you going to do?'

'I'm going to open a little seaside cafe. Believe it or not, I'm a bloody good cook and I've found a little place that's ideal. I'll cook breakfasts and lunch, then afternoon tea and scones – and close in the evenings. I don't want to wear myself to a frazzle. Once I'm established if I think an evening trade would work, I could give it a try too.'

'And where is this little cafe?'

'On the Isle of Wight. Bembridge. Nice little spot. Mind you it might just be a holiday trade, I'll have to see, but hopefully my cooking will be good enough to keep open in the winter with just local trade. Oh, Daisy, I can't wait to walk out of this door for the last time.'

'I shall miss you, Stella. I'll be out of here too as soon as I can. But not for a bit, sadly. The punters are dropping off now. I'm no longer a novelty.'

'But you *are* different, Daisy love. You still maintain that air of innocence; you've not lost that, despite everything.'

Daisy laughed harshly. 'Not outwardly maybe but inside I hate what I've become.'

'It's just a job. Look at it like that and it becomes easier. But don't hang around too long or you'll never leave! You may have to lower your sights a little. The shop you want may have to become one room to begin with. Have you thought about that?'

'No, to be honest. I've always looked at the bigger picture.'

'Then think about it, please.'

As she walked home, Daisy thought over Stella's words. It certainly would be a way to get out of this life sooner than she thought. She would seriously consider it. After all she had to start some-where. If Agnes would work for her, she would only have to buy two sewing machines and a limited amount of material. She'd sit down and work out her finances.

She was so wound up with her thoughts that she was unaware that she was being followed until she was roughly grabbed from behind.

'Hey! What do you think you're doing?' she cried as she struggled.

'I'll have you one way or another.' Ken Woods dragged her into a side alley. 'I was prepared to pay, but no, you bitch, you thought you were too good for me. Well now I'll take you for free!'

Daisy fought for all she was worth as the man tried to kiss her, but he was a big man and powerful. His wet mouth covered hers and she gagged. She could smell the stale alcohol on his breath. When he stopped, she balled her fist and with as much strength as she could she punched him in the face.

He cursed her and grabbed for her breast.

Daisy brought her knee up sharply and caught him in his genitals with as much force as she could muster.

The man cried out and doubled up with pain – and she fled. She ran until she had to stop for breath, clutching her side as the cramp hit her. She listened carefully but could hear nothing. Leaning back against the wall she slowly recovered. With trembling fingers, she lit a cigarette, drawing deeply on the nicotine in an effort to calm herself. Then looking around carefully, she began to walk home, constantly looking over her shoulder, ready to run should Woods appear again.

Her hands were still shaking as she tried to put the key in the lock of her front door and she prayed that her mother wouldn't be sitting by the fire when she entered, knowing that her blouse had been torn in the struggle.

Fortunately for her, Vera was in the kitchen. She called to her as she went upstairs to change. 'Hello, Mum, put the kettle on. I've decided to call it a night.'

Upstairs, she took off her damaged garment and put on a different one, pushing the torn blouse to the back of a drawer. She washed her face and tidied her hair. Still shaken by the incident, she took a deep breath and walked downstairs.

'What are you doing home so early?' asked Vera.

'Business was so slack I thought I'd come home,' explained Daisy.

'Nice of Harry to let you off,' her mother said.

'Harry?' For a moment Daisy forgot that her mother thought she was still working behind the bar. 'Oh, yes, Harry. He didn't mind. There was barely enough trade to keep him going.'

'You all right love? You look a bit pale.'

'I'm just a bit tired that's all,' Daisy hastily replied. But Woods had scared her and she knew that somehow she had to get out of working as one of Flo's girls . . . and soon.

Vera sat quietly by the fire and glanced over at her daughter. Something was wrong but obviously Daisy wasn't going to confide in her. Vera was concerned. Daisy had changed so much over the past weeks. She'd lost her joyful disposition. Even when Fred had been at home and things were difficult, Daisy had always managed to be cheerful, but lately she'd lost that happy frame of mind. It wasn't just tiredness, there was more to it than that, Vera was sure. Her attitude to life had hardened. She'd become cynical. She had gained in confidence but with that came a certain harshness, which was quite unlike the young girl she was used to. Perhaps the loss of her father had done that, but of this, Vera was not at all sure. She didn't like the change, that was certain, but was at a loss as to how she could approach Daisy.

'I'm off to bed, Mum,' said Daisy, and the moment for further conversation was lost.

At the Solent Club the following evening, Daisy confided in Harry and told him of her encounter with Ken Woods.

As he listened, Harry was angry. He'd taken to this young girl and it broke his heart to see her used by the men she took to her room. But when he heard about her lucky escape, he was livid.

'That bastard!' he exclaimed. 'I'll have something to say to him!'

'Oh, Harry, don't do that or you'll make things worse. He's not a man to be crossed.'

'I don't care! He can't get away with this. He was going to rape you, girl, and who knows how badly he'd have hurt you. He has to be stopped!' He was called away to serve a customer.

Daisy was now very worried. If Harry interfered how would Woods react? The menace in his voice when he attacked her was terrifying; Harry might get hurt if he tackled the man. She would go to Flo and tell her. She was the one to deal with the situation.

Flo was dismissive. 'If you had taken him on as a client, you wouldn't have put yourself in any danger, but oh, no, not you, madam. You made your own rules and now see where it got you!'

Daisy was horrified by the coldness of the other woman. 'You don't give a damn do you?' she cried. 'All that is important to you is how much money you make.'

'I run a business; it was your choice to join my girls and you'll have to face any consequences. It has nothing to do with me. As long as Ken Woods behaves himself in my club, what he does outside is none of my business.'

'But what about Harry? He says he's going to have words with him?'

'I shall tell Harry on no account is he to interfere or he'll be out of a job!'

Daisy couldn't believe what she was hearing. 'You are a heartless bitch, Flo!'

The woman ignored her.

She would tell Harry herself not to do anything, Daisy decided. He'd worked in the bar for years. She couldn't let him jeopardize his position.

But Harry was not at all fazed by the news. 'Flo won't sack me,' he said with a wry smile. 'I know too much, so don't you worry about me, love. I won't come to any harm either from Ken Woods or Flo Cummings.'

But Daisy couldn't help but worry.

Harry had lived and worked around the dock area of Southampton all his life and knew his way around. He collected information. People who came into the bar chatted and confided in him, knowing that he kept everything to himself. He knew most of the business people who worked and owned businesses and also was on talking terms with a few villains as well. This way he knew all the dodgy dealing that went down. He was well aware that Ken Woods used to skim off the top from the many items that came to be stored in his warehouse. Information that the police would be only too happy to know.

So it was with confidence that he visited Woods' warehouse the next morning. He knocked on the man's office door and walked in.

Ken looked up from his desk, surprised to see who was calling on him.

'Hello, Harry. A bit out of your usual habitat aren't you? What can I do for you?'

He didn't beat about the bush. 'You can leave Gloria alone! I heard about you attacking her the other night; bit desperate weren't you? After all you can have any woman in the club. It's not as if you are short of a sexual gratification.'

The man's eyes flashed angrily. 'What I do is none of your business! Had that little bitch given me the time of day, I wouldn't have touched her.'

Harry leaned over the desk. 'You ever lay a finger on her again, Ken Woods, and the police will be informed about your habit of creaming off the top of your goods and the stuff you hide in your warehouse, that's illegal.'

The man's face flushed with rage. 'You dare to come in here and threaten me? Want to be found floating in the dock one night, do you?'

Harry just stared at him. 'In a safety deposit box at my bank I have a large envelope to be opened after my death. It's all written down there, my friend, every single detail about your business, so any ideas you may have about my demise would be foolish. Frankly I don't give a shit about your dodgy dealings, you'll get caught one day, but you touch that girl again and I'll see you go down for a long time!'

Woods stared at Harry's retreating figure as he walked out of his office and cursed under his breath. There was no way he could call the man's bluff; he had too much to lose. He'd wait a while, but he was going to have that girl one day – however long it took. No woman was going to treat him with such disdain and get away with it.

Fifteen

After her debacle with Ken Woods, all Daisy could think about was getting out of the Solent Club. She'd worked out her finances and if she could find a room somewhere at a cheap rent, she figured she could just about do it. With this in mind, she put an advertisement in the local paper and a few newsagents who placed such adverts in their windows. She then called on Agnes and put her proposition to her.

'When I find a room, will you come and work with me?'

'Like a shot. The workroom hasn't been the same since you left and if I have to put up with that Jessie much longer, I'll smack her in the face!'

Daisy laughed at the idea. 'Oh, Agnes, I'd pay money to see you do it.'

'Don't tempt me! Any idea when this will happen?'

'It will depend on any answer I get from the adverts I've placed around, but as soon as I do, I'll let you know, but not a word to any of the others,' warned Daisy. She hugged herself. 'I can't wait to get back to sewing.'

'Working behind the bar getting you down?' asked Agnes.

'You could say so, and I love my sewing and just long to get back to normal.'

'Now your dad has sadly gone, then you don't have the expense of the nursing home, which must make life financially a bit easier, but you did a fine thing there, Daisy. You're a good daughter. Your dad would be proud of you.'

If only she knew, thought Daisy. And that night when she had a punter who treated her roughly, despite looking like a young gentleman, she asked herself how much longer could she do this? And then later, when Bert Croucher walked into the club, she froze, waiting for his mate to walk in as well, but Croucher remained alone.

As he poured the man a beer, Harry asked, 'Where's your mate then?'

'Haven't seen him for a couple of days. I did catch sight of him yesterday morning coming out of the bank. He was limping a bit I thought, perhaps he's had a fall, but he was gone before I could catch up with him.'

As Croucher walked back to his seat, Harry grinned to himself. He was probably limping after being kneed in the balls, he concluded, and that gave the barman immense pleasure.

Daisy was well aware that the butcher was watching her throughout the evening as she took her punters upstairs. His constant gaze unnerved her somewhat and she was pleased to see him go, towards closing time.

'Want me to walk you home, love?' asked Harry as Daisy was ready to leave.

She was about to refuse, but she suddenly changed her mind. 'If you take me to the end of my street, that would be great,' she said.

Despite the fact that she held Harry's arm as he kept up a constant conversation, Daisy felt unnerved and kept glancing behind her. Although she couldn't see anyone apart from the occasional seaman heading for the docks, she felt as if somewhere in the dark, they were being followed.

At the end of her street, she bade goodnight to Harry.

'I'll just stand here and watch you to your door, love,' he said and Daisy was grateful. When she put her key in the door, she turned and waved to Harry, and let herself into the house. But a few minutes later when she peeped out of the corner of the curtain, she thought she saw a shadowy figure standing down the street a way, but couldn't see who it was in the dim lighting. Locking the front door and checking that the back one was secure, she went to bed.

The week went from bad to worse for Daisy. She'd had to drop her prices and be less choosy with her punters to make any money at all, which delighted the other girls.

'Not such a good catch now are you, ducky,' said one. 'You're spoiled goods now, just like the rest of us. Pretty soon you'll be pleased to take anyone!'

Daisy ignored her even though she spoke the truth. It was becoming very apparent that men coming into the club were now used to seeing her and to them she became another of the girls . . . no one special. Flo had started booking her appointments without asking her and, to make the money she needed, Daisy couldn't argue, but for every man who laid his hands on her, she made herself think only of the money.

But the final straw was when she returned home one night and found Vera sitting by the dying embers of the fire, in tears.

Daisy rushed to her side. 'Mum, whatever is the matter, are you ill?'

Vera looked at her and sobbed, 'Daisy how could you?'

The look of anguish on her mother's face made her go cold. 'Whatever do you mean?' she asked fearfully.

'How could you become one of Flo Cummings' girls?'

Daisy was speechless.

'I met Mrs Cummings in the grocery store this morning. She said how sorry she was to hear about your father and then she told me how hard you had worked to pay for the nursing home. She told me she knew it hadn't been easy for you to decide to work the other side of the bar and she admired you for doing so. She also went to great lengths to tell me it was nothing to be ashamed of!' Then she burst into tears.

Daisy closed her eyes in despair. Then she tried to explain to her mother that Fred had said he wanted to stay in the nursing home until the end. 'We couldn't have given him the care he needed, Mum. At least his last days were with people who could help him with the pain. At home he would have really suffered. I couldn't let that happen.'

'But at what cost, Daisy, at what cost? And why didn't you leave once your father had gone? Why stay on?'

'I need the money to open my own business, how else could I get it?' she asked defiantly. 'My reputation was already in ruins, so I had nothing more to lose.'

'What about your self-respect?'

'I lost that with my first punter!'

'Oh, Daisy, don't talk like that. I can hardly bear to think of what you've done.'

Now Daisy was angry. 'You think I enjoy it? I hate every minute. Every time a man touches me, I feel dirty! Every time I take his money, I feel dirty! Believe me, Mother, I've lost far more than my self-respect but I'd do it all over again for Dad, if I had to.'

Vera wiped her tears. 'I know you did it with the best intentions,

and I know your father benefited by it, but to be honest had he
known how you earned the money, he wouldn't have budged out
of this house!'

'Yes, well he didn't know did he?'

'And I thank God for that, but I know. When is it all going to
end?'

'I've advertised for a room to rent so I can set up a small workshop. Agnes is going to work with me and as soon as I can get a
place, I'm leaving the Solent Club for good.'

'But will you get any clients?' asked her mother.

'With my reputation do you mean?' said Daisy wryly. 'Well,
Mum, not everybody knows what I've become, but I'm a bloody-
good seamstress and I know the right people to contact. I'll get
work all right. These clients are only interested in good clothing,
nothing more. And I'll have you know one of my wealthy clients
wanted to come into partnership with me.'

'But she didn't know where you've been working!'

'That's where you're wrong. I told her. She was still willing but
I turned her down.'

'Why ever did you do that when it would have given you the
opportunity you wanted?'

With a sigh Daisy explained. 'She comes from a wealthy family
and should it ever get out that I worked for Flo Cummings, I
didn't want her to be involved in a scandal, not from her background. It wouldn't have been fair.'

'Oh Daisy, another sacrifice you had to make. Life really isn't
fair is it?'

Daisy knelt beside her mother. 'It won't be for much longer.
We'll soon be able to put all this behind us and start again. Now
come on, it's late. Off to bed with you.'

Vera cried herself to sleep. She was well aware of the sacrifice
her daughter had made but she couldn't shake off a feeling of
shame. Her Daisy was a whore. It was a mother's nightmare.

Downstairs, Daisy sat staring into what was left of the fire, silent
tears trickling down her cheeks. She was devastated that her mother
had found out that she'd been working as one of Flo's girls. She
loved Vera dearly but knowing her mother so well, Daisy knew
that Vera would be shamed by the knowledge. Whereas Daisy had
steeled herself to cope with the situation, she doubted that her
mother would ever get over it. No matter what happened if she

managed to start afresh, her mother would always know how she earned the money to do so.

With a deep sigh, she brushed away her tears and went to bed.

Spurred on by her mother's revelation, Daisy decided to make the rounds of the estate agents in the hope that one of them would know of a decent room to rent. The first three hadn't anything on their books, but took her address in case in the future they had something to offer. She decided to try one more and then call it a day.

As she opened the door and walked in, the man behind the desk looked up. To Daisy's acute embarrassment she recognized him as one of her regular punters.

'What on earth are you doing here?'

'I'm looking to rent a room,' she told him.

'Setting up on your own?' he asked archly.

'Certainly not!' she exclaimed. 'I'm a seamstress by trade and I want a large room to open as a workroom.'

'My, but you're full of surprises!'

'It has to be big enough to house two sewing machines, a table for cutting out and enough space to receive clients.'

'And if I find you one, can I be one of your clients?' he asked with a sly smile.

'I don't make clothes for gentlemen,' she replied, ignoring his implication.

'If you find such premises, does that mean you'll be leaving the Solent Club?'

'Yes it does.'

'That would be such a pity,' he said: 'I would miss being with you. Perhaps if I find you such a place, we could come to an understanding and I could come to you privately.'

She felt demeaned and angry at his suggestion and turned towards the exit. 'Never mind, I'll go elsewhere,' she snapped and walked out, slamming the door behind her. As she walked away, Daisy was shaken by the meeting. It hadn't occurred to her that she could perhaps encounter her clients outside the club. By being selective in the beginning, she had chosen several men who were in business in the town and who came from decent backgrounds and no doubt in the future she would meet others. How embarrassing that would be! But it was one of the perils of choosing to work in the club and the possibility would have to be faced. She just hoped she wouldn't be with her mother when it happened.

Later that evening, the man from the estate agency came into the Solent Club and asked for Gloria. When she walked over to him, he smiled at her. 'Are you free?' he asked.

She couldn't refuse him as she needed the money.

Once in the room he removed his tie and shirt then said, 'I have a proposition.'

'And what is that?' she asked.

'I'll tell you after,' he said as he removed his shirt and trousers.

Eventually, he lay beside her and said, 'After you left my office this morning I thought I could solve your problem of finding a workshop. I have a nice flat on my books; it has a large front parlour that would be admirable for your needs.'

'But I couldn't afford a flat,' she protested.

'You wouldn't have to. I'll pay the rent, you can use the room and live there and I'll be free to visit you when I want to. I'll treat you well, give you money and look after you. What do you say?'

'You don't understand!' Daisy retorted. 'I want to give up this way of life. I want to be Daisy Gilbert, seamstress, not Gloria, whore!'

He chuckled quietly. 'Daisy, so that's your real name. I find that rather sweet and you wouldn't be a whore, you'd be my mistress.'

She got off the bed and started dressing. Looking at her would-be benefactor she said, 'Mistress? It's just a different name. I'm sure you meant it kindly, but no thanks.'

'If you change your mind, you know where to find me,' he said and he too started to get dressed before paying for her services.

Sitting at the bar later, Daisy thought about the man's offer, knowing that several of Flo's girls would have jumped at the chance of being a man's mistress as opposed to working in the club, but that wasn't what she wanted. She wanted a normal life back. And that was no way to get it.

Sixteen

It was a further two weeks before Daisy heard any news about a room to rent, but one morning there was a letter on her mat from a newsagent saying he'd one advertised and she hurried off to see it.

The room was large and at the back of a shop with its own side entrance. It was in decent condition and large enough for her needs. The shopkeeper said it was surplus to his requirements and he would welcome a rental for its use. Daisy was thrilled as it was just what she was looking for.

They chatted about the going rate, but after her experiences, Daisy was now a hardened businesswoman and she managed to bargain for a better price than he was asking. Eventually they shook hands on the deal and she arranged to take it over a week hence.

As she walked away she felt as if a weight had been lifted from her shoulders. At last she could put the past behind her and get back to the work she loved, but there was a lot to be done, meantime.

She visited a place that sold second-hand treadle sewing machines and purchased two. She bought a long foldaway table and asked for it to be delivered when she opened and she then contacted Agnes.

The two girls met after Agnes finished work to plan the new venture.

'You'll have to give Madam a week's notice,' said Daisy, 'and we may not have any work for a short time, but Mrs Portman said she'd come and bring her friends. I'll get in touch with my private clients and meantime make a few things to show people when they call.'

'Oh, Daisy,' cried Agnes, 'how exciting. I can hardly wait! It'll give me great pleasure to leave London Road. I really hate it there now; the atmosphere is so bad in the workroom and Madam Evans seems so bad-tempered all the time. But then she's lost business since you left.'

'I'm sorry to hear that but that was her own fault,' said Daisy. 'She paid for her mistake.'

'You can contact the ladies who have left her,' Agnes suggested.
'I don't know where they live.'

'I can get that information for you,' said her friend with some glee. 'I have my book of measurements and inside are the clients' names and addresses. I'll bring it round on Sunday if you like?'

'That would be lovely,' said Daisy with a broad smile. 'After all it's not like I'm pinching them from her if they've already left.'

'Exactly!'

After the girls parted, Daisy rushed home to share the good news with her mother.

'That's wonderful news,' said Vera. 'When do you open?'

'I take over the shop in a week's time and Agnes will be joining me. She's giving me addresses of some old clients and Mrs Portman in Brockenhurst said she'd come so I must let her know. Hopefully it won't take too long until we start making money.'

'I'm delighted for you, love,' said her mother, but her enthusiasm was somewhat muted.

Knowing her mother as well as she did, Daisy was certain that Vera was remembering how she made her money which enabled her to do all this, but that was unfortunate and her mother would have to learn to accept the fact. Nothing was going to spoil her happiness at achieving her goal.

That evening at the club, Daisy spoke to Flo and told her she would be leaving at the end of the week. She decided to see the week out which would earn her a bit more money to go into the kitty. After all, she had nothing to lose now and it would be more money to buy materials for the new garments.

Flo Cummings was astonished at the news. 'Why are you leaving?' she asked.

'I'm going back to my sewing, but this time I'm working for myself!'

This put Flo in a dilemma. Whatever she'd said to Daisy about not now being any different from the other girls, wasn't strictly true. She was still of value to her, but on the other hand, she loved the clothes that Daisy had made for her and being a woman proud of her appearance she was torn between a business loss but a more personal gain.

'Well this is a surprise,' she told Daisy. 'However your heart and soul was never in this game, but you are a superb seamstress; I wish

you good luck. If I come to you, will you take me on as a client?'
She was uncertain of the response.

'Why not, Flo,' said Daisy, 'after all as you've said to me many
a time, business is business!'

Flo Cummings burst out laughing. Whatever Daisy might think,
these past months had made her a shrewd woman, so it hadn't
all been a waste, even though she really wasn't cut out to be a
whore.

'Let me know where you are and when you open and I'll be
round.'

'I'd better warn you, Flo, I'll be expensive!' said Daisy with a
sly smile, which only brought forth more laughter.

'I wouldn't expect anything else,' laughed Flo. 'You'll do all
right, girl. You're made of the right stuff and have the talent to
go with it.'

Daisy then went over to Harry and told him she'd be leaving
and why. The barman beamed from ear to ear and he gave her a
big hug. 'That's the best news I've had for a long time, girl. I
couldn't be happier for you if you were my own daughter.'

At the Manor House in Brockenhurst, the atmosphere was completely
different. Grace Portman stood by the large window, holding a
telegram in her hand, staring across the vast grounds, yet seeing
nothing. Her mother, visiting for the day, bustled into the room.

'The vicar has left a note about the church bazaar,' she said,
'and he wants you to get in touch with him before the weekend.'

Grace didn't move. 'Hugh's dead!' she exclaimed.

Victoria Hargreaves stared at the rigid back of her daughter and
asked, 'What do you mean, he's dead?'

Turning round to face her mother, she held out the telegram.
'He's dead, killed on active duty.'

Her mother took the telegram and read it. Then enfolding Grace
in her arms she said, 'Oh, darling, I am so sorry.'

But Grace didn't cry. She strode angrily across the room. 'Stupid
fool! That's typical of Hugh, so gung-ho about everything. He
couldn't wait to go to the front with his men. I wanted a baby
but all he would say was, "We'll wait until the war is over, darling,
then we'll start a family". He wouldn't be moved on the subject
– and now it's too bloody late!'

And the tears began to flow.

'I longed for children. Had we had one at least I'd have something of his to hold. Now there is nothing. Nothing!'

Victoria poured a glass of brandy from the side table and gave it to Grace. 'Here drink this, you're in shock and it will do you good.' But her mind was racing. There would be a funeral to arrange . . . but would her son-in-law's body be sent home she wondered? She'd ring her husband and ask him to come over. Grace would need all the help she could get to help her through this terrible time.

The news of Daisy's departure soon spread among the clientele of the Solent Club and she was kept busy during her last few days. But this time as she took each man to her bed, she counted every penny equating it to another roll of cloth or a batch of patterns to be bought for her new business.

The more gentlemanly of her punters voiced their regret at her leaving, but some took delight in using her and treating her like a meal to be devoured, greedily. She smothered the hate in her heart for such men and counted the pennies. But deep down she despised and regretted what she had become.

When at last she said goodbye, the girls who had been furious at her for taking some of their punters were more than pleased to see her go, but dear Harry was quite emotional about her leaving.

'I wished you had never come here in the first place, love, but I'm really going to miss you. I'll call in and see you from time to time, if that's all right with you. Just to make sure you're alive and kicking.'

She gave him the address of her workshop and said, 'You come any time you like. I shall miss you too, so make sure you call in often.'

As she walked home, there was a definite spring in her step. From this moment her past would be put behind her. Once again she would be Daisy Gilbert, seamstress. How great that felt. She only wished she knew where Steven was so she could tell him her good news. He was the only man she would remember. He had been so kind and thoughtful when he paid all that money to take her virginity. He had made love to her with great tenderness and she had felt safe in his arms . . . after that didn't really bear thinking about.

As she rounded a corner, she collided with a man. It was so unexpected, she screamed in fright.

'It's all right, Gloria, it's only me.'

As she looked into the cold eyes of Bert Croucher, her legs began to shake.

'I hear you're leaving the Solent Club?'

'Yes that's right,' she said, trying not to show her fear.

'Shame,' he said. 'I really wanted to be with you, but Flo wouldn't let me. Don't suppose you and I can come to some arrangement?'

Daisy's stomach turned at the thought. 'Sorry, Mr Croucher, but those days are behind me now,' and she tried to walk past him, but he caught her by the arm.

'If you change your mind, call into the shop.'

She pulled her arm away. 'I am no longer in that business,' she said and hurried away. She wanted to run, but she could feel his gaze following her so just walked quickly, hardly daring to breathe until she reached her house and let herself in. Once safe in the confines of her home, she leaned against the wall until her limbs stopped shaking.

'You all right, Daisy?' called her mother from the kitchen.

'Yes, I'm fine,' she answered as she took off her coat. She sat in the chair and lit a cigarette, a habit she had acquired when working. It used to calm her down and she really needed calming after her encounter with the butcher.

'You look a bit pale, are you sure you're all right?' asked Vera as she walked into the living room.

'Yes, Mum. I've been rushing that's all.'

'I'll make you a cup of cocoa before you go to bed. I expect you're looking forward to your new business?'

Daisy smiled. 'Not half! I can't wait until the morning. My sewing machines arrive, and the patterns and material. Agnes and I'll clean the place and then the next day we can start making a few garments. I'll write to my old clients and the ones that have left Madam Evans, then I'll write to Mrs Portman and tell her the good news. She promised to bring me lots of trade.'

But when Daisy's letter arrived at the Manor House, it was put aside with others from people who had written to Grace with their sympathy at her loss. She'd opened one or two but couldn't face the others and they had been put to one side – Daisy's among them.

Seventeen

Daisy and Agnes worked all day long, washing down walls and paintwork, scrubbing floors and arranging the sewing machines in the best place and putting the table up, ready to start cutting out garments the following day. Then Daisy sat and wrote letters to various clients, stopping to mail them on the way home. Tomorrow the sewing would begin.

The next two weeks passed quickly as Agnes and Daisy worked non-stop, making garments for display. Despite advertising in the local paper and writing to her previous clients, orders were slow coming in and Daisy began to worry. She'd budgeted carefully. She had enough money to pay Agnes' wages and the rent for the premises for three months, but after that if they didn't have much business — she was in trouble.

One or two of her private clients called and ordered something, but she'd heard nothing from Grace Portman, which was a surprise. Grace had been so enthusiastic about her starting up and Daisy had relied on her promise of customers.

Grace had been occupied. The army had sent the body of her husband home and she and her parents had a funeral to arrange. Clara Portman, her mother-in-law, a controlling woman, had tried to take over the arrangements, but Grace would have none of it.

'I'm more than capable of arranging my own husband's funeral,' she informed her, sharply. There was no love lost between the two women.

Clara had not been pleased at her son's choice of bride. At the time of their engagement she'd said to Charles her husband, 'The girl may be good looking, but she's strictly middle class!' She had hoped that Hugh would choose one of the daughters of her lady friends who came from the upper echelon of society, not a mere general practitioner's daughter! And the fact that her daughter-in-law had a rod of steel running through her, enough to show her independence and run her own life, had not sat well with Clara Portman and now she was pushed out of arranging the funeral.

Hugh was buried at the local church with full military honours, his coffin draped with the Union Jack with his hat and medals on the coffin beside Grace's flowers. On seeing this Clara was infuriated.

'Our flowers were put with all the others, not on the coffin where they should be!' she complained to her husband, who remained silent at her outburst. Charles Portman liked his daughter-in-law and was secretly full of admiration for the way Grace handled his difficult wife.

Giles Bentley walked up to Grace as she left the church. 'I'm so terribly sorry for your loss, Grace.' And he tucked his arm through hers. 'If there is anything I can do, you only have to ask you know.'

His closeness was comforting. Giles was an easy man to be with. He seemed to have a capacity to be there at the right time, quiet and yet with a presence.

'You can come to my rescue at the wake,' said Grace. 'I'm dreading it.'

'I'll come to the rescue when I think you need it, will that do?'

'That would be wonderful.'

The Manor House dining room held a splendid buffet with which to feed the mourners. The cook had worked extremely hard to do her late employer proud and Clara, prepared to be critical as she walked into the room after the funeral, had to admit that the buffet was excellent.

Grace coped well with the guests, and Giles, as promised, stepped in to rescue her from overzealous mourners, but as the time wore on she wished they would all go home, including her mother-in-law. She said as much to Giles, so he walked her through the crowd and out into the garden. He fetched her a glass of sherry and they both sat down at the top of the steps leading to the garden.

'Here, drink this,' he said. 'It will do you good. Everyone will be going soon and then you can breathe. You've done very well; Hugh would be proud of you.'

'And you have been my knight in shining armour, coming to

my rescue. Honestly some people are so depressing. I know it's a funeral but . . .'

He chuckled softly. 'Ah well, some do like to play Uriah Heap at such times. It's like a drama to them.'

'But I wanted them to tell me about Hugh when he was alive – to share their memories and some did of course, but so many were full of doom and gloom. One woman came up to me like a black widow spider and in a sad voice asked me how I was feeling. I said I was fine as long as no one asked me! Thankfully you honed in on those and came to my rescue.'

'I could always tell by the expression on their faces,' he explained.

Grace drank the sherry and stood up. 'I'd better go and play my part,' she said. And he let her go.

Her own mother, Victoria, came over to her and asked, 'How are you holding up, darling?'

'I've really had enough; I just wish everyone would go. If I have to listen to Clara much longer there may be another funeral to arrange! She keeps telling me what to do with my life now that I'm a widow and how the responsibility of running Manor House and all that goes with it is too much for me. Dear God! Who does she think has been running it since Hugh went away?'

'Ah well, dear, Clara wants to get her fingers in the pie again. You be careful she doesn't want to move back in and take over.'

'Over my dead body! Oh Lord, what a terrible thing to say, today of all days! She hated moving out when we got married, she wanted to remain the lady of the manor, but it was Hugh's father's decision for Hugh to take over and run the estate when he retired. He said he wanted to enjoy what was left of his years. I bet the old trout gave him a hard time over that decision.'

'Look, darling, people are beginning to leave. It'll soon be over then you'll be able to relax.'

'But tomorrow is the reading of the will and that woman will be back again! I need another drink,' said Grace and walked away, thanking people for coming as she took another glass of sherry from the maid.

Unaware of all this drama that Grace Portman was having to face, Daisy was sewing an intricate piece of embroidery and beading on an exquisite evening blouse. Agnes looked up from her own sewing to watch her.

'That is going to be beautiful,' she said. 'None of us back in London Road could ever match your expertise.'

'But you are superb at pin tucks,' Daisy replied. 'I used to find them so fiddly.'

'Ah well, we're a good team,' Agnes said. 'I just hope we get some more business soon.'

'It takes time, Agnes. Word has to get about that we are now open for business. You see, it will all happen at once and we won't know where to turn.' But inside she was praying that this would come to pass.

Ken Woods had heard about Daisy leaving the club and opening up in Bernard Street. He walked past the premises one morning on his way to the bank and saw the notice on the door. *Gilbert. Gowns à la Mode.* He smirked to himself. A la Mode! Bit swish for a whore. But at least he knew where she was and he had a score to settle with that girl. Well he could wait for his opportunity. He'd keep an eye on the place, meantime.

Bernard Street was a busy place, near the docks and the Docks railway station. It was here that the passengers for the transatlantic liners arrived and the many troops waiting to be shipped to the front. It was also essential to ship horses abroad. It was quite a sight to see them wending their way through the streets leading to the ships waiting for them. Some days when she took a break to rest her eyes, Daisy would watch the parade of animals, thinking how sad it was that they would have to suffer enemy fire too.

It was also here that troops returning from the Western Front in hospital ships were sent to the various hospitals for treatment. In the spring many had returned after suffering from gas attacks. The Germans' new and deadly weapon.

Without the aid of gas masks, the troops' only protection was to hold wet cloths to their faces, coughing and choking, as they went into battle – and now they were being shipped home. Some, never to recover.

Daisy, walking to work, observed the ambulances making their way to the station from the dockside, her heart heavy at the thought of so many wounded and those lives lost in this terrible war. She'd seen some who had returned earlier, not fit enough to work and now reduced to selling boxes of matches from trays slung round their necks and had thought how dreadful it must be for those men to be brought so low, after fighting for their country.

There was no facility to make tea or coffee in the workshop, but nearby was a cafe and Daisy used to go along there mid morning for a tray of tea for two, when she and Agnes would take a break. It was on one such morning she saw a soldier coming towards her who looked familiar. As he neared she recognized her old boyfriend, Jack Weston

'Jack,' she said as she stopped beside him. 'How are you? I had no idea you'd joined up.'

His response was a little cool. 'Hello, Daisy. I joined up after we parted; there seemed little to keep me here after that. Are you still working as a barmaid at that awful place?'

'No, Jack. I have my own business. I have a small workroom just along the road,' she told him with great satisfaction.

He looked surprised. 'Well good for you. I'm pleased to know you eventually came to your senses. It's just a great pity it took you so long!'

She ignored the barb. 'How are you?' she asked.

'I've been on leave, but I'm due back in a couple of days.'

She was sorry to hear this. 'Is it really bad over there?'

'Worse than you could ever imagine,' he said quietly.

'Oh, Jack, I am sorry. Let's hope it will all be over soon.'

'We all pray for that,' he said. 'It was nice to see you, Daisy. Good luck and take care.'

As she said goodbye, she was filled with sadness. She and Jack had planned so much together and it had all fallen apart. But seeing him now, Daisy realized that it was like meeting up with an old friend – nothing more. They both had changed of course, but then circumstances did this to people and both of them had suffered – in different ways.

The following day, Flo Cummings called into the workroom and after looking at the patterns and material, ordered a gown to be made. As Daisy was checking her measurements, Flo said, 'If you fancy coming back and working a couple of nights, I can still find work for you.'

'No thank you,' said Daisy, as she wrote down the measurements. 'I've given that life up. Anyway I'm far too busy.' There was no way she'd let Flo know that business was slow.

'I'm pleased for you, but bear it in mind. It's always good to have another string to your bow.'

When the woman had gone, Agnes asked, 'Was she trying to get you back behind the bar again?'

'Something like that,' Daisy said, wondering what Agnes would think if she discovered how she'd been making her money the last few months. She certainly hoped it would never come out in the open. She would hate to lose such a good seamstress; she was integral to the success of her business.

Before the week's end, one or two of Daisy's private clients called and booked work, but Daisy knew that she needed more business to maintain the overheads and the wages for Agnes. One or two people working nearby had said how much they would like to wear her garments, but sadly they were not earning enough money to pay the prices. Daisy didn't want to lower her standards and use inferior materials. That's not what she'd built a reputation on and if she wanted to appeal to the upper classes, where the real money was, she'd have to stick it out.

To Daisy's great surprise, the next day Jessie, the seamstress with the loud mouth from Madam Evans' establishment, knocked on the door and walked in.

'So this is where you're hiding yourself,' she said.

'Good heavens, Jessie! What on earth are you doing here?' asked Daisy.

'I wondered if you needed a good seamstress?'

Agnes gawped at the girl. 'You've come here to ask Daisy for a job?'

'Yeah that's about it and why not?'

Agnes flew into a rage. 'You cheeky bugger! It was you and your big mouth that got Daisy the sack. How dare you come here and ask her for a job?'

'Don't get your knickers in a twist, Agnes. Anyway, I'm not asking you, so mind your business!' She turned to Daisy. 'Well, do you need another girl or not?'

Looking at the girl coldly she replied, 'I do not and if I did, you would be the last person I'd employ . . . not because of your being the cause of my dismissal, but because you are not good enough to work on my garments.'

Agnes sat back in her seat wearing a big grin.

Jessie looked furious. 'There's no need to be like that.'

'Madam Evans fired you didn't she?' Daisy enquired, and knew she was right by the flush on Jessie's face.

Agnes chipped in. 'Well it wasn't before time. You were the reason her business dropped off. If Daisy hadn't left, the clients would still have come, so you see, it's all your own fault.'

'I don't have to stay here to be insulted!'

Daisy walked to the door and opened it. 'No you don't,' she said. 'Please leave, you're not welcome here.'

The girl stormed out.

'Well,' said Agnes, 'the neck of the girl! Anyway, she's out on her ear. I wonder how she likes it?'

With a chuckle Daisy said, 'I really don't care but I did enjoy showing her the door.' And they both laughed heartily. 'Right, let's get back to work, we have to get on.'

As she sat sewing, Daisy recalled an old saying of her mother's. 'What goes around, comes around'. In Jessie's case it seemed to have worked.

Eighteen

Ken Woods walked around his spacious warehouse with two lists in his hands. He dealt in commodities. Whatever the market required he would buy in bulk and sell at a profit. War destroyed many people in various ways, but there were always the few who profited in such difficult times – and he was one of them.

In his store were blankets which he sold to the army, and various pieces of army equipment while in his cold store were hung sides of beef, pork and lamb. This too he sold to the army camps, which were full of troops with mouths to feed, as they waited to be shipped abroad.

One list was for the customs and his clients, the other was listed goods which he filtered off the supplies and sold at a huge profit and pocketed the money. It was fraud on a large scale. He walked up and down checking everything, wearing a smile of satisfaction as he mentally made a tally of the money that would be going into his coffers. This was a good month and that evening he had arranged to meet his friend, Bert Croucher, at the Solent Club. He felt the need to celebrate – and he wanted a woman. Marriage for him was not on his agenda. Taking a woman out and spending money on her, courting her, to him was a waste of time. If he wanted sex, he paid for it. No preliminaries, no waiting to see if the woman he was wining and dining could be persuaded to succumb to him. Oh no, if he wanted a fuck, he paid and no questions asked, no nonsense. It was cheaper in the long run to pay a whore.

Woods was the first to arrive. He ordered his usual whiskey and ginger ale and sat at a table, eyeing up the talent. His enthusiasm waned somewhat when he realized that he'd had all of Flo's girls many times. He wanted fresh blood, not the same tired women, pretending to find him attractive. He knew all their patter by now, it was all false anyway, but that wasn't what he paid for and he could well do without it. All he really needed was an enthusiastic and wanton woman between his legs. He contemplated trying the brasses walking around Canal Walk, just to make a change, but here at least you had the use of a room which was included in the price – as long as you bought a few drinks – as opposed to an alleyway and a brick wall. He was getting too old for that; he needed a modicum of comfort whilst he satisfied his sexual urges. No, he'd stay put and have one of the girls here. At least they were clean. The brasses in Canal Walk were not so fussy. Bert Croucher arrived as Woods contemplated which girl to use that evening, but he was in no hurry. He'd have a few drinks first.

Croucher sat beside him. 'Well, Kenny, how are you doing?'

'Just fine. I've had another delivery of meat; do you want any lamb or pork?'

'I'll have both,' Bert said. 'You know I'll take all you can spare.' Croucher had his own fiddle. He sold meat to hotels and hospitals, which had so many mouths to feed with the massive influx of the casualties of war. All meat sold at an inflated price of course. The war had caused shortages on all fronts, so he had a ready market for his goods too.

Woods lit a cigarette and swallowed the contents of his glass. 'God I needed a drink tonight, I've been that busy. Sup up and I'll get us another.' He went up to the bar and placed his order with Harry.

'I miss that lovely Gloria,' he remarked.

Harry looked at him wryly. 'Do you now?'

'It was always a pleasure to be served by her . . . I'd have liked to have her serve me in a different way, if you know what I mean?' the man smirked.

With a cold glare, Harry leaned forward and said, 'Don't forget our conversation in your office will you?'

Woods' expression changed. 'Don't threaten me, Harry,' he said menacingly. 'The girl's no longer here, so what are you worried about?'

'I know you of old, you bastard. If I hear you've been worrying her, I'll be down on you like a ton of bricks!'

'I find this fatherly interest in the girl very touching, Harry . . . or is it something else? Do you fancy a bit of the other, perhaps?'

'For once why don't you try and keep your mind above your trouser belt,' snapped the barman as he walked away.

Woods returned to his seat, chuckling quietly.

'What was all that about?' Croucher asked.

'Never mind, it is just a bone of contention between Harry and me.'

Later that evening Ken took a girl upstairs, but all the time he used her, he kept thinking of Gloria. She was the one he wanted to be with and he would have his way one day, no matter what. Harry could threaten all he liked; he'd make sure the barman wouldn't be able to carry out his threat – one way or another.

Daisy was just about keeping her head above water. There was enough work available to pay the rent and Agnes' wages and a little over, but she wasn't making the money she'd hoped for. It was a great disappointment to her. She still hadn't had an answer to the letter she wrote to Grace Portman and she found this hard to understand. After all, the woman had said that had only Daisy gone to her about the expense of her father's medical fees, Grace would have helped her. Perhaps after all, the woman thought it better not to be involved in any way, but getting her gowns made in the shop wouldn't involve her family in a scandal, so it couldn't be that. It was a mystery. She would write again, Daisy decided, because she badly needed the extra work to be a success. That evening, she sat down and wrote to Grace Portman once again.

It was now several weeks since the funeral of her husband and Grace was keeping busy. After a great deal of trouble arguing with her mother-in-law that she was perfectly capable of running the affairs of the estate and with encouragement from her father-in-law, she had eventually been left alone to do so, with the help of the estate manager whom she had hired as soon as Hugh had been shipped abroad. Things were running smoothly, but she was still having to cope with her loss. She put away the accounts, and sat back, gazing out at the garden, contemplating her marriage.

Frowning, she thought if she were honest, marriage to Hugh Portman had been a disappointment. At nineteen when she first met Hugh, she'd been impressed by the young handsome officer and swept off her feet. Their first night spent in France seemed, to her innocent mind, very undignified. It wasn't the kissing and caressing, she'd quite liked that, it was all the huffing and puffing and groans that Hugh uttered as he made love to her – it was like an animal. And when he'd shuddered above her, she thought he'd had a fit, and then when he collapsed on top of her, for one awful moment she thought he'd died! How naive she'd been. Nothing much had changed. Sex for her certainly wasn't a pleasure but a duty to be endured. But Hugh had been a good man and in her way, she had loved him. Now he was gone and she had to get on with her life.

The maid brought in the mail on a silver tray. 'This just arrived, Madam.'

Grace thumbed her way through the letters, laying aside the ones she recognized until she came to one that was handwritten and was unfamiliar. She put the others aside and opening the envelope, read it. She was very surprised to see it was from Daisy Gilbert and looked at the contents with interest. Frowning she put it down and in a drawer of the bureau took out a bundle of letters and cards she'd received after Hugh's death and which she'd not been able to face looking at. Among them was an unopened envelope with the same handwriting. She quickly read it.

'Oh, Daisy, I'm so sorry,' she murmured. And she rang for the maid. 'Tell Brooks to get the car out,' she said. 'I need to go to Southampton.'

Daisy and Agnes were busy working when there was a tap on the door and Grace Portman walked in. 'Hello, Daisy,' she said.

'Mrs Portman! You got my letter then?'

'I am so sorry not to have replied to your first letter, but I didn't open it until this morning.' Seeing the puzzled expression on Daisy's face she said, 'I'd better explain.'

'Agnes,' said Daisy, 'would you go to the cafe and get a tray of tea for us, please.'

When they were alone, Grace told Daisy about the death of her husband.

'Oh, Mrs Portman, I'm so very sorry. Had I known that, I wouldn't have bothered you.'

'That's all right, Daisy. I'm very pleased that you did, but your first letter came just after Hugh died and it was put away with the many cards of condolence that arrived, and I just couldn't face reading them. Now tell me. How are you doing?'

'To be honest, not as well as I hoped.'

'Do you have just this room?'

'It was all I could afford,' Daisy explained.

Looking around Grace asked, 'Have you anywhere to display your gowns?'

'Sadly not. I advertise in the local paper when I can afford to.'

As Agnes returned and poured the tea, Grace said, 'You need a shop with a window, then people will be able to see your beautiful work for themselves.'

Sighing, Daisy said, 'That would be nice, but this was as far as my money would stretch.'

Knowing how Daisy made the money to finance her one room, Grace concluded that it was enough to enable her to leave her old profession as soon as it was possible. She sipped her tea and mulled over the situation.

'Well my circumstances have changed,' said Grace. 'Now I feel in a position to help you.'

Daisy gave her a warning look. 'Have you forgotten why I refused your offer before?'

Choosing her words carefully as Agnes was busily sewing nearby, Grace said, 'No I've not forgotten, Daisy, but now I have only myself to consider. I am in charge of my life. I have an estate manager working for me, so the Manor House and all its surroundings are being run properly and I feel free to choose how I run the way I live!'

Daisy chuckled. 'There was a definite note of defiance in your voice then, Mrs Portman.'

Laughing quietly Grace said, 'Well my mother-in-law tried to dictate to me, but she soon realized that I have a mind of my own.' Finishing her tea, Grace said, 'I think we need to meet and discuss this together and make plans, don't you?'

'It sounds very interesting,' Daisy agreed.

'Can you spare the time to come and have a bite to eat now, and we can talk at the same time?'

Agnes, who had been listening, chipped in. 'You go, Daisy. There's no fittings today and the work you're doing can wait another few hours. I'll be here if anyone calls.'

'Thanks, Agnes.' Turning to Grace, Daisy said, 'Right, let's go then.'

Brooks drove them to a hotel in the town and the two of them sat down and ordered lunch. 'I want to finance you,' said Grace without delay. 'You'll take forever to get established where you are.'

'But you must get a return on your money,' Daisy insisted and then with some concern asked, 'Will you get any trouble from the family by investing in this?'

'I won't be using any of the Portman money, Daisy, I'll be using my own, an inheritance from my grandmother, so I can certainly choose how I spend it. And once the business starts to make money, I'll take a percentage. I'll also do the accounts. I'm good at figures and it will give me an interest. What do you think?'

'I think it's a miracle!'

'If it's agreeable to you, Daisy, I'll go round the estate agents and look for suitable premises. At the moment you have just Agnes working for you, but you'll need more staff, another two girls I would say.'

Daisy looked worried. 'I'm not at all sure we will have enough work for extra girls, after all we need to pay them wages and if they're not doing anything . . .' Her voice trailed off.

'We'll have plenty of work. I'll rally my friends and get my mother to do the same. I promise you, you'll have plenty to do and then it's by word of mouth.'

'There are two good seamstresses at my old place,' said Daisy, 'who I know, through Agnes, are less than happy working there. I could pass the word along.'

'Excellent!' said Grace. 'If they are agreeable, tell them to keep it quiet and we'll be in touch as soon as there is a shop for them to work in. What else would we need?'

'Two more sewing machines, more material and another couple of tailor's dummies for a start.'

'Make a list when you get home, Daisy, and meantime I'll look for a suitable shop. How marvellous! I'm so excited,' she exclaimed.

'I'm a bit stunned, Mrs Portman, to be honest.'

'If we are to be partners, you must call me Grace.'

Daisy looked startled at the possibility of such familiarity with a woman of such standing, but when she looked into the smiling eyes of the animated woman opposite her, she knew it would be just fine.

'All right – Grace,' she said and they both burst into gales of laughter, much to the surprise of the other diners.

Daisy returned to Bernard Street in great style she thought as Brooks drove back to her workroom. Grinning at Grace as she alighted from the vehicle, she said, 'I could get used to this.'

'One day, Daisy, one day!' laughed Grace. 'I'll be in touch,' she said and waved as she was driven away.

Daisy almost ran into the workroom to pass on the good news to her faithful assistant. Agnes listened with baited breath as Daisy told her of the plans she and Grace had made for the future of *Gilbert. Gowns à la Mode.* They had decided to keep the title.

Agnes promised to talk to Rose and Doris, the two seamstresses that they'd worked with before. 'They're good workers,' Agnes said, 'and clever with their needle. Oh, Daisy, won't it be great for us all to be together again?'

'It will,' she agreed, 'and Grace has promised us lots of work.' She clapped her hands in glee. 'Oh, Agnes, I'm so happy!' The two girls danced round the workroom together.

Grace was so thrilled with her plans she wanted to share her excitement, so she saddled up her horse and rode over to the neighbouring farm to see Giles.

He was just going into the house when he heard the sound of hooves and turned to see Grace enter the yard. 'Good heavens, what a lovely surprise,' he said.

Over a cup of tea, Grace told him of her plans.

'What a perfectly splendid idea,' he said. 'I wish you both lots of luck.'

'Clara will have kittens!' she said, laughing gleefully.

'My dear Grace, you must live your own life. Mrs Portman has had hers for goodness' sake.'

'Oh, Giles, you do say the right things at the right time.'

'As a matter of fact I don't. There are times when, believe me, diplomacy is not a word I would use. Let me know if I can be of help. Hugh would be proud of you.'

'Now you are being diplomatic! You know as well as I do, Hugh would be furious with me. He would say I was going into trade, as I'm sure his mother will too. If I'm honest, there were times when he was far too much like his mother for comfort!'

Giles' laughter echoed. 'I do know what you mean. Hugh and I were close as kids and I told him he was a pompous twit one day. It came to blows.'

'I didn't know that! He never told me.'

'Of course not, because I beat the hell out of him!'

When Grace rode home, she was still smiling at the thought of Hugh and Giles, as boys, thumping each other.

That evening, Daisy told Vera, her mother, the good news. But Vera only looked concerned.

'What if it ever gets out you worked for Flo Cummings, what then?'

Daisy was furious with her. 'You just can't forget can you, Mum! I'm trying to forget those days. If it comes out so what? The women I deal with won't give a hoot. All they want is to wear my clothes. I haven't got some dreadful disease you know! They won't pick anything up from me!'

'Oh, Daisy, what a terrible thing to say!' Vera was appalled.

Daisy glared at her. 'I thought you'd be pleased for me.'

'I am, of course I am. How could you think otherwise?'

'You've got a funny way of showing it, that's all I can say.' And she rushed upstairs to her bedroom, slamming the door behind her.

Vera sat in the chair by the hearth. It wasn't that she was unhappy about Daisy's news, good heavens the girl deserved a break after the sacrifices she had made, but these things had a habit of crawling out of the woodwork and biting you when you least expected it. She just hoped it wouldn't happen to her daughter.

Nineteen

It was six weeks later that *Gilbert. Gowns à la Mode* opened in East Street, a busy thoroughfare in the town centre. Resplendent in the wide bay window were two mannequins, one wearing an exquisite evening dress with heavy beading on the bodice and a day gown of the finest silver-grey material, with its long draped skirt and fitted bodice. It was in the latest fashion and was being much admired by passers-by and prospective clients, invited to the opening.

True to her word, Grace Portman had found the premises, had them decorated, bought more sewing machines, material and all that had been on Daisy's list. Then she'd rallied round her friends and those of her mother, and sent personal invitations to the wives of prominent businessmen in the town, to ensure that the day the new shop opened there were plenty of clients – and the local press.

Glasses of sherry were being served as the women who had gathered were inspecting the garments which had been made during the interim period, and were now hanging on dress rails inside the reception area of the shop. Daisy and her faithful band of workers had sewed for long hours to prepare for the opening. Grace Portman, wearing one of her gowns made by Daisy, had cut the ribbon across the door, declaring the establishment open. The cameras flashed and the orders poured in.

Daisy insisted that Grace deal with the press. She didn't want to give an interview and, as she explained to her partner, it would be better for her to remain in the background, under the circumstances. When they were established, it would be different. Grace thought she was very prudent and agreed.

Grace Portman discovered she had a flair for sales and she worked the room, selecting gowns she thought would particularly suit each individual. With her well-modulated voice and demeanour, her opinion and obvious taste, she was an important contribution and the ladies shopped enthusiastically.

Giles Bentley arrived, carrying two bouquets of flowers and was greeted warmly by Grace, who introduced him to Daisy.

'Congratulations,' he said and handed the flowers to them. 'I thought this appropriate for the occasion.'

'Oh, thanks so much, Mr Bentley,' beamed Daisy.

'Giles, please and you are more than welcome. How did it go?' he asked.

'Better than we could ever have hoped,' Grace told him. 'We have sold many items and have orders for many more.'

'Well done both of you. I'm delighted for you.' He had a sherry and took his leave. 'I'll be in touch, Grace. So nice to meet you, Daisy.'

Daisy nudged her friend. 'Where have you been hiding him, might I ask?'

Grace blushed. 'I haven't, he's an old friend of the family, that's all.'

Towards the end of the day, when it was time to close, they all got together to discuss the many orders in the book.

'I didn't refuse anyone,' said Daisy, 'but we are going to be really pushed to fill the orders, and there is a waiting list.'

'What do you suggest?' asked Grace.

'We need outworkers. Those women – like my mother – who can make the collars and sleeves, things like that which can then be sewn in by the girls working here.'

'You'll have to arrange that, Daisy,' said Grace. 'I wouldn't know where to start.'

'I know a couple,' said Agnes, then the other two girls came up with names of women who were good enough and would be pleased with the extra money, but who were unable to work full-time. And it was arranged that the girls got in touch with them and ask them to come for an interview with Daisy.

'When the press print the pictures of the opening tomorrow, we're likely to have even more clients visiting us,' Grace remarked, 'but never mind, if they realize they have to go on a waiting list, it'll make them even more eager!' She chortled with delight.

'Oh, Grace,' she said when they were at last alone. 'How can I ever thank you?'

'Oh, come along, Daisy, we've helped each other. It's given me an interest which I really needed after Hugh passed away. I'd have gone mad otherwise.'

'I think we need to get a receptionist,' Daisy suggested. 'I can't keep leaving my work to take care of the clients.'

'I'll do it!'

Daisy looked at Grace in horror. 'You can't possibly do it, not a lady of your breeding. It wouldn't be right!'

'What rubbish! My father is a GP in the town, he's not the lord of the manor or anything like it.'

'Maybe so, but *you* are the lady of the Manor House in Brockenhurst. What on earth would your mother-in-law say?'

'She'd probably have a fit!' And Grace burst out laughing. 'It would be worth doing it for that alone.'

'Mrs Portman, you are a wicked women!'

In the edition of the local paper the following day, there was a whole page spread, with pictures of the opening of the new gown shop in East Street. There was a lovely one of Grace, cutting the ribbon with the name of the shop in full view, and the written interview with her where she expounded the talent of Daisy Gilbert, her partner – and her workforce. There were no pictures of Daisy, but the women in the background eyeing the display were obviously from the upper echelons of society and the reporter had interviewed several of them. It was a great advertisement, read by many and received by a few with different reactions.

Madam Evans, whose business was failing rapidly, was jealous. Harry the barman was delighted. Flo Cummings looked at the pictures with mixed emotions and Ken Woods was delighted that he now knew where Gloria, as he thought of her, had moved to. When he'd discovered that her workroom in Bernard Street was no longer occupied, he'd been livid.

But there was no one who was more angry at this public display than Clara Portman.

At the dinner table she shook the offending paper at her husband, Charles. 'Have you read this?' she demanded.

'Yes, as a matter of fact I have.'

'How could she take part in such a vulgar display? Bandying the family name about like that!'

He gazed across the table at his wife and said, 'I think it's a splendid idea myself. Grace needs an interest to help get her over the loss of Hugh.'

'But she's gone into trade!' Clara was outraged.

Charles glared at her. 'You seem to forget, my dear, that your family fortune was made originally in the slave trade!' Throwing down his napkin, he left the table and his wife, whose face was puce with anger.

Vera had looked at the picture with motherly pride, but also with some trepidation. The women in the picture were obviously wealthy and she was afraid that Daisy's past might come out into the open. Her daughter had already been through so much, she couldn't help but fret that sometime in the future, just as Daisy had achieved her dream, it could all collapse about her. If it did, she doubted if Daisy would ever recover. But she kept such thoughts to herself.

Flo Cummings made a visit to the shop the next morning, pausing to look at the models in the window. There was no doubt about the talent of the girl. She opened the door.

'Good morning,' said Grace. 'Can I be of assistance?'

Flo was taken aback to be greeted by such a well-bred person and recognized her as the woman in the picture, Daisy's partner.

'I want to place an order for a couple of gowns,' said Flo.

'I'm so sorry, but at the moment we are unable to take any more work, but I can put your name on the waiting list if you wish?'

This floored Flo, as she'd expected to be measured up on the spot, choose her material and arrange her first fitting. 'That won't do at all,' she retorted. 'I'm an old client of Daisy's. I'm sure if you call her, she'll accommodate me.'

Sensing that there was no other way to deal with the woman, Grace asked Daisy to step out of the workroom for a moment.

'Hello Flo,' said Daisy, 'what can I do for you?'

'I'm told there's a waiting list, but as I'm an old customer I'm sure you can make an exception.'

'I truly wish I could, Flo,' smiled Daisy, 'but I've already filled my book. There is no way at all I can fit you in. We're up to our necks in the workroom. I'm really sorry.'

Flo's eyes narrowed. 'I remember once I helped you out in the past when you needed a helping hand, so can't you do the same for me?'

Daisy stared hard into the other woman's eyes. 'I'll never forget what you have done for me, Flo – in every way – but if I get a cancellation I'll give you a call. You'll have to forgive me but I've so much work I can't stay for a chat, I'm sure you'll understand. Business comes first.'

Grace stood by and watched the interchange with great interest. So this was Flo Cummings, the owner of the Solent Club. The woman who had been the means of leading Daisy down the slippery slope. Using the girl's desperate situation to suit her own ends. During their chats when setting up the business plans, Daisy had confided in her every sordid detail of her life as one of Flo's girls. This woman was wicked to have taken such an advantage of one so innocent.

Looking at her Grace asked politely, 'What would you like to do; now you know the situation?'

'I'll leave it!' snapped Flo and stormed out.

Daisy appeared when she heard the shop door close. 'Thank goodness she's gone.'

'I thought you handled her very well,' said Grace with a grin.

'She'll get fed up with waiting and I'll never have enough time to fit her in . . . unless the business is slack,' she smiled. 'If that happens I'll take anyone's money.'

'She's a hard woman,' Grace said, quietly.

'I used to think she was my friend,' Daisy admitted, 'but I was wrong. I was worth a lot of money to her, once upon a time.'

'Those days are gone, Daisy, and are best forgotten.'

'I managed to bury them pretty deeply, but they are never truly gone, alas,' said Daisy as she returned to her work.

One other person had read the local paper, but had not realized that one of the partners in this new venture was someone familiar, until he went into the Solent Club for a drink that evening.

'Hello, Steven,' said Harry. 'I haven't seen you for ages.'

Steven ordered a pint of beer and said, 'I promised myself I'd never come in here ever again.' He gazed around, saw the girls sitting at the far end of the bar and asked, 'Is Gloria about?'

'No, lad. She left some time ago.'

'Really, why?'

'She opened up a little workshop; our Gloria is a brilliant seamstress it seems and now she's just opened her own business. Here, it was in the paper.' And he picked up the edition with the opening of the shop and handed it to the young man.

'I saw this on the ship,' said Steven. 'But it says that a Daisy Gilbert is the part-owner.'

'That's our Gloria's real name,' said Harry. 'She's doing really well so I'm told.'

Steven sat and drank his beer, thankful not to find his Gloria sitting waiting for a punter. It had been his one dread. He'd vowed not to return and had kept away for many a month, but not being able to get her out of his mind, had wandered back to the bar this evening.

Picking up the paper, he made a note of the address of the establishment. He sat drinking his beer, thinking back to the night he had spent with the young girl who had trusted him enough to let him be her first lover. He thought himself that and not a punter. That would have demeaned their evening. There was no way he ever could think of her as a common prostitute, she was much more than that to him. She was a beautiful girl, an innocent in the ways of men and he had felt privileged to have been the first one – and now he longed to see her again.

Twenty

Daisy was alone in the shop at the end of the following day. The staff and Grace had left, but she had stayed behind to prepare some work for the morrow. The outside bell rang, which startled her. Who on earth could it be? Leaving the workshop she walked into the reception and was astonished to see Steven Noaks standing outside. With her heart thumping, she unlocked the door.

'Steven. What a surprise! Please come in.' She locked the door behind him.

'I saw the light on and hoped you'd still be here.' He looked around at the exquisite gowns displayed with open admiration. 'My goodness, are these your designs?'

She flushed with pride. 'Yes, they are. How on earth did you find me?'

'Harry showed me the spread in the paper. I'd actually read it on board. My steward brought it in with the daily papers after we docked. Of course I didn't realize that Daisy Gilbert and Gloria were one and the same person.'

'No, I imagine not. How are you, Steven?' She gazed at him with affection.

'More to the point, how are you?' He took her hands in his and added, 'I've thought about you so often.'

'And I've thought about you too,' she confessed.

He caressed her cheek. 'It's so good to see you here and not at the Solent Club.'

'Those days are behind me, Steven. I'm carving out a new life for myself, thanks to my partner, Grace Portman.'

'Come and have dinner with me . . . Daisy. I'll have to get used to that name.'

She looked longingly at him, remembering how he had held her in his arms, had been her first and only real lover. And here he was, holding her hands, gazing into her eyes with the same expression as when he took her to bed that very first night at the Solent Club.

'I'd like that very much,' she said quietly.

★   ★   ★

He took her to a select restaurant in the High Street and when they'd ordered he asked, 'How much longer did you stay at the club after I left?'

She felt her skin grow cold. 'Far too long. My father died but I stayed on to earn enough money to start my business in one room with one assistant, then Grace came along . . . well you've seen the shop.'

'Oh, Daisy, I can't bear the thought of you being there after I sailed.'

'Please don't think about it, Steven. It's all in the past. The only thing I want to remember was our night together. That was very special and I'll always be grateful to you for that.'

He tried to blot out the visions of other men and the intimacy they had shared with this lovely girl, who, it seemed to him, gazing at her now, still had such an innocent air about her, but in his heart he knew differently and he couldn't bear it.

'Tell me about you,' she urged, anxious to change the subject.

He told her of the trips to New York, the passengers leaving England to start a new life in America before the ship was commissioned to carry troops. They discussed the war, wondering how much longer it would continue, the tremendous loss of lives, skirting around the way they had met and the life they both knew she had lived.

Eventually Daisy said she had to leave. 'My mother will wonder where I am,' she explained.

'How is she coping after the loss of her husband?' he asked.

'She has her good and bad days, we both do, but Dad's no longer in pain, which is a good thing.'

At the door of her house they paused. Steven was desperate to see her again, but was fighting a battle within himself. He was finding it impossible to blank out the images of the men Daisy had taken to bed and he knew if he wasn't careful it could come between them. He needed time to sort himself out.

'It was great to see you again, Daisy, and I'm so thrilled that you are doing well. I wish you every success.' He drew her into his arms and kissed her longingly. Then he walked away without a backward glance.

Daisy watched him, confused and hurt. During their evening, she'd felt the affection in his voice, his look, his touch. But the sudden departure after the passion of his kiss was like a bucket of cold water thrown in her face. She couldn't understand it. Putting the key in the door, she entered the house.

'That you, Daisy?' Vera called from the scullery.

'Yes, Mum. Sorry I'm late.'

Vera emerged wiping her hands on a glass cloth. 'I was getting worried about you,' she said.

'I worked late,' said Daisy. 'I needed to prepare the work for tomorrow, then I went out for a meal with a friend. Did you finish those collars and cuffs I gave you?' Her mother with her sewing skills was now one of Daisy's outworkers which gave her a small wage and independence.

·'They're on the side table.'

Daisy inspected the work. 'This is excellent,' she said smiling at her mother. 'Perhaps I should get another sewing machine in the workroom and move you in full-time!'

'If you were short of staff I'd do it for you willingly, you know that,' said Vera, 'but at the moment, I'm happy as things are. I still have free time to see my friends.'

Knowing that such meetings with other widows and house-wives were helping Vera recover from her loss, Daisy was pleased to let things stay as they were. She and her mother were getting along well these days. Vera had seemed to come to terms with her past and no longer referred to it, which made things so much better.

At the Manor House in Brockenhurst, no such understanding existed between Grace Portman and her mother-in-law, who had descended on her that evening, uninvited. When the maid showed Clara into the living room, Grace stood up to greet her – ready for battle.

'Good evening, Clara, and what have you come to complain about this evening?'

The hostility oozed out of every pore as Clara glowered across the room. 'How very rude of you, Grace. Have you forgotten your manners?'

'Have you forgotten that your interference into my life is un-acceptable?'

'You, Grace, seemed to have forgotten that you are the widow of my son who died a hero and who would be turning in his grave knowing that you, a Portman, are working in a common gown shop!'

'You seem to forget that this same gown shop is a business in which I have shares. Hugh was never against making money as I recall and believe me, our clients are far from common. Some of them have graced your table many times in the past! And let's face it, Clara – you would *never* deem to mix with the *hoi polloi*.'

There was no answer to this as Clara Portman was well aware that some of her associates and friends had indeed become clients of her daughter-in-law's gown shop and were full of praise for the work involved, which only infuriated Clara even more.

'It's unseemly, that's all. What really worries me, Grace, is that spending so much time in Southampton, the running of the estate will suffer.'

'Oh for God's sake!' Grace turned away, furious with the woman, then turning back, she tried to speak calmly. 'The estate is in good hands. The farms are doing well and are in profit after I made a few changes, the Manor House is in good repair, the grounds are well cared for and your family name is unsullied! These are all under my careful jurisdiction. You have nothing to worry about, so please leave me alone to get on with my life in any way I please.'

'Well if you are going to be so unpleasant I'll leave.'

'What a good idea. I'll see you to do the door myself!' And she ushered the woman out of the house.

Returning to the living room, Grace poured herself a stiff brandy. 'Interfering old bitch!' she murmured as she sipped her drink. 'Why the hell can't she leave me alone?'

Working at the gown shop had given her a new lease to her life and what's more she really enjoyed it. In many ways it made up for the fact she had no children; she nourished the business as she would have done a child, looking after the financial welfare side of things, buying materials at the best prices, bargaining hard with the manufacturers. A skill she didn't know she had. It was all very satisfactory.

At the weekends, she and Giles would ride out into the country and she enjoyed his company. With him, she could forget her worries, the responsibilities of overseeing the estate and sometimes Giles would advise her when she was in doubt about a decision.

He teased about this. 'You really don't need my input you know; you're about the most capable woman I've ever met.'

Pulling a face she said, 'Oh dear, that doesn't sound very feminine.'

'Believe me, Grace, it doesn't take away an ounce of your femininity. Not one bit!'

She blushed at the compliment. 'Come on, I'll race you to the edge of the meadow!' and they both kicked their horses into a gallop.

These outings, she realized, were important to her and she looked forward to them after a busy week at the shop. There was nothing more exhilarating than a good gallop with the wind blowing through your hair and a nice companion to race. It set her up nicely for a busy week ahead.

Harry the barman called into the shop one day to see Daisy, who introduced him to Grace. 'Harry here used to look after me like a father when I worked at the Solent Club,' she told her.

Grace took to Harry immediately. 'I've heard so much about you from Daisy. I'm delighted to meet you.'

Daisy showed him over the workroom and the work in progress. Pride shone from her eyes as she did so. 'Come on, Harry, I'll make you a cup of tea and we'll go into the office and you can give me all the gossip.'

They sat down together. 'How's Flo?' she asked.

'Same as always, she was really pissed off when she couldn't get her stuff made,' he told her with great glee. 'She came back to the club in high dudgeon, cursing you up hill and down dale!'

'I wasn't being difficult, Harry. I honestly *couldn't* help her. I'm booked up for weeks in advance and I have a waiting list which I did offer to put her name on, which she declined. But I have to say it did give me great pleasure to turn her down. She stormed out of here in an awful temper.'

His gaze was full of admiration as he smiled at her. 'Well, Daisy, girl, you have done really well for yourself and I'm right proud of you.'

'Thanks, Harry. It was my dream to work for myself; it made the struggle worthwhile I suppose, although I wish I could have financed it in a different way.'

'You did what you had to do, Daisy.' He sipped his tea. 'Have you seen anything of Ken Woods?'

She frowned. 'No, why do you ask?'

He shrugged. 'He still has an unhealthy interest in you, asks me have I seen or heard from you on a regular basis.'

Daisy felt her back go cold, remembering how the man attacked her and her lucky escape. 'Do I need to worry about him do you think?'

He looked pensive. 'To be honest I'm not sure. I did have a talk to him, but he really is a nasty piece of work. Just keep your eyes peeled, that's all.'

After Harry had left, Daisy returned to her sewing, but she couldn't get the warning she'd been given out of her mind. She'd always secretly feared that Woods was unfinished business but as the weeks passed she'd forgotten about him . . . until now.

She'd heard no more from Steven, which was a great disappointment, but in her heart she knew it was because of her time spent at the Solent Club. No man would be able to face these facts and be able to forget she'd been a whore. And if she were to meet a man with whom she fell in love and wanted to marry, she'd have to be truthful about her past, which she realized would probably preclude her for ever from marrying and having a family of her own. This saddened her, but at least she had her work.

The success of Daisy Gilbert's business had become an obsession with Ken Woods. He read the local paper every evening and saw the advertisements for the gown shop that appeared fairly regularly. He'd strolled by on several occasions, observing the comings and goings of the well-heeled clients, the fashions displayed in the window, the opening and closing times. He'd watched as Daisy locked up and left the premises on several evenings, usually with at least one of her assistants. Every time he saw her, he became even more frustrated that the one time he'd caught her alone, she'd made her escape . . . and he made his plans.

Twenty-One

It was Friday evening and Daisy had stayed behind in the workshop to finish some beading on a bodice, so that the following day it could be sewn into the skirt, as the client was coming into the shop on the Monday for a fitting. When she'd finished, she tidied up her table, laying the garment across Agnes' workbench. She sat for a moment and rubbed her eyes, weary after so much close work. Then putting on her coat, she turned out the lights, realizing just how late it was from the darkened street beyond. Unlocking the main door from the inside, she opened it and stepped on to the street. Before she had time to lock the door, she was grabbed from behind and pushed back into the reception area, lifted off her feet and carried through to the workroom.

Unable to scream as her attacker had her mouth covered, she kicked out, scratched and struggled for all she was worth – to no avail. Then she heard the voice of her attacker. A voice she knew only too well – and it filled her with terror.

'Think you could escape me for ever did you, bitch!'

She could feel the hot breath of Ken Woods on her neck. 'Let me go, you bastard!' she cried.

He laughed harshly. 'Not until I get what I came for,' he threatened and spun her round. Pushing her up against her worktable and grabbing her by the throat, he said, 'You do as I say or I swear to God, I'll squeeze your neck until you can't breathe.'

In fear of her life, she gasped, 'All right, all right, just let me go.'

He eased the grip round her neck. 'That's more like it. You behave yourself and we'll get on just fine.'

While he was talking, Daisy was frantically feeling around the tabletop behind her until her fingers found the long scissors used for cutting material. 'All right, Mr Woods,' she said, trying to keep the fear from her voice, 'let's get on with it. I imagine that you want me to get undressed?'

Filled with confidence at her swift acquiescence, he released his hold on her and stepped back.

Daisy pointed the scissors at him. 'Now get out and leave me alone!'

He looked at the scissors and then at her and laughed. 'Don't be so bloody stupid; you haven't the nerve, so don't pretend. Now stop messing about and let's get on with it.' His eyes narrowed. 'I've waited too long as it is.'

'Keep away or so help me I'll use these,' Daisy cried.

He snarled at her, 'You little bitch! You – threaten me! Come here.' He stepped forward to grab at her.

With lightning speed, Daisy plunged the scissors into him.

Woods cried out, staggered back, clutching his chest – and fell. Daisy rushed to put on the lights, then looked at the figure on the floor. She gasped as she saw how the blood oozed from the man's shirt as he lay motionless and looking at her hands, Daisy screamed when she saw they were covered in blood where she'd held the scissors. She dropped them, wiping her hands down the front of her dress and fled from the workroom, through the reception area and out into East Street, still screaming and ran straight into the arms of a passing policeman.

'It's all right, Miss,' he said, then seeing the blood on her dress asked, 'What the hell has happened here?'

But terror had robbed her of her voice. Daisy just pointed into the shop. The policeman led her to a chair in the reception area and told her to sit still until he came back. Then he walked into the workroom.

The next few hours passed in a haze for Daisy Gilbert. She was aware that other members of the police force arrived and an ambulance. She vaguely remembered being taken to the police station and being led into an interview room and given a cup of tea. Then, later, Grace Portman's voice could be heard somewhere outside. Eventually, a solicitor came into the room to speak to her.

'My name is Edward Davidson. Mrs Portman has hired me to defend you, Miss Gilbert.' He sat opposite her. 'Perhaps you would like to tell me what happened.'

By now, Daisy, still in shock, was able to collect her thoughts well enough to tell him of the events that had taken place.

'Is he dead?' she asked fearfully.

'I'm afraid so.'

Daisy put her hands to her head. 'Oh, my God!' she murmured, unable to truly believe what had happened. 'I didn't mean to kill him,' she whispered. 'I just wanted to get away.'

'Did you know your attacker?' he asked.

'Yes,' she said.

'How did you know him, was he a boyfriend of yours?'

'No he certainly was not!' Then she told him how she had worked at the Solent Club. The whole sad story came out. The man listened impassively.

'This is a clear case of self-defence,' he said. 'You'll have to give the police a statement now. Just tell them what you told me. I'll be here with you while you do it.'

'Will I have to go to prison?' she asked.

'Let's not think about that at this time,' he said.

'Will you please get in touch with my mother. She'll be worried sick.'

'I'll ask Mrs Portman to go to her. I'll go and arrange for her to do so now and I'll tell the police you are ready to give them a statement. I won't be long.'

Left alone, Daisy began to shake. However could this have happened just when things were going so well? She felt the tears begin as she tried to control her trembling limbs. Thank God her father wasn't alive to witness this terrible affair. But how on earth would her mother take the news?

Grace Portman knocked on the door of Daisy's home and waited. When the door was opened she said, 'Mrs Gilbert? I'm Grace Portman, Daisy's partner; may I come in for a moment please?'

Vera was thrown when she saw the well-dressed stranger standing before her and as she invited the lady inside, her stomach tightened. Something was terribly wrong, she could tell by the expression on the woman's face.

Grace gave Vera the bad news as kindly as she could, knowing that any mother would be devastated under the circumstances. 'I've hired a good solicitor for Daisy,' Grace told her. 'He's with her now.'

Vera's face was sheet white as she listened. 'The man's dead you say?'

'I'm afraid so.'

'I must go to her,' Vera said, getting to her feet.

'I have my car outside,' Grace told her. 'I'm sure Daisy will be pleased to see you. Please try not to worry too much, she's in safe hands. The solicitor is a very clever man, and he'll look after her.'

They drove to the police station in silence.

When the two women arrived at the police station they were told that Daisy, after giving her statement, was now being examined by a doctor.

'Is she hurt then?' Vera asked.

'It's just routine,' she was told.

Turning to Grace Vera asked, 'How is it that you're here?'

'I'm the key holder with Daisy, so when all this happened they rang me at home and I got my driver to bring me here immediately. We must be brave for Daisy, as she'll be in a state, of that I'm certain.'

'I bet it's got something to do with working at that bloody club!' Vera exclaimed. 'I knew no good would come of it.'

Grace tried to placate her. 'That's not strictly true, Mrs Gilbert. A lot of good came from it. Daisy was able to care for her father in his last days, and save to start her own business.'

Vera just sat, simmering and worrying.

Eventually the two women were able to see Daisy, who flew into her mother's arms. 'There, there, love,' Vera said as she held her.

They sat down together and Daisy told them what had occurred. 'I thought he was going to kill me!' She buried her head in her hands. 'What will happen to me now?' Then turning to Grace, 'What about the business?'

'Don't you worry about that. We have a good team of girls; we'll manage until you come back.'

'Oh, Grace, what if they send me to prison?'

'Why would they? You were fighting for your life.' But nevertheless, Grace Portman was worried.

Edward Davidson came into the room. 'I'm afraid that Daisy will have to spend a night in the cells as she'll be in court tomorrow.'

'What does she have to go to court for?' asked her mother.

'Just to give her name, address and her plea which of course will be not guilty. I'll try and get bail for her.'

'And if you can't?' Grace asked.

'Then I'm afraid she'll be kept in on remand until the trial.'

Grace caught hold of Daisy's hands and squeezed them. 'We'll do what we can to keep you out, Daisy. You just have to be strong and brave. You can do it, I know you can. I'll take your mother home and bring her to the court tomorrow.'

'Thanks, Grace, I won't forget your kindness.'

'What tosh! We're partners and we stick together through thick and thin.'

As Vera was driven home she looked at Grace and said, 'Do you think she'll get bail? Now give me your honest opinion.'

'Honestly, Mrs Gilbert, I don't know. We'll just have to keep our fingers crossed.'

Grace was so worried that she asked her driver to take her to Giles' farm. She needed some support and he was the only one she could turn to.

When Giles opened the door he was surprised to see Grace as it was so late, but then he saw the expression on her face.

'Grace, what on earth has happened, you look terrible. Come inside.'

She sipped at the brandy Giles insisted she drink while he dismissed the driver saying he would see Mrs Portman safely home and, when he returned, she told him what had transpired.

'Oh my God! How dreadful . . . the man's dead you say?'

She nodded. 'I can hardly believe it.'

'Poor Daisy. Is she all right?'

'Badly shaken and now to have to go to court, I am so worried for her. The solicitor is a good man, but I am frightened of the consequences.'

The two of them talked long into the night until Giles insisted he take her home. 'You need to get some sleep,' he urged. 'I'll call round to see how it went tomorrow evening.' And he drove her home.

The following morning in the courtroom, Daisy stood before the magistrate and gave her name and address. She froze when she heard the next words.

'You are charged with the murder of one Kenneth Woods. How do you plead, guilty or not guilty?

'Not guilty,' she replied clearly.

Her solicitor got to his feet. 'My Lord, this was clearly a case of self-defence on the part of my client and we request bail. Miss Gilbert is not a threat to the public.'

The judge looked over the top of his glasses at Edward Davidson. 'We can't be sure of that; she was certainly a threat to Mr Woods!'

'But that was because she was fighting for her life, my Lord.'

'That yet has to be proved, Mr Davidson. Bail is denied.'

As Daisy was taken down the steps of the witness box, she looked frantically around for her mother and Grace, who were sitting absolutely stunned by the judge's decision.

Seeing the distress on Vera's face, Grace caught hold of her hand. 'Daisy will need us more than ever now.'

Vera was speechless and sat wiping the tears from her cheeks.

Edward Davidson came over. 'I am sorry, Grace, but I didn't really think they'd let Daisy out until the trial. I'll do my utmost to get it on the list as soon as is possible. I promise. Come with me and then you can see Daisy before they transfer her.'

Daisy Gilbert sat alone and forlorn at the table in the holding room, with its stark walls and barred window, a policeman in attendance. She looked up as the door opened and Grace came in with her mother. She didn't get up and hardly moved so shocked was she at the thought of going to prison.

Vera bravely fought back the tears and sitting down, she took her daughter's hands in hers and with a forced smile, she spoke.

'Now love, try not to take this too hard. I know it's awful news, but Mr Davidson will try and set the trial for as soon as is possible. He's a good man and I trust him.'

'If there's anything that you need,' Grace said, 'you just have to let me know.'

Daisy gazed at her. 'You should have listened to me; I told you my past would cause you embarrassment. This will all come out in court, then where will you be with your family name and connections?'

'As if I care!' Grace was astonished that she could think of her plight, with everything else hanging over her. 'You listen to me, Daisy Gilbert. This will be a hard time for you, but believe me, once it's all over it will be a nine-days' wonder and things will return to normal. You see.'

'It won't be a nine-days' wonder for me. I killed a man.'

'It was an accident, Daisy, and don't you forget that,' urged Vera.

Leaning forward, Grace said, 'Who knows what might have happened if you hadn't defended yourself? It could have been your body in the morgue, not Ken Woods', don't forget that, Daisy.'

'Sorry ladies, your time's up,' the constable announced.

Vera hugged her daughter, then as Grace did the same, she whispered to Daisy, 'Don't you worry about your mother; I'll see she's all right. Chin up, Daisy Gilbert, you are a survivor and don't you forget it!'

As the door shut behind them, Daisy wondered just what was ahead of her now? She'd had to face up to being one of Flo Cummings' girls and now a prison inmate. Life could be cruel, but at least she knew that Grace would look after her mother and that was a relief. But how long was she to be shut away for? She could only wait and wonder.

Twenty-Two

Daisy, now on remand, was taken to Holloway prison with other female offenders. When she was told where she'd be held until her trial, she was shocked. She'd read about several suffragettes being imprisoned there and eventually force-fed. She couldn't even begin to imagine what it would be like.

On her arrival, she was searched thoroughly and none too gently by the stern-faced policewoman. 'Handy with a pair of scissors I hear, Gilbert,' she said. 'Well you won't be using any in here.'

Looking at the woman, Daisy knew instinctively that declaring she'd used them in self-defence would be met without any understanding. Her belongings and contents of her handbag were listed, which she had to check with the warder as it was written and then sign the paper to say she agreed with the contents. She was then given soap and a towel, a change of underwear and a well-worn but clean nightdress, which was threadbare in places, made to undress, and take a bath.

'And don't take all day, we have a queue waiting,' she was told. 'When you've finished, get dressed and wait outside the cubicle.'

The cubicle had only half a door so that the prison warders could look over the top to watch what was going on, so there was no privacy at all. Daisy was allowed to dress in her own garments as she was awaiting trial. She was issued with a sheet, two blankets and a pillow, then led along a stone corridor, with cells either side and shown into one near the far end. The place was stark and uninviting. Footsteps echoed on the stone floors, but it was the rattle of the keys worn at the waist of the warder that seemed to her to encapsulate her loss of liberty.

Inside the cell were bunk beds, a small table, two chairs and in the corner, a bucket with a lid. On the bottom bunk was a book and a dark-grey cardigan which Daisy recognized as prison garb, having seen other inmates dressed in prison uniform as she walked to her cell.

'Yours is the top bunk,' she was told. 'When the bell rings, go to the floor below and join the queue for food. Now we don't put up with any trouble, so be warned. Cause a disturbance and you'll be very sorry!' The warder left her alone.

Daisy stood in the middle of the cell and looked around. Space was limited and she wondered who slept in the other bunk. She sat down at the table, feeling completely lost. Hearing footsteps approaching she looked up as a woman walked into the cell. She was tall, thickset and imposing. Her hair was dragged back from her face in a tight bun; her prison pallor was a testament to her environment. She didn't smile.

'Who are you?' she demanded.

'Daisy Gilbert.'

'What you in for?'

'I'm on remand awaiting trial.'

'What for?' Her expression didn't change.

'I killed a man, but it was self-defence.'

'Of course it was!' The sarcastic tone wasn't wasted on Daisy, but what was the point of arguing?

'I'm Belle Harding and I don't put up with any untidiness. This place isn't big enough to swing a cat. Understand?'

'Fully. I'm Daisy Gilbert – and I won't be bullied!'

Belle looked at her with a glimmer of interest. 'So you've got some spirit then. You'll need it in here.'

'Have you been here long?' Daisy ventured.

'Yes,' was the curt reply and Belle washed her hands and lay on her bed.

Daisy was at a loss. It was quite obvious that her companion was not going to chat, so she could do nothing else but wait for the bell to ring for lunch. When it did, Belle got off her bunk, walked to the cell doorway, turned and said, 'Well don't just sit there, come on.'

Daisy followed her down the steel staircase, watched how Belle picked up a tin plate, a knife, fork and spoon and joined the queue. Daisy did the same.

The food was served by women in prison garb. A runny stew was slapped on the plate followed by mashed potato and some peas. In a small basin was served some kind of sponge and thin custard. No one spoke; neither did they show any interest in the new inmate.

Daisy followed Belle and sat at a long bench table which was partially occupied. Some of the others nodded to Belle, gazed at Daisy, then started to eat.

'This your new cell-mate then, Belle?' asked one.

She nodded.

'What you in for?'

'I'm waiting for my trial to come up,' Daisy answered.

'That's not what I asked. What are you in for?' the prisoner demanded.

Daisy stared straight at her and answered, 'Murder!' Out of the corner of her eye, Daisy saw Belle try to hide a smile.

There were no more questions.

The murder of Ken Woods and the arrest of Daisy Gilbert made headline news in the local paper. Grace Portman read them and was appalled at such publicity. Poor Daisy, now everybody who read the paper knew she had worked at the Solent Club. She had no place to hide.

The seamstresses had arrived the morning after only to be turned away by the police from the crime scene, but were told to return the next day. Grace had been there to tell them the terrible news.

'Now we have a business to run,' she explained. 'So far, we can manage without Daisy and I expect you all to do your utmost to keep up with the work and then when Daisy returns she won't have a backlog of work to face.'

Agnes was very concerned about her friend. 'Is she going to come back, Mrs Portman?'

'Of course she is! Daisy was fighting for her life, had she not been she would most probably be dead. And by the way, I'll have no gossip from here. We all owe a lot to Daisy Gilbert for starting this business and I will make sure she has one to return to. Do I make myself clear?'

'Yes, of course,' they all agreed.

'Was she hurt?' asked Rose.

'She's a bit battered and bruised, that's all physically, fortunately, but she is suffering from the trauma of it all, as you can imagine.'

Again Agnes intervened. 'Don't get me wrong, Mrs Portman, but do you think we'll still have any customers? Will all this scandal chase them away do you think?'

'I have given this matter considerable thought, Agnes, and the possibility is that we may indeed lose some, but consider this, the ladies who come here do so because of the quality of our work. Others will still come to be able to glean any inside information

. . . sadly that's the way of the world. Some we will lose. But once it is all over and Daisy returns, it will be forgotten about in time. We just have to hang on long enough.'

'Don't you worry about that, Mrs Portman,' said Agnes. 'We'll keep the home fires burning so to speak,' and looking at the others she added, 'won't we girls?'

They all agreed with great enthusiasm.

Grace was quite overcome with such loyalty. 'Thank you, ladies, I really do appreciate that.'

But back at the Manor House, Clara Portman, her mother-in-law, was incandescent with rage when she swept into the Manor House that evening, waving the local paper at Grace.

'I suppose you've read all this? What a dreadful scandal! And our name is emblazoned all over with this Daisy Gilbert. Hugh must be turning in his grave!'

Grace looked coldly at her. 'Is that all you can think about, Clara? Have you no pity at all for poor Daisy who was attacked and might have been murdered herself?'

The look of astonishment on Clara Portman's face was something to behold. 'Pity? You must be joking! This girl worked at the Solent Club and we all know what sort of place that was. Oh, please. I can't believe you are that naive.'

'I have no intention of discussing this any further with you, Clara. It's none of your business.'

'Of course it's my business and I hope you'll have the good sense to sever all ties with this girl.'

'I most certainly will not!' Grace was livid. 'Daisy Gilbert is my friend and partner and I am standing by her side through thick and thin. She'll be fine eventually and the business will thrive, of that I am certain.'

Clara glared at her daughter-in-law. 'Then you're a bigger fool than I thought.' She strode to the door. The expression on her face when she turned towards Grace was filled with vitriol. 'I always knew that Hugh made the wrong choice when he took you as his bride. Well he wouldn't listen to me, but if he were alive now, he'd know that I was right.'

Grace, weary from the verbal onslaught, poured herself a brandy. Clara's taunts were of no consequence to her. She would do as she thought was right. Her concern was for Daisy, and although she'd tried to fill the staff with confidence, she wasn't really certain that the business would hold up. However she would rally all her friends and get her mother to do the same in the hope that together they could keep the business running for the time being. The result of the trial would make the difference.

The front-page spread was read by many and some with a vested interest. Flo Cummings knew that her business now was in dire trouble. When Daisy came to trial she would certainly tell of her days of being one of her girls and Flo could face a charge of living off immoral earnings . . . this was cause for great satisfaction for Bertha Grant, the wife of the landlord of the White Swan. Her husband's mistress could be sent to prison. What a shame that would be. The woman laughed heartily at the thought.

Steven Noaks read the account with horror. His lovely Daisy was in prison on a charge of murder. He could hardly believe it. He remembered how sweet and innocent she'd been when he was the first man to make love to her, the softness of her skin, the trust she'd placed in him and how later she'd overcome her past and opened her own business. He was due to sail that morning so was unable to go and see her. How on earth was she coping with being in prison? He had seen Ken Woods at the Solent Club and thought him a nasty piece of work. Whatever must have happened at the gown shop for Daisy to have done such a thing? As the ship's funnels sounded announcing their departure, he couldn't get her out of his mind.

Harry the barman was deeply distressed. In his heart he guessed that the frustrated Woods, despite the warning that Harry had given him, had let his frustration boil over and no doubt visited the shop to have his way with young Daisy. She must have had to put up a fight against him and that was the culmination of it all. How sad, just when things were turning out right for the poor girl. All this publicity could only harm her business surely. What would the future hold for her then . . . supposing she *was* released after the trial?

Bert Croucher was furious when he read the paper. Bloody Woods! He couldn't stand being turned down. Well now he was dead and it served him bloody well right! He had lusted after Daisy himself, even going as far as following her home some nights. He had hoped to persuade the girl to go with him, but she'd turned him down. But not Woods, oh no! That wasn't good enough for him. Serve the bugger right. But he couldn't help but wonder if Woods met his death before he'd had sex with the girl . . . or after?

While all this was going on, Daisy Gilbert was spending her first night in Holloway prison. She and Belle had settled in bed at lights out. Daisy was exhausted and hoped that a good night's sleep would make her feel able to face the next day, but that was not to be. It was like being in bedlam.

To begin with, there were arguments which could be overheard, and some women were crying. Others were telling them to shut up. Another began to scream to be let out; she wanted to go home to her children.

When Daisy made a comment about that and how sad it was, Belle said, 'She'd have a job, she smothered both of them – that's why she's in here.'

Eventually, Daisy buried her head under her pillow and closed her eyes, praying she wouldn't be in this godforsaken place too long.

Twenty-Three

During the next few weeks, Grace's predictions about the business were proved correct. A few of their clients did cancel their orders. Others came in for fittings hoping to hear any kind of gossip about Daisy and the murder, but the girls were up to such ploys and gave nothing away. Grace's friends came along as usual and friends of her mother's. Some made a point of ordering further garments, to show their solidarity. But the one thing Grace had not bargained for were the new clients. Those who thought it some kind of thrill to be wearing the clothes of a woman who was in prison with a murder charge hanging over her! It was a perverse kind of thrill which neither Grace nor the staff could understand.

'They're like a bunch of bloody vultures!' Agnes exclaimed after measuring one such client. All they want to know is about the murder, where did it happen, was there much blood? It makes me want to puke!'

Her outrage made Grace laugh. 'I know what you mean, Agnes, but think of the money! We need every penny we can make at the moment to make up for our losses.'

'I know, Mrs Portman, but honest to God, I have to keep control of myself because all I want to do when they start is stick a pin in them. If they want blood then let it be some of theirs!'

'For goodness' sake, Agnes, don't ever do that, but I know what you mean. I want to slap them for obviously deriving so much pleasure from another woman's downfall. Women can be such bitches.'

'Mrs Portman! Such language and you, such a lady!' They both doubled up with laughter.

Three weeks later, Grace made the trip to Holloway prison to visit Daisy. She'd asked Vera Gilbert if she wanted to come but Vera had a heavy cold and was confined to bed for a few days, but she did ask Grace to take some fresh clothes to the prison, as Daisy had written asking for another skirt and two blouses. So after packing up the garments and making sure the woman was all right, Grace went alone.

As she made her way through several gateways of the prison, the ominous clanging of them as they closed behind her made her feel sick to her stomach. She waited in an anteroom with other visitors, after handing over the package at the reception to be searched, and was fascinated by the mixture of people around her. Some were obviously poor, clutching the hands of small children with runny noses. Others were well dressed with a certain air about them which placed them as members of a much higher society. No one spoke.

Eventually they were led into a hall with long trestle tables and chairs set out. Across the room she could see the inmates behind barred gates, standing with the warders, waiting to be let inside to see friends and family. There was a potent air of expectation.

The gates opened at last and Grace sat up straight, staring at the line of prisoners, searching for Daisy. When she saw her enter the room she waved. Daisy's face lit up with pleasure as she hurried over and sat opposite her friend.

Grace reached over the table and grabbed Daisy's hands in hers. 'How are you?' she asked.

Pulling a face Daisy said, 'All things considered, I'm fine. How are you? How's the business, or don't we have one any more?' Although Grace had written to her, Daisy wasn't sure if she had been trying to cheer her up rather than tell her the truth.

'I'm well and so is the business. The girls are marvellous, working hard of course, and we're ticking over nicely.'

'Honestly, you're not just trying to be kind?'

'No, Daisy, I wouldn't lie to you. I'm not saying we've not lost a few clients but we've had some new ones so that's sort of balanced the scales.'

Daisy raised an eyebrow and sardonically remarked, 'The new ones have come for a thrill I expect.'

Grace was astonished at her perception. 'How could you possibly think that?'

'I've learned quite a bit about human nature in the past, Grace, and even more since I've been inside.'

'How are you coping? Is it as awful as I imagine?'

'Probably worse, but I've learned to keep myself to myself and to stand up to anyone who tries it on. I'm working in the laundry and that's like being in a hellhole, it's so hot. But I'm getting by. Mum writes to me. She told me she was in bed with a cold. Her chest is a bit weak after taking in so much laundry in the past – and drying it inside during wet days didn't do her much good I'm afraid.'

'I went to see her,' Grace told her. 'She's all right. I took her some medicine and a bit of food and the lady next door is looking after her. She'll be up and about in a day or two so don't worry.'

'You're so good, Grace, I don't know what I'd do without you.'

'What rubbish! Have you heard from Edward Davidson?'

'Yes, he came to see me last week. He's doing his best to bring the trial forward. He said he could pull a few strings, call in a few favours.'

Smiling, Grace said, 'He's good at that.'

With a frown Daisy confessed, 'I'm dreading going to court. I'll have to tell about being one of Flo's girls. That will destroy my mother.'

'Your mother's made of stronger stuff than you realize, Daisy. It won't be pleasant – of course it won't be, but when it's all over, then you can get on with your life. You've been through so much, it doesn't seem fair.'

'You think I've suffered! You should hear about some of the women in here!' She then told Grace about some of the other prisoners and their sad stories. Eventually the visiting time was over.

Grace hugged Daisy. 'You take care. I'll write and let you know how things are going.'

'Thanks, Grace, for everything. How's your mother-in-law?'

Laughing, Grace said, 'Don't ask!'

The following morning after breakfast, Daisy made her way to the laundry with Belle. The two women had soon settled down to a coexistence of some sort. Daisy learned quickly that Belle didn't do conversation or gossip but kept herself to herself. She didn't like questions and didn't ask any of Daisy, after she discovered what she was being charged with on that first day. But strangely, she was a comforting presence. The other inmates kept out of Belle's way, making sure not to upset her which made Daisy think she was a force to be reckoned with.

The heat and steam in the huge laundry room was intense. The women working there were permanently bathed in sweat. Large machines washed the linen and towels, huge mangles took the strength of two women to turn the handles while another fed the sheets through. Long lines of sheets hung over racks of wood, suspended over the room, drying, reminding Daisy of the laundry hanging around her own house when her mother used to take in the local washing. And the large presses for ironing them were dangerous. It was all too easy to burn your hand as you fed the linen through, then pull down the cover to steam out the creases. It required great concentration.

Only the previous day a fight had broken out between two women and one had forced the hand of the other on to the pad and pulled down the lid. The woman's screams could be heard all over the prison.

One or two of the inmates had picked on Daisy when first she worked there. Women guarded their position in the laundry jealously and a newcomer was met with hostility. Belle quietly warned Daisy to keep a watchful eye on them.

Despite this, one day Daisy was taken by surprise. One woman in particular had taken against her for no apparent reason. In prison it didn't seem to need one. As Daisy was passing the machine that did the washing, the woman cannoned into her. She felt her arm sear as it touched the side of the machine, and cried out. Looking up she saw the woman grin. This infuriated Daisy who was suffering severe pain and knowing that strength was her best weapon, she turned on the woman. 'You bitch, you did that on purpose!' She glared menacingly at her. 'I warn you to be very careful. I'm in here on a charge of murder, so don't push me too far!'

The woman had backed off. Belle looked over at Daisy and nodded her approval. But Daisy, soon after, had to go to the hospital for treatment – an incident she kept from Grace and her mother. And when she was allowed her one bath a week, she made sure that she was in the next cubicle to Belle. Somehow the nearness of her cell-mate made her feel safer.

The days seemed endless to Daisy. She went from her cell to the dining room three times a day and, in between, to the laundry. The exercise period was for one hour after lunch. The quadrangle was bare and women gathered in groups, chatting or arguing. Some walked round the perimeter to get some form of exercise and others stood in pairs with the woman of their choice. Lesbian relationships flourished here with those who were inside for a long spell. Daisy had learned very quickly to ignore them, or chance being challenged about her interest. The young pretty girls were at their most vulnerable, but here, everyone had to tread carefully as the wrong look, the wrong move could escalate into a near riot.

She herself had been approached by one of the women one day as she was coming out of the bathroom. The woman, big and butch, had sidled up to her.

'I've been watching you, darling. You need someone to watch out for you in here, what with your good looks, you could find yourself in deep trouble.'

'No thanks. I'm perfectly able to look after myself.' The woman stepped nearer and caught Daisy by the arm.

Belle stepped out of her cubicle at that moment. 'Fuck off, Charlie. Daisy doesn't want you pawing her or you'll be the one in trouble. Do I make myself clear?'

The woman just glared at Belle but she walked away.

'Thanks,' said Daisy. But Belle remained silent.

But Charlie wasn't that easily deterred, she'd been inside too long. She waited for an opportunity to catch Daisy alone, and the following day she followed Daisy into the toilet block and waylaid her.

Pushing Daisy up against the washbasins, she pinned her arms behind her back and lifted her skirt. 'Never been with a woman have you, pretty thing. Well let me show you what you're missing.'

Daisy was enraged! It was bad enough to have had to sell herself to men, she was not about to be assaulted by a woman. She headbutted Charlie, catching her on the bridge of her nose. The blood spurted everywhere and Charlie let out a cry of pain. Daisy pushed her away.

'You try and touch me again and so help me, I'll kill you!' Thrusting the woman from her, Daisy rushed outside.

Oh my God! She realized just what she'd said. She was on remand for murder for Christ's sake and she'd just threatened to kill someone else! She hurried back to her cell.

Belle was sitting on her bed and looking up saw the blood on Daisy's face. 'What the bloody hell happened to you?'

Daisy poured some water into the washbasin and washed her face. She then told Belle what had happened.

Her cell-mate was furious. What infuriated her more was the fact that Charlie had ignored her warning. This was a bad reflection on Belle's position in the hierarchy of the inmates.

'Where is she?' she demanded.

'I left her in the toilet block.'

Belle stood up and walked purposefully out of the cell.

Daisy, now that her anger had abated, was shaken. Wasn't it bad enough that Ken Woods had attacked her and now in here she wasn't safe from the same kind of violence? How long would she be inside this madhouse before she became as bad as the other inmates? She lit a cigarette to calm her nerves.

Belle soon returned with a look of satisfaction. 'You won't have any more trouble,' she announced.

'You found her then.'

Belle nodded.

'What did you do?' Daisy asked.

'You don't want to know,' Belle said firmly, so Daisy didn't question her further. But the following day she heard that Charlie was in hospital after apparently falling down a flight of stairs.

Eventually Edward Davidson arrived to visit Daisy with the news that her case was being sent to trial in two weeks' time. Although she couldn't wait to leave Holloway, the idea of appearing in court with her past revealed to all and sundry, chilled her to her core.

Edward tried to cheer her. 'Yes, it will be the talk of the town for a while, until something else comes up, but take my word for it, Daisy, it will soon fade into the background and be forgotten.'

'But to be known as one of Flo Cummings' girls will stay with me forever. I'll never be able to live that down.'

He smiled benignly. 'If we were to look behind all the curtains of the grandest houses in Southampton, you would be shocked at the many skeletons in their cupboards.'

'That's probably true, but at least they are still private.'

They spent the rest of the afternoon going over his defence. 'I have managed to get a really good barrister to defend you in court.'

Daisy's eyes widened with surprise. 'A barrister? Aren't you going to appear for me?'

'I'll be assisting,' he told her.

'But I can't afford a barrister!'

'Grace Portman has instructed me to hire him. She insisted on it.'

Daisy put her hand to her head and closed her eyes. Grace to the rescue once again. How would she ever be able to repay her?

As if reading her mind, Edward said, 'When this is all behind you, Daisy, you'll soon regain your reputation as the clever seamstress and designer that you are. You'll see, your business will flourish and both you and Mrs Portman will be successful. That's what she believes – and so must you.'

She looked up at him and with a fearful look asked, 'Do you honestly think the court will find in my favour?'

'Absolutely! I have one star witness who will testify that this man, Woods, kept after you when you worked in the Solent Club and because of this he did fear for you.'

'Who is prepared to go into a witness box and swear to that?'

'Your friend Harry, the barman. He was so concerned for your safety that he went and saw Woods himself, to warn him off.'

She was overwhelmed by this revelation. 'And Harry would do all that for me?'

'Indeed he will, and he is also prepared to tell the court the only reason that you became one of the girls was to pay for the fees for your father's nursing so he'll be a good witness as to your character.'

She thought for a moment and said, 'But prostitution is illegal. What happens to the Solent Club when all this comes out in court?'

Laughing heartily Edward said, 'It will be closed! Mrs Cummings has already got rid of her girls, trying to show that the club is just for drinking, but it's far too late. The police will have a heyday. Flo has had a good run, she greased a few palms in the past and gave a few free visits to the odd copper to keep him quiet, but once it comes up in court, she'll be finished.'

'And poor Harry will lose his job.'

'Don't you worry about him, Daisy my dear, he's already left and is working in a pub in the docks. He's a wise old bird have no fear. Grace herself is willing to stand as a character witness if we need her.'

'On no account must she do that!' Daisy was adamant. 'She has already done too much but I cannot let her drag her family name through the courts. Please, Edward, stop her at all costs.'

'Very well, Daisy, if you insist.'

'I most certainly do.'

Gathering up his papers he put them away in his briefcase. Rising to his feet, he shook her hand. 'See you in court, my dear.' He smiled and said, 'Please try not to worry, you are in good hands.'

Returning to her cell, Daisy sat on the chair by the table and sighed. Belle looked over at her.

'Trouble?' she enquired, which was unusual.

'My case comes up in two weeks' time,' Daisy told her. 'I'm dreading it.'

'At least you'll be a free woman after.'

Forgetting that Belle didn't like to be questioned, Daisy asked, 'How much longer will you be in here, Belle?'

'Until they take me out in a box,' she stated as if it was of no importance.

'Oh, Belle, that's terrible, I'm so sorry.' Daisy didn't know what to say.

The other woman shrugged. 'At least I escaped the rope.'

Daisy looked at her with horror.

Belle rolled a cigarette and, for the first time, held a proper conversation with her cell-mate.

'I caught my husband in bed with his mistress . . . in my bloody bed would you believe? So I blew my top and killed the pair of them. I got off on a lesser charge of manslaughter as it wasn't premeditated, but I got life. I've got used to being here by now.'

Daisy was speechless. No wonder the others kept out of her way; she had nothing to lose if they ever caused her grief and she retaliated. The old saying 'strange bedfellows' came into Daisy's mind. It was never more true than at this moment.

Twenty-Four

In the morning of the first day of her trial, Daisy Gilbert dressed carefully in a clean skirt and blouse, packed her meagre belongings and waited for a warder to collect her from her cell. She'd scarcely eaten at breakfast, but had managed some bread and a scraping of butter. Now sitting at the table in her cell, she was full of uncertainty. Would she be returning here tonight? Edward had told her that the trial would take several days. She fought the feeling of nausea that swept over her.

A warder appeared at the door of the cell. 'Right, Gilbert, we're ready for you now.'

Belle looked at Daisy and with a half smile said, 'Good luck.'

Too full to say much, Daisy tried to smile back. 'Thanks . . . for everything.'

The drive to the Old Bailey in the Black Maria seemed endless, but eventually they arrived and Daisy was hustled into a room where her solicitor and a man in gown and wig stood waiting for her.

Edward took her hand and squeezed it. 'This is Quentin de la Hay, your council. He wants to have a few words with you before we go into court.'

The barrister shook her firmly by the hand and in a deep, well-educated voice, went over various parts of her statement, filling in the details which he would use in her defence.

Then holding her gaze he said, 'I will lead you in my questions, Miss Gilbert, and you'll have no difficulty in understanding what I want to know. Just answer simply and truthfully. You will be cross-questioned by the prosecuting council and I want you to remain calm when he does. It is his brief to make out that you are guilty of this unfortunate incident, so just answer clearly, and again tell the truth. Don't let him confuse you or bait you. Just answer a direct question, don't comment otherwise. If you aren't sure, stop and think before you reply to his questions. I will be there to protect you, have no fear.'

Daisy could feel her heart racing and her nerves tingle with the anticipation of what was ahead of her. 'I'll do my best,' she said.

He took her by the hand. 'Try not to worry, there's a good girl. I'll see you in court.' He left Daisy and Edward alone.

'I'm scared to death,' she confessed to the solicitor.

'No one likes going to court, Daisy. But you're in very good hands, I promise.'

'Is my mother here?'

'Yes, she's with Grace Portman. You'll be able to see them later.'

Soon after this, Daisy was called into court. She walked up the stairs and took her place in the dock, where she was told by the policewoman to sit on the chair that was there.

Daisy looked around. She saw her mother and Grace sitting together, looking somewhat pensive, although they both smiled and waved at her. She noticed that Giles was sitting on the other side of her friend. The barrister, in his gown and wig, nodded to her. She looked up suddenly as the jury entered and took their places. She returned their looks of curiosity and thought I suppose they are looking to see if I have the look of a murderess, but what would one look like?

'All rise,' called the clerk of the court as the judge entered and took his seat, resplendent in a red robe and wig.

Both barristers spoke to the jury, laying out their case, before sitting down. Quentin de la Hay called his first witness.

Harry Blake, the barman, walked into the court and entered the witness box, where he was sworn in. He was smartly dressed in a dark-grey suit, white shirt and striped tie.

'Are you Harry Blake, of 20 Union Street, Southampton?' asked Daisy's barrister.

'I am.'

'Were you once employed as barman at the Solent Club in Bernard Street?'

'Yes, sir. Until recently. I had worked there for three years before that.'

'Please tell the court how you know the witness, Miss Daisy Gilbert.'

'Daisy came to work as a barmaid because she needed the extra money to pay the fees at a private nursing home for her father, who was dying.'

'How do you know that?'

'She told me. She used to confide in me a lot.'

Daisy watched her friend, full of regret that he had to appear in court on her behalf. But he appeared to be very comfortable while giving his evidence.

'While she was working behind the bar did she meet the deceased, Ken Woods?'

'Yes, sir, he was a regular customer.'

'Did he have anything to do with Miss Gilbert, other than be served drinks by her?'

'No, sir. He did used to pester her, asking her out, but she refused. I warned her about him, because he was a bad lot.'

'Objection!' The council for the prosecution rose to his feet.

'I am trying to establish Woods' character and any association he might or might not have had with the witness, my lord,' said de la Hay, referring to the judge.

'I'll allow it.'

'Why did you feel the need to warn Daisy Gilbert?'

'Well Woods could be very rough with women, it was a known fact,' continued Harry.

'Isn't it true he used to pay for the services of the various hostesses in the club?'

'Yes, sir. In fact he was only allowed to pay for one of the girls on the understanding that he treated her without any rough stuff and I didn't want Daisy mixed up with him.'

'Did Miss Gilbert always work as a barmaid?'

Harry hesitated, glanced over at Daisy, then said, 'No, sir.'

'What else did she do?'

Taking a deep breath Harry said, 'She worked during the day as a seamstress and when her boss found out she worked as a barmaid in the Solent Club, she fired her, so Daisy was in a state because she wasn't earning enough to pay her father's fees.' He stopped talking.

'And what did she do about it?'

'She gave up bar work and became a hostess.'

Smiling at Harry, the barrister posed his next question. 'That must have pleased Ken Woods because now he had access to her.'

'Well no he didn't, sir, because she refused his offer.'

'Offer, what offer?'

'Daisy was a virgin, and there was a bidding war as to who

would pay the most to be her first punter.' He ignored the buzz that went round the court at this revelation and continued. 'But Daisy made it very clear to Flo Cummings, the owner of the club, that on no account would she accept any offer from Ken Woods.'

Daisy hid her head in her hands, not daring to look at her mother or the members of the jury.

'How did he react to that?'

'He was bloody furious! Begging your pardon. He swore he'd have her one way or another.'

'Isn't it true, Mr Blake, that you paid a call on Ken Woods in his office to warn him off?'

'Yes, sir, I did. Woods don't take kindly to rejection and I was worried as to what he might do. Daisy Gilbert is a good girl and was forced into this position only because she wanted the best for her dad, a man with only weeks to live. Then she told me that Woods had grabbed her when she was walking home one night. Luckily she got away, so I thought I ought to have a word with him.'

'Did he agree to leave Miss Gilbert alone?'

'Yes, sir, he did but I never trusted the man and told Daisy to keep a look out for him.'

'Thank you, Mr Blake. No further questions.'

The council for the prosecution rose to his feet. Smiling at Harry he said, 'A good girl? Surely no *good* girl would put herself in a position to sell her body to all and sundry?'

Harry stared back at the man. 'Only a *really* good girl would make such a sacrifice for her own father.'

'Why didn't she decide to bring him home, then she wouldn't have had to make such a sacrifice? Surely that was the only real solution? The decent thing to do.'

'She was going to do that until one day when she visited the old man and he told her that he wanted to stay put as it would be too much for her mother to cope with and Daisy then felt she had no choice. I tried to talk her out of it, but her father's welfare came before her own reputation.'

No matter how he tried to tarnish Daisy by his cross-questioning, Harry always had an answer and eventually the barrister ended his examination and Harry left the witness box.

Daisy heard the next witness called and was astonished when Stella walked into the court. Under questioning she told the same story as to why Daisy became one of Flo Cummings' girls and how reluctant she was to do so. And once again the prosecutor had little room to manoeuvre.

Then the call for a lunch break came and Daisy was taken back to the room where she spoke with her representatives before her mother and Grace joined her.

Daisy ran into her mother's arms. 'I'm so sorry you had to hear all this,' she cried.

'Now then, less of this. There's no reason for you to be ashamed, you did what you thought was right for Dad. Now eat some of these sandwiches and drink some coffee, you'll feel better then.'

Grace and Daisy chatted about the shop to stop them thinking about the return to the court. The business was going along nicely it seemed, with the girls working hard, all anxious to know the result of the case, longing for Daisy to be released and for things to get back to normal.

When the court resumed, Daisy once again took her place in the dock.

Several people were called to attest to Woods' dodgy reputation. Names given to the barrister by Harry, who with his expert knowledge of the seedy characters who would be willing to testify, were useful towards building the case for Daisy's benefit. It seemed a long day to all concerned and it was with some relief when it came to a close.

'Try and get a good night's sleep, Daisy,' Quentin told her, 'because tomorrow, I'm putting you in the witness box.'

Daisy felt her stomach sink at the thought.

'I'm pleased as to how things went in there today,' he said. 'Your friend Harry was a great witness as I thought he would be, but tomorrow is important. Don't wear any make-up. Keep your hair simple as I want you to look as innocent as possible. And don't worry; I'll take care of you.'

Giles had taken Grace and Vera to a hotel for a meal after they had chatted with Daisy. He felt they both needed some sustenance after such a long day. He and Grace tried to cheer Vera, without much success. The case hung heavily over them all.

Daisy was taken to spend a night in a cell of a local police station to save the journey to and from Holloway. At least it was quiet, apart from a drunk who was kept in overnight to sober up. He soon fell asleep and so eventually did Daisy.

In the morning she was taken to the bathroom to freshen up before travelling back to the Old Bailey.

The court resumed again and Daisy was called to give evidence. She stood in the witness box and took the oath, her hands trembling. She gripped the edge of the box to give herself some support.

Quentin rose from the table and smiled as he walked towards her. He went through his evidence about Daisy's reasons for working in the club, then asked, 'Did you enjoy working behind the bar?'

'Yes, sir. Harry the barman was good company and he showed me the ropes as I'd not done this kind of work before. And Mrs Cummings, the owner of the club, had offered me the job so I could earn extra money for Dad.'

'Isn't it true that you are a very talented seamstress and designer?'

'Yes, it's what I do best.'

'Would you say you were an asset to your previous employer, Madam Evans in London Road?'

'Definitely! After she fired me, she lost a lot of business I was told.'

'How did you feel when you lost your position?'

Daisy looked straight at him and said, 'I was distraught. I needed my wages to help pay for the nursing home fees for the care of my father.'

'What made you become one of the hostesses?'

'When she knew I'd been fired by Madam Evans, Mrs Cummings said I could make a great deal of money by doing so. As my money as a barmaid wasn't enough, I had to give the offer some serious consideration – and I eventually said yes.'

'Eventually?' asked Quentin. 'Did you have to *think* about the offer?'

Daisy's cheeks flushed. 'Of course I did! Do you think it was easy for me to become a whore? I hated every moment of it! Although the money I earned prolonged the life of my father, I felt dirty and cheap.' She straightened her back and defiantly said, 'But I would do it all over again for my dad!'

There was a murmur of approval among the people in the courtroom watching the proceedings.

'But when your father eventually passed away, why didn't you stop working as a hostess? Surely that was your opportunity to stop?'

'Yes, I suppose anyone would think so, but I had no other job to go to and I wanted my own business. I had already lost my reputation and it was the *only* chance I had of saving enough money to do so. I thought it worth the disgrace.'

'But you didn't save enough money to open the fine establishment you now have in East Street, surely?'

'No, I had only enough to rent one room with one other seamstress. But now I have a partner which allowed me to move to East Street.'

'And is the business a success?'

Daisy smiled. 'I'm happy to say that it is.'

'So it was worth the sacrifice you made to achieve this?'

Daisy looked at the ground as she pondered over this question. 'In one way it was, but it was a great price to have to pay. And now with all the publicity, I may well have reason to regret it even further.'

'What do you mean?'

'With my past laid bare for all to see, who knows if I'll still have a business?'

'Let's move on. Tell me what happened on the night of the murder.'

Daisy described how Woods had caught her locking up and how he carried her into the workshop.

'Why didn't you call for help or scream to attract attention?'

'I couldn't! Ken Woods had his hand over my mouth, then he held me by the throat and started to throttle me, demanding I have sex with him. I was terrified that he was going to kill me.'

'What happened next?'

Taking a deep breath, Daisy explained. 'I was groping around my worktable at the back of me and I felt the scissors I used for cutting out – and I grabbed them.'

'What were your thoughts as you picked them up, Daisy?'

'All I could think about was getting away from him.' She fought back the tears that brimmed. 'I thought if I threatened him with the scissors, he'd back off – but he didn't. I didn't mean to kill him!' she cried, her voice full of anguish. 'It was a terrible thing to do. I just wanted to get away from him, that's all.'

'Thank you, Daisy. No further questions.' The barrister sat down.

The prosecuting council stood up and walked towards the witness box and Daisy Gilbert knew he would try to discredit her and was afraid.

Twenty-Five

The council for the prosecution faced Daisy. 'A very touching story you do tell, Miss Gilbert. You would have the court believe that you were an innocent girl, caught up in this wicked world, all for the sake of your sick father.' He waited for Daisy to answer but she just looked at him and remained silent, remembering the advice she'd been given, only to answer any direct question put to her.

He continued. 'Wouldn't it be true to say that instead you were a deliberately calculating young woman?'

She frowned, not knowing where this was leading. 'I don't understand the question.'

'Then let me explain. When you eventually agreed to become a whore' – he emphasized the word – 'wasn't it true that you made certain demands of Mrs Cummings, the owner?'

'What demands?' asked Daisy.

'Oh come, Miss Gilbert, don't try and play the innocent with me! You stipulated that you would choose your clients and that you alone would set the price for your services?'

'Yes, that's true.'

'Hardly the actions of such an innocent, wouldn't you agree?'

Daisy met his contemptuous gaze and said, 'Because I *was* such an innocent doesn't mean that I was a fool!' There was a sound of people chuckling and the judge looked up and frowned at the public gallery.

'I was very much aware of the interest shown by the men in the club in my virginity. Several had tried to tempt me to sell it to them when I was working behind the bar.'

'You turned them down then?'

'Of course I did. I was a barmaid then – not a whore!' She snapped back the name at him.

'So when did you decide to be your own agent, so to speak?'

'You forget, sir, that I am a businesswoman. I understand supply and demand. If I had to resort to such a thing, I wanted to earn as much money as I could while I was of any value.'

'That's a very cold way of looking at it, wouldn't you say?'

'It was the only way I could cope with losing my reputation and having to let men use me.'

'Use you?'

'What else would you call it, sir? It certainly isn't love! You are there to satisfy a man's sexual appetite.'

He cast a wry expression in her direction. 'But couldn't such an experience be enjoyable? Didn't you learn to enjoy your work? Indeed wasn't that the real reason you stayed on after the death of your father?'

Daisy just glared at him and slowly shook her head. 'You have no idea have you? How could any woman enjoy being treated like a piece of meat, without any feelings – and have to listen to men utter obscenities as they work their frustrations out on you? No, sir, I did *not* learn to enjoy my work. But I counted every pound they paid me, because every one would enable me to buy another length of cloth and it meant I was that bit nearer to opening my own business. This would enable me to earn a living and take care of my mother. It was the only way I could endure such treatment, and that's the truth of the matter!'

He moved on to the night of the murder. 'I do believe that Ken Woods took you by surprise on the night in question but when you picked up the scissors, you must have known that they were a lethal object, after all you used them every day.'

'I didn't give it any thought, other than to use them to get away.'

'Yet you deliberately stabbed the man! You must have known how dangerous to the victim that was?'

'I wasn't aware of using them in any particular way. I just knew it was my only chance of getting out of his clutches.'

'By killing him, you mean?'

Daisy's eyes flashed angrily. 'I never even thought of that. I didn't mean for the man to die, just to let go of me!' She suddenly felt faint and grabbed the rail on the box.

Quentin leapt to his feet. 'My lord, the witness needs a glass of water, she's unwell.'

Daisy was handed a glass and drank the contents.

'Are you able to continue, Miss Gilbert?' asked the judge.

'Yes, my lord, I'm all right, honestly.'

'No further questions,' said the council and sat down.

Daisy left the witness box and returned to the dock where she was able to sit down. Despite what she told the judge, she did feel unwell and wiped the perspiration from her forehead. The wardress, carefully watching her, leaned forward and gave her some smelling salts to use.

'Don't breathe in too deeply,' she whispered.

'Thanks,' said Daisy and took a sniff. It helped clear her head and she felt revived.

The judge spoke. 'This would seem a good time to break for lunch, gentlemen. The court will reconvene at two thirty this afternoon.'

Daisy breathed a sigh of relief as she was led down the steps and back into a room, where her barrister and solicitor were waiting.

'Well done, Daisy,' said Quentin de la Hay. 'You did very well.'

With a grimace she said, 'He tried to make me out a hard case.'

'Yes, but you coped with that in fine style,' Edward said with a nod of approval.

'So what happens now?' she asked.

'We both do our summing up and then the jury go away and try to reach a verdict.'

'There are a few old boys on the jury who wouldn't take kindly to me being a whore,' Daisy remarked. 'They looked very straight-laced to me.'

'You can never tell,' Edward murmured. 'We'll just have to wait and see, but remember Quentin has to give his summary last.'

'At least my mother didn't have to face a witness box.'

Edward surprised her. 'She wanted to, but I knew you'd be very upset if we called her and we didn't think it really necessary to put her through that.'

'My mother was prepared to do that for me?'

'Yes, Daisy, but we had enough witnesses to testify to your good character, we felt.'

Daisy let out a deep sigh of relief. It would have broken her heart to see her mother standing in the witness box and being cross-questioned.

Edward sent out for some sandwiches and coffee for the three of them as they waited for the court to reconvene.

When it did, Daisy took her seat in the dock and listened to the council for the prosecution stand in front of the jury and try to prove that Daisy Gilbert was *not* the innocent young girl she claimed but a calculating minx and more than capable of murder. He called for the jury to find her guilty as charged.

As he sat down, Daisy felt sick. Surely the jury wouldn't be swayed by his eloquent delivery. She studied the faces of the twelve men sitting in judgement of her and her blood ran cold.

Quentin de la Hay stood up and walked slowly over to the jury.

'My learned friend speaks convincingly and puts his case to you very well. Of course it is his brief to bring in a guilty verdict, no matter what. It doesn't matter that Daisy Gilbert is innocent of the charge.' He glanced over at her. 'This lovely and talented girl is a victim of circumstances. As an upright citizen of this town, she worked hard as a seamstress, the sole breadwinner of her family with a sick and dying father. Her mother took in washing to add a few shillings to her daughter's wages which were spent mostly on medication for Fred Gilbert. Times were hard for them all.'

He walked up and down as he spoke. The eyes of the jury following his every move.

'It was becoming difficult for Mrs Gilbert to manage her husband as he became even weaker with the tuberculosis that ravaged his body – and Daisy longed to get him into a nursing home where he would be cared for properly. To this end, you have heard how she worked as a barmaid at the Solent Club to earn extra money, which enabled her to move her father into such care.'

He looked particularly hard at the jurors. 'Then when she was fired because of her work as a barmaid, she made the supreme sacrifice and became a hostess. Can we even begin to understand how difficult this was for her? A well brought up young lady, instilled with a strong moral sense? Of course we can't because we have never been in that situation. Yet because of the love she had for her father, she did so. I think this shows amazing bravery on her part!' His gaze held those of the older members of the jury.

'You heard her say how dirty it made her feel and yet she managed to keep her father in the nursing home until his death. A place he said he was happy in and wanted to end his days.' He paused. 'Perhaps you think it wrong of her to stay on to finance her business . . . which to begin with was one room, two sewing machines and one assistant. But I ask you, gentlemen, what choice did she have? She had no job to go to. How was she to earn a living? No, she knew she had to now provide for her mother and to work for herself was the only option, so she stayed until she'd saved enough money . . . then she left. It takes a lot of courage to be so focused, being used by men, as a means to an end.'

He paused again. 'However we are not here to make a judgement on the way she earned her money, that was only to show how Daisy Gilbert met the deceased, we are here to decide if she is capable of murder. You have heard various testimonies as to the sort of man Ken Woods was. He was a hard character known for the force he had used on women, and already he had pestered Daisy Gilbert in the Solent Club and then when his advances were refused, attacked her once before, in the street, where she was fortunate then to make her escape. Not content with that, he cornered her again as she was locking up her shop.'

Once again, he stopped in front of the jury. 'Unless you are a woman, you can't begin to know how terrified Daisy must have been to once again be held captive by such a man. She was terrified and thought she was about to be killed.' He walked away, then turning back he asked, 'What was she supposed to do? What would any of us do? We'd fight back of course! Which is precisely what Daisy Gilbert did. Managing to grab hold of anything she could, she felt the scissors on the table, and with these she struck out blindly in an effort to escape. Unfortunately for her, in doing so, she struck a fatal blow. Had she not done so, I doubt that we would be here today. Instead, Daisy Gilbert would have been dead and buried by now.'

He waited for the jury to consider his words then he continued. 'Daisy Gilbert is a fine woman who has suffered a great deal for the good of her family and then when eventually things were going well for her, this dreadful incident happened. It was not of her making and beyond her control. She was faced with a man who was set on his course to violate her, maybe even take her life, and now she stands before you. Innocent of the charges brought before you. How could you possibly send her to the gallows? You must find her not guilty and let her get on with her life. She's certainly earned that freedom.'

He walked back to his seat and sat down.

Daisy, hearing the word gallows . . . froze. She had never even considered the fact that she might have to face the death penalty! Oh my God! she thought. It was possible if the jury found her guilty that the judge could place the black hat upon his head and order her to be hanged. She started to tremble.

Seeing her distress, the female warder placed a hand on her shoulder. 'Take a deep breath, Gilbert. You don't want to collapse now. It won't look good.'

The judge was making his summary to the jury, but Daisy didn't hear a word as she fought to control herself. She was vaguely aware of the jury leaving the courtroom and then was told to stand as the judge went to his chambers while the jury decided on their verdict.

Daisy was led down the steps to meet with her solicitor and barrister and where she was given a drink of water.

'How long will we have to wait?' she asked nervously.

'You never know,' Edward told her. 'It could be hours and as it's getting late, if they take their time, it could be tomorrow before we get a verdict.'

At that moment the clerk of the court walked in to tell them that the jury needed more time and, as it was getting late, the case would be held in the morning at ten o'clock.

Daisy was distraught. She wanted it over and done with – whatever the verdict. Edward tried to comfort her.

'Try and get some sleep, Daisy. It will all be over tomorrow.'

She looked at him, her face pale and drawn. 'Have I got any chance at all?'

'A very good one and I want you to believe that.' He rose to his feet and picked up his briefcase. 'I'll see you tomorrow. Keep the faith,' he advised.

But that night in the holding cell, Daisy was finding it very hard to keep the faith. She'd watched carefully as Quentin spoke to the jury and had been unable to gauge the response to his plea for a not guilty verdict. Would she ever walk back into her shop in East Street again? If she was found guilty, how would her mother manage?

She tried to sleep but dreamed she was standing on the scaffold, a rope being placed round her neck. She woke up screaming.

Twenty-Six

Standing in the washroom of the police station the next morning, Daisy Gilbert looked at her reflection in the mirror. The deep circles under her eyes showed her lack of sleep and her pale face was etched with concern. This morning would mean either her freedom, long incarceration or . . . much worse. She dressed slowly, her trembling fingers having great difficulty doing up the small buttons of her blouse.

She was given a mug of hot tea and some toast by a policewoman and told to try and eat it. 'You'll need your strength for the courtroom,' she was told. Looking at the grim expression on the woman's face, Daisy wondered if she knew something that she didn't?

The public gallery of the court was full to capacity. The local and national press were gathered, smelling a good story for their newspapers. Grace and Vera sat, holding hands, both fearful of the verdict and when the jury walked in and took their places, Grace tried to read their expressions in the hope of gleaning something that would help her to judge their conclusion, but they all looked so serious she felt her heart miss a beat.

Daisy was led up the steps to take her place in the dock and eventually the clerk of the court announced the arrival of the judge. Everyone stood as he walked to his chair and sat down.

The judge fiddled with his papers for a moment and then staring over at the jury asked, 'Have you reached a verdict that you all agree upon?'

The foreman stood up. 'We have my lord.'

'Do you find the defendant guilty or not guilty of the charge of murder?'

Everyone held their breath and not a sound was heard.

'Not guilty!'

The court erupted. The members of the press ran from the room to report to their editors, Grace and Vera jumped to their feet and hugged each other and Daisy just stood as if frozen to the spot.

'Miss Gilbert,' said the judge, 'you are free to go.'

It was then that her legs gave way. The policewoman caught her and lowered her to the seat. 'Congratulations, Miss, you are a free woman.'

Edward came over to her. 'Daisy, are you all right?'

She looked at him with a dazed expression. 'Can I go home now?'

'You certainly can. I suggest we go to the nearest hotel for a very stiff drink. You look as if you need a brandy.'

Outside in the corridor, Daisy clung to Grace and her mother and then turned to Quentin de la Hay and shook his hand. 'Thank you so much,' she said.

'It was my pleasure, Daisy. Believe me it was a privilege to be part of all this.' He smiled at her. 'Now you can get on with your life. You'll be the centre of local gossip for a while, but ignore it, because in time no one will remember. I promise.'

A little later as they sat round a table in a nearby hotel, Daisy was handed a glass of brandy and told to sip it slowly, then Grace ordered a bottle of champagne and some sandwiches. Looking at Daisy she thought it prudent to get some food inside her because she looked so drawn. Edward had joined them and they all chatted merrily about nothing in general, trying to give Daisy time to recover. Every one of them had been under a certain amount of tension, but none more than Daisy herself.

Vera caught hold of her daughter's hand. 'You all right, love? Only you look so pale. You're not going to faint on me are you?'

With a wry smile Daisy said, 'No, I'm fine, honestly. It's just that I'm trying to get used to being free and able to go where I like. You have no idea how strange it feels after being shut away in a small cell.'

Vera tried not to think about it. 'It'll be lovely to have you back home . . . I have missed you so much.'

It was then that Daisy started to cry.

Edward softly said, 'That's the best thing she could do, it will release all her tension. She'll feel much better after.'

And she did. After the tears had stopped flowing, Daisy felt as if a huge load had been lifted from her shoulders. But she couldn't help thinking about Belle and the years still stretching ahead for her without any release and she realized just how precious her freedom was. It was something that everyone took so much for granted until it was taken away from you and she vowed to make the best of every minute of her future.

'You need to take a rest now,' Grace said. 'It will take a while for you to settle down to normality.'

But Daisy would have none of it. 'No fear,' she said. 'I will come into the shop tomorrow and take a look around. I'll be back working in it in a few days' time. That's all I need, a couple of days, then I'll be just fine.' Seeing the look of uncertainty on her friend's face she said, 'I need to work, Grace.'

'Then you must do what you think is right for you, Daisy. I for one will be delighted to see you back in the workroom and so will the girls.'

When she arrived home that night, Grace rang Giles to tell him the good news.

'That's wonderful. Are you all right, Grace?'

She felt her eyes fill with tears. The day had taken its toll on them all. 'No, Giles, to be honest, I'm not.'

'I'll be right over,' he said.

When he arrived he took one look at the anguish on her face and took her into his arms. She burst into tears.

'That's right, Grace my dear, have a good howl. You've been a tower of strength to everyone else, but now you can let go.'

When eventually she recovered, she told Giles what had tran-spired in the courtroom.

'When the jury entered after their deliberation, they all looked so very grim, my heart sank,' she said. 'For one terrible moment I thought they were going to give a guilty verdict. It was almost too much to bear for us, so God knows how Daisy felt.'

'I can't even imagine,' he said. 'How was she when you left her?'

'Shaken, relieved, confused. That poor girl has been through so much, it's unbelievable.'

'And you, dear Grace, have been wonderful the way you handled her defence, looked after her mother and ran the business. I think you are an amazing woman.'

'Stop it, Giles, or you'll start me off again!'

The staff all showed their delight when Daisy went into the shop the following day. They greeted her so warmly that Daisy was overcome. 'Grace told me how hard you all worked and looking around I can see how well you've all done.' She inspected a garment. 'This is superb.'

Agnes beamed at her. 'Well we couldn't let you or Mrs Portman down now, could we? After all, clients come to us because we are the best.'

Daisy walked around inspecting the work on hand and was delighted. Agnes showed her a gown which needed the skirt shortened when the client came in for a fitting this morning. And when Grace showed her the bookings she was even more pleased.

'So are we making any money?' she asked Grace.

'Enough. We are paying our suppliers on time, covering our costs and paying back a little of the money put up to finance the business, so by the end of the year we should do a little more than break even and next year should see us in profit.'

At that moment the expected client came into the shop for her fitting. She was one of the new brigade of customers. Her eyes lit up when she saw Daisy.

'I read in the paper that they let you out!' she declared with the utmost glee. 'Wait until I tell my friends I met the murderess herself!'

Daisy froze for a moment and then she said, 'I am so happy that I have enlightened your day, madam. I was looking at your gown in the workroom. I'll get one of the girls to cut away the extra material on the skirt because you wouldn't want me to approach you with a pair of scissors in my hand, would you?' She stood in front of the woman and stared at her.

The woman went white as if the blood had drained away from her and her eyes widened with shock. Daisy smiled at her, then walked out of the room.

Grace followed her, chuckling. 'That was very naughty of you,' she said, 'but the bitch deserves it.'

Daisy looked at Grace and grinned broadly. 'Sorry, couldn't resist it, but believe me she would have got a thrill from it and no doubt will dine out on it for months.' She burst out laughing. 'Oh Grace, you have no idea how much I've learned about human nature these past months. I used to think my reputation would ruin my business, but you know, in some perverse way it might just improve it!'

*   *   *

During the weeks that followed, Daisy got used to the stares and nudges of people who recognized her when she went into a shop. She ignored the whispers as she passed and just smiled. In time, the clients that had left returned one by one after discovering that they couldn't find the expertise in the stitching or the fashionable style elsewhere. When Daisy attended any of them, she was polite and made no mention of their return.

'Good morning, Madam,' she would say. 'How nice to see you. Now what can I do for you?' And so the clients were not embarrassed.

Her name was once again in the local news when Flo Cummings was up before the court, charged with living off immoral earnings. Although Daisy wasn't called as a witness, the previous facts of her being one of Flo's girls, and the consequences, were again mentioned.

'Is there to be no end to all this?' Daisy cried as she read the paper in the reception area of her shop.

'Try not to get upset about it, Daisy,' urged Grace who was counting the day's takings. 'It was bound to happen, Edward did warn you.'

'I know, but to be truthful, I'd forgotten. It's just that at last people were beginning to forget my past and accept me, but now it's shoved down their necks once again. And then there's my poor mum. The neighbours will be having a good gossip behind their damned curtains. They've only just stopped twitching them every time I walk into the house.'

'Your mother will cope don't you worry. Let's face it; you've both been through worse. Anyway, Flo will be the main topic of conversation, not you.'

Daisy couldn't help but grin. 'You know I thought she was such a friend, but all I was to her was a little gold mine.' And she started to laugh.

'What is it?'

'I know one person who will be delighted by the turn of events.'

'And who might that be?'

'The wife of the landlord of the White Swan. Flo was his mistress for years and his wife and Flo both used to get their gowns made at Madam Evans. We had to be careful they weren't booked in for fittings at the same time. She hated Flo and chose the most expensive material in the shop, making her husband pay through the nose.'

Bertha Grant was sitting reading about the case in the local paper with a broad smile. 'Serves the bitch right!' she muttered under her breath. 'I hope they send her down for a long stretch.' She thought she might take herself along to the court tomorrow and see for herself what was happening. How she would enjoy watching Flo standing in the dock. Nothing would give her greater pleasure and how she would crow about it to her husband. Oh my, vengeance was sweet!

The following morning, Bertha dressed in her finest outfit and most stylish hat, extravagantly trimmed with feathers, and made her way to the court, finding a seat in the front of the public gallery. She found the proceedings most interesting and was absolutely delighted when Flo Cummings at one time glanced up at the public gallery and saw her sitting there. The look on the woman's face was a thing to behold. First the surprise, then the anger tinged with embarrassment. Bertha just raised her eyebrows and cast her a look of utter disdain. It was better than a night at the theatre and when Flo was sent down for two years, Bertha could hardly contain her pleasure. And she made her feelings very clear when she returned to the White Swan.

'You're all dressed up this morning,' her husband Jim remarked. 'Been somewhere special?'

'You could say so. I've been sitting in court watching your doxy go down for two years!' She couldn't hide the smile of satisfaction. 'She'll have no use for the expensive gowns you bought for her in there!'

'You really are a first-class cow, Bertha.'

'At least I don't live off immoral earnings.'

'That's quite true, and I'm certain you have never had an immoral thought in your head; if you had, you might be more satisfying in the bedroom!' With that stinging remark, he walked out of the room.

All of Bertha's feeling of euphoria was destroyed. It was as if she'd received a blow to her solar plexus. She'd never found sex to be anything but a duty, but her shortcomings put in so many words was hurtful and demeaning. And of course she couldn't deny it was because of her lack of enthusiasm that Jim had turned to Flo Cummings . . . a thoroughly immoral woman! And now she wondered, without his mistress, would her husband find another to take her place? She took the hatpin out of her hat, which she threw across the room in anger. The pleasure she had wallowed in so much this morning, was now gone.

When Daisy heard of the verdict handed out to Flo Cummings, she felt no sympathy. She'd played with the law for so long and so successfully, but at last it had caught up with her. The club was closed, the girls dispersed to wherever. She thanked God that Harry had found work elsewhere and Stella had her cafe on the Isle of Wight; as for the others, they would drift off to another establishment or take to the streets. They − like her − would have to get on with their lives as best they could. And if they had saved their money as she had, they might be able to start a new life, out of the same business, because Daisy couldn't honestly believe a woman became a whore by choice. How could they?

Twenty-Seven

A few days later, Daisy had slipped out of the shop to buy a certain shade of cotton, when she saw a man coming towards her in army uniform, walking with a crutch. She was surprised to recognize Jack, her former boyfriend. She was even more surprised at his icy reception when she greeted him.

'Jack! How lovely to see you, my but you look as if you've been in the wars.'

'Hello, Daisy,' he said with a distinct coolness in his voice. 'I was wounded a couple of months back, but I'll soon be fine. I read all about you in the local paper.' He looked at her with disdain. 'How could you sell yourself like that? I couldn't believe that you became one of Flo Cummings' girls. You should have listened to me when I told you to give up working as a barmaid in the Solent Club, then you would never have had to face a jury charged with murder!'

Her back hackles rose. 'You forgot to mention that I was found not guilty! You'll never understand, Jack, and I am certainly *not* going to stand here and make excuses for my behaviour. Get well soon.' And she strode away, head held high. Pompous ass, she thought. How high and mighty he did sound. She didn't have to answer to him or anyone! But his cruel remarks had hurt her. This would be the way all men would think of her, and there was little hope of her having any kind of relationship with the opposite sex. No man would want to marry her knowing that other men had known her intimately and that she'd killed a man even if it was in self-defence. Oh well, if that was the price she would have to pay – so be it. She at least had her career. That was something. She didn't tell Grace of her encounter when she returned. She would put it behind her along with everything else in her life that was unpleasant.

Vera too had suffered a backlash from her friends after Daisy's case came to court and she had given up most of them. So many voiced their distaste over Daisy's way of life and Vera had met all of this with anger as she defended her daughter and when Flo's case was written of in the paper, she again met the stares of her neighbours with contempt. They all were entitled to their opinion as long as they kept it to themselves. But she did wonder if Daisy would ever meet a man who could see beyond the scandal and love the girl for who she was, a girl with a good heart. She hoped so, but deep down, she doubted it. She of course kept such thoughts to herself.

With more time on her hands now, she took in more work for Daisy. She was a fine needlewoman and her work was much appreciated and admired by Daisy's workforce and the clients. It meant that Vera was earning more money and that gave her independence. It was good for her that she wasn't entirely dependent on her daughter for every penny. They did however depend on each other for company. At the end of the day Daisy would come home, tired after a long day and the two of them enjoyed their time together. The difficult past brought the two closer and they were a great comfort to each other.

'We're like a couple of old maids, Mum,' said Daisy one evening. 'All we need is a couple of cats!'

'Not bloody likely!' Vera exclaimed. 'Think of the hair and what if they clawed at my sewing.'

Daisy laughed. 'I was only joking, Mum.'

They decided to go to the Palace of Variety on the Saturday evening, to give themselves a treat. It was a good programme with jugglers, a sword swallower, a comedian and finishing with a singer. It lifted their spirits and they came out of the building talking about the acts, when Daisy saw two men in naval uniform. As they turned, she saw one was Steven Noaks. He stopped when he saw her and came over to them.

'Daisy!' He smiled and said, 'How lovely to see you.'

She introduced her mother and he introduced his friend. 'We're just going for a drink,' said Steven. 'Would you two ladies care to join us?'

Daisy glanced at her mother, who shrugged. 'Thank you, Steven, we'd like that.'

The four of them sat in the saloon bar of the nearest hostelry. Steven's friend was in deep conversation with Vera and Steven gazed fondly at Daisy.

'You are looking well.'

'Thanks. How long have you been in port?' she asked.

'We docked this morning and decided we were in need of some entertainment other than the pub. How are you?'

'Fine now,' she said hesitantly, not knowing how much he knew about her arrest.

'I read about you in the papers just as we sailed. I was so sorry to hear of your troubles. It must have been dreadful for you.'

'It was, but I really don't want to talk about it, Steven. I'm trying to put it all behind me. I'm working hard and I'm happy to say the business is holding up. My unsavoury reputation doesn't seem to have done too much harm, I'm happy to say.' She gave a wry smile, remembering how he left her the last time. How he kissed her passionately then walked away. She'd not heard a word from him since and she wondered how much her reputation had changed things between them.

The two men walked them home but declined a cup of coffee or tea.

'Sorry, Daisy, but we are on night duty in an hour,' Steven explained, 'but I'll be in touch.' He kissed her on the cheek, shook hands with her mother and said goodnight.

Once inside the house, Vera made a pot of tea. 'Nice couple of blokes,' Vera said as she poured the hot beverage.

'I didn't know the other chap,' Daisy said, 'but I knew Steven from the Solent Club. He's a nice man.'

Just how well did Daisy know him? Vera couldn't help but wonder, but she said nothing more and the conversation about the men ended.

Bert Croucher was at a loose end. Now that the Solent Club had closed, he'd had to find another venue in which to spend his Saturday evenings. He'd tried the Horse and Groom in East Street, but it was rowdy on a Saturday with the inevitable fights breaking out. It was also the favourite drinking spot for the local ladies of the night. At least here he was free to pay for their services, unlike the Solent Club where he was barred from using the whores. But he still lusted after Gloria, or Daisy Gilbert as she was he learned after reading about the murder of his old mate.

He knew all about her business and how talented she was and she seemed to be doing well. She wouldn't be interested in him; she'd made that quite clear. Well he was doing very well himself in the butcher's shop. He could even afford a wife if he so wished.

Daisy Gilbert wouldn't be interested in him as a punter, but how would she react to an offer of marriage? It was respectable and she would share his bed as Mrs Bert Croucher. He smiled to himself and thought after all, no ordinary decent man would want her after the Solent Club. Well he didn't mind that at all, which made him quite special, he mused. Yes, he wasn't a bad catch; he could provide a home, money for clothes, and a good living too. After all, he wasn't a bad-looking bloke; he dressed well, and what more could a girl ask for – especially one who had been a prostitute.

On Wednesday, his half day, Croucher had a bath, went to the barber's for a haircut, picked up his best suit from the cleaners and prepared to propose to Daisy Gilbert. On the way to her shop, he bought an extravagant bunch of flowers. He arrived just as she was closing.

Bert opened the door of the shop and entered. He was taken aback by the classy interior, the beige carpet, chairs covered in velvet, and a small desk. It was simple but tasteful. He began to feel a little out of his depth. The well-dressed woman behind the desk spoke.

'Good afternoon, sir. Can I be of help in any way?'

Blimey! He thought, what a classy bird, so well spoken. Daisy had really come up in the world. 'I would like a word with Miss Gilbert, please.'

'And who shall I say wants to see her?'

With a coy smile he said, 'If you don't mind I'd like to make it a surprise.'

Grace rose from her seat and walked into the workroom. 'Daisy, there's a gentleman bearing flowers in reception wanting to see you. He won't give his name; he says he wants to surprise you.'

Daisy immediately thought it was Steven and rushed into the reception. When she saw her visitor, she froze to the spot.

Bert Croucher rose somewhat awkwardly from the chair which seemed lost beneath his large frame.

'Hello, Daisy,' he said. 'I bought these for you,' and thrust the flowers at her.

She had no choice but to take them, but she looked at him very warily. 'Thank you.'

For a man who could look menacing, Bert was unusually shy. 'I expect I'm the last person you expected to see,' he ventured.

'Yes, I was surprised. What can I do for you?' Her mind was racing. What on earth was he doing here? And where the hell was Grace?

Grace was in the workshop, thinking she would give her friend some privacy.

'I don't suppose we could go somewhere where we could have a private conversation?' he asked.

Daisy was horrified at the thought. She was afraid of this man and no way on earth would she be alone with him.

'I'm sorry but we are very busy at the moment,' she quickly replied, 'but there isn't anyone here at the moment.' She glanced behind her but the door to the workroom was closed.

Bert Croucher cleared his throat. 'Well, Daisy, I wanted to offer you a home.'

She was completely puzzled by this. 'But I have a home.'

'I know that. I mean a home with me – as my wife?'

He looked at the shocked expression on her face. 'I know this offer will come as a complete surprise to you, but I've been thinking. As you are aware, I've always fancied you, and I thought if you agreed I could make an honest woman of you. After all I doubt you'll get an offer of marriage from any man after your past . . . but I don't mind that!' He hurried on now he'd started. 'I can provide for you, Daisy. My business is doing well; you'll have plenty of money for housekeeping and a good allowance for clothes. I'll take care of you. What do you say?' He stood before her with a satisfied smile, pleased with himself. Certain that she would see his point of view – and be grateful to him.

Daisy Gilbert was shaken to the core. Who did Bert Croucher think he was speaking to her in such a condescending manner as if he was saving her from herself? But she also knew that this man could be dangerous and she would have to pick her words carefully.

'Thank you for the flowers, Mr Croucher, and for your offer of marriage, but I must refuse. I am running a successful business as you are and I do not plan to marry any man. I shall remain a spinster and be happy to do so.'

This was not the response he was expecting at all.

'But there is no need for you to be a spinster. I'll happily take you on,' he said angrily.

Daisy could feel her own anger rising. 'I don't want to be "taken on", thank you very much,' she snapped.

'Now you listen to me, girl,' he began.

Her eyes blazing, Daisy interrupted him. 'No, you listen to me!

I'm sure you meant well, but I don't want to be your wife, now is that quite clear?'

His demeanour changed. His eyes narrowed and his mouth tightened. 'You'll get no better offer. No man will want you as his wife with your past; I was prepared to overlook that.'

'And I am prepared to overlook your impertinence, but it's time you left my premises, Mr Croucher, as I do not intend to argue with you . . . and take these with you.' She shoved the flowers back at him. 'Good day to you!'

He went out slamming the door behind him.

It was then that Grace appeared.

'Are you all right?' she asked when she saw her thunderous expression.

'No I bloody well am not! That damned butcher had the temerity to offer me marriage as no other man ever would, knowing my past, but he didn't mind that and was prepared to take me on! Really!'

'Who is this man?' asked Grace.

'He was a friend of Ken Woods. A nasty piece of work if ever there was one.'

'Will he cause you any trouble?' Grace looked worried.

Daisy frowned. 'To be honest I don't know. He was furious at my refusal; I thought he was going to take the door off its hinges when he left.'

'I heard the door slam, that's why I came through. Oh Daisy, what are you going to do?'

'I don't see I can do anything, after all he hasn't done anything wrong. I'll just have to hope he'll calm down and accept what I said.'

But she was worried, knowing the man's reputation.

Twenty-Eight

Bert Croucher strode angrily down East Street, pushing pedestrians aside, still clutching his bunch of flowers. How dare that bitch dismiss him like that! There he was, offering her respectability and she turned him down. Who the hell did she think she was? He tossed the flowers into the gutter. A shabby street urchin stopped and picked them up, before running away.

Croucher called into the Horse and Groom and ordered a large whiskey. He sat and fumed as he drank it down before ordering another. That girl needs teaching a lesson. She would learn to her cost it didn't pay to treat Bert Croucher that way, he thought, as he sat sulking in the corner.

At the end of the day, Daisy had another male visitor, but this time she was happy to see Steven Noaks enter her shop and was thrilled after he'd looked around and was obviously impressed.

'Hello, Daisy, this really is very smart I must say.' He walked over to inspect the gowns, displayed. 'These are beautiful, so much intricate work and so stylish. You are indeed a talented young woman.'

'Thank you,' she said, smiling happily. 'To what do I owe the pleasure of your visit?'

Walking over to her he said, 'I wondered if you would like to come out to dinner this evening?'

Daisy was delighted at the invitation. 'I'd love to,' she replied.

'I'll come and pick you up about seven this evening then.'

'Do you remember where I live?'

'Yes indeed I do. I'll see you later.'

Grace emerged from the workroom as he was leaving. She gazed at the uniformed young man with curiosity. Seeing the happy expression on her friend's face she said, 'I can see that this time you have no concerns about this visitor.'

Gleefully, Daisy said, 'No. Steven and I are old friends; he's taking me out to dinner this evening. I must rush home and get changed.'

★　　★　　★

As she dressed for her date, Daisy wondered if this time he would ask to see her again or would he just walk away at the end of the evening as he had done before? She had no need to hide her past from him, after all he'd been the one to pay for taking her virginity and she remembered just how he'd made love to her. The gentle way he'd treated her. Was she wrong when she thought there had been a certain feeling of affection there too? She hoped not because she'd thought of him often and had longed to see him again. Now that he had returned, was she foolish to hope that he was here to stay?

During dinner, Steven didn't mention the Solent Club or the fact that she'd been taken to court accused of murder. She wondered if it was to spare her feelings or was it because he didn't want to think about it? She tried to push such thoughts to the back of her head and enjoy his company.

They discussed the past sinking of the *Lusitania* by a German submarine and the loss of so many lives, several of them women and children.

'Aren't you afraid when you cross the Atlantic?' she asked.

'At the moment, the *Mauritania* is being used as a troopship; we have to carry men who are fighting in the Gallipoli offensive. It's vital we get them there and we pray that it will be a safe journey. We do have superior speed which is a help. We don't have a choice I'm afraid.'

He questioned her about her business. 'I'm amazed to see you doing so well; how did it all come about?' he asked.

'After Dad died, I stayed on at the Solent Club' – there she'd mentioned it – 'until I had enough money to start work in one room. Then Grace Portman offered me a partnership after I wrote to her. Her money allowed us to move into proper premises and expand. I was able to employ more staff – and so we grew.'

'How do you know Grace?'

'She was a client of mine when I worked in London Road. I was amazed that a lady of her breeding wanted to finance me, I must say, but it seems to be working very well.' She paused. 'I did tell her about my background when she made her offer, as it seemed only fair.'

'That obviously didn't daunt her in any way,' Steven said.

'No, she's an unusual woman. I'm very lucky.'

Steven sipped his wine, looking at Daisy over the rim of his glass. 'You too are an unusual woman.'

'Me?' she said with surprise.

'Yes, you. You have been through so much and yet, you've managed to overcome all that . . . and now you have your own business. I think that's very unusual.'

'But I am still a woman with a past, Steven. It will be there to haunt me the rest of my days. Someone will always remember and bring it up. I have to live with that and so will those who are a part of my life.'

'That sounds like a warning, Daisy.'

She smiled softly as she gazed at him. 'I think it's something you should be aware of. I would hate for you to be affected by it and talked about, just because you have taken me out to dinner.'

He chuckled as he looked at her. 'That's really very sweet of you, but you forget, I was part of your past.'

'Do you think I've ever forgotten that for a moment?' she said. 'What you did for me that night was something very special. But it's what happened after that has me marked as a scarlet woman.'

'But, darling Daisy, you were a reluctant sinner! You did what you had to for your father . . . and then for yourself. It was a valiant thing to do.'

'That's not how many people look at it; to them I was a common whore!'

He took her hands in his. 'I don't ever want to hear you describe yourself that way again. I *never* thought of you in those terms and I *never* will!'

It meant so much to hear this from him, that Daisy was overcome and couldn't speak. But she knew that sadly others wouldn't agree with him. She could live with it – but it was a lot to ask from another.

'That makes *you* a special person too,' she said, trying to lighten the conversation. 'Are you in port for long?' she asked trying to change the subject.

'Yes, as a matter of fact I am. The ship has to go into dry dock, so I'll be around for a few weeks. Of course I'll have to be on duty some of that time. Perhaps you would like to come on board one day. I could give you a tour of the ship.'

'Oh, Steven that would be wonderful! I've often wondered

what an ocean liner looked like and what it would be like to sail on one. Are you sure it would be all right for me to go on board?'

'Absolutely! I can show you around and then we could have lunch in my cabin.'

'Really? I can't tell you how exciting that would be.'

He was amused by her enthusiasm. 'When it's your workplace you forget that to others it can be so interesting. It will give me the greatest pleasure. How about this coming Sunday; then you won't have to take any time off from your business?'

'Oh, yes please.'

He looked fondly at her. 'It doesn't take a lot to please you does it?'

Her eyes widened. 'You have no idea just what a treat you're offering. Steven Noaks, you have become blasé!'

He laughed loudly. 'Me? Never! You forget that I've been at sea for a long time.'

When later he walked her home, he kissed her with great longing as he held her close. 'It's so good to see you again, darling Daisy. I'll pick you up at eleven o'clock on Sunday morning.' And he kissed her yet again.

When Daisy walked into her living room, she was in a state of euphoria. She could still feel the imprint of Steven's lips on hers, the feel of his strong arms as he held her. She didn't know when she'd been so happy.

Vera looked up from her sewing. 'Well it's obvious to a blind man that you've had a good evening.'

'I've just spent a very enjoyable meal in good company. Steven is a purser and he's taking me over his ship on Sunday for a tour and then lunch. Imagine, Mum, what it must be like to be a passenger on such a liner?'

'That's for people with money and not for the likes of us, I'm afraid,' Vera remarked with her usual down-to-earth logic.

But Daisy would not be daunted. 'Who knows? Maybe one day if the business is successful, we could afford a trip.'

'On the Isle of Wight ferry maybe,' Vera retorted.

'Oh Mother! You must have a dream. Something to strive for in life, or how would we ever survive?'

'Ah well, love, I've been around a lot longer that you. I only want enough money to live on and pay the bills . . . and to be healthy,' she added. 'That's enough for me.'

Daisy leaned down and hugged her. 'At least we can do that already, thank goodness.'

And that was all down to her daughter, Vera thought as she continued to sew. She was pleased to see Daisy so happy, my God she deserved it after what she'd been through. Folding her work carefully, she prepared for bed. Putting out the lights, the two of them went upstairs.

As Daisy lay in her bed she wondered what Steven was thinking. He couldn't have kissed her as he had done without some kind of feelings for her. But were they enough? Anyway, she'd enjoy every moment without expecting anything, then she wouldn't be disappointed. She turned over and settled down – and fell asleep with her fingers crossed.

At the Manor House in Brockenhurst the same evening, Grace Portman received an unexpected visitor. Frank Baker, Hugh's batman, called to see her. He was still in uniform, but looked gaunt and unwell. She ushered him into the living room and poured him a brandy.

'I'm so pleased to see you,' she told him. 'I often wondered what happened to you.'

He told her briefly about the action he'd seen. 'I've been invalided out of the army and am waiting to sign off. My lungs are shot from the gas attacks we had.' He started coughing, then apologized. 'Sorry about that, it catches me unawares at times.' He sipped his drink. 'I was with your husband when he died, Mrs Portman.'

Grace felt the blood drain from her face. She was just beginning to start the day without thoughts of her husband being uppermost in her mind and now she was faced with the fact of his demise.

'Did he suffer?' she asked quietly. 'Only they wouldn't allow us to open the coffin.'

Baker hesitated. How could he tell her that her husband was blown up by an exploding bomb and severely injured? 'No, Mrs Portman, he didn't feel a thing. It was very sudden.' At least that was the truth. 'He was a fine officer, very brave and held in high regard by his men. I thought you'd like to know that.'

'I always worried that he would take unnecessary chances,'

she admitted. 'Hugh was a bit gung-ho, if you know what I mean?'

The man smiled. 'He was fearless it's true, but he was too good an officer to be foolish.' He drank his drink and rose to his feet. 'I must be on my way but I just wanted to come and see you and tell you about the Captain.'

'Where are you staying?' Grace asked anxiously as she was concerned for his health.

'In the village with my family.'

'Then I'll get my man to drive you home.' As Baker went to refuse, she insisted. 'It's the least I can do.' She rang the bell for the maid and instructed her to tell the chauffeur to bring the car.

When she was alone, she thought about Hugh. She was pleased to know that he hadn't taken any chances during his time abroad. That had been a great relief. She wondered just what he would have thought of her being in business and allowed a slow smile to creep across her features. He would have had a fit! She, however, had found it an ideal way to get on with her life and cope with being a widow.

When eventually she went to bed, she felt a sense of closure after Frank Baker's visit. At least she knew that Hugh hadn't suffered and that meant a great deal.

Twenty-Nine

It was a bright sunny day when Steven called for Daisy on the Sunday to take her for a guided trip around the *Mauritania*. She looked up at the four funnels and was astonished at the size of the ship and although it was wearing camouflage paint in an effort to confuse the enemy, the ship still had a kind of majesty about it. She was thrilled as they walked up the gangway thinking how marvellous it would be to do this as a passenger.

The interior had of course been utilized for the use of the many troops being carried, but it was still possible to see the beautifully hand-carved wood panelling in the first-class public rooms and Daisy was very taken by the dome skylight in the first-class dining salon.

Eventually Steven took her on to the bridge. All she could think about as she looked out over the bow of the ship from what seemed a great height, was what on earth it would feel like to be standing there in mid-Atlantic when there was a rough sea? It must be terrifying!

She relaxed soon afterwards in Steven's cabin. As befitting his position as purser, his cabin was spacious with a sitting area with a table and chairs and a couple of armchairs, as well as his bunk in the far corner.

'Gosh! This is bigger than some people's homes!' she declared.

At that moment the steward appeared and smiled at her before he laid the table and then served them lunch. He opened a bottle of wine, poured it, then left them alone.

Daisy grinned broadly as she looked at the food and sipped her wine. 'This really isn't a bad life you have, is it?'

He agreed. 'It can be a privilege, but then again a seaman spends a lot of time away from home, which makes life lonely if you are married. Your wife would have to understand this. It's a lot to ask of a woman.'

'I understand that,' said Daisy, 'after all Southampton is a seaport and many families I know have someone who goes to sea. But if you are in love, you'd accept your man's way of life. Being a seafarer's wife is a hell of a lot better than being married to our poor soldiers out there fighting. At least you wouldn't be worried about your man being killed in action.'

'Yes, that's true. When I see the troops leaving the ship I do wonder just how many will return.'

They finished their meal and sat in the armchairs drinking coffee until Steven said, 'It's time for me to get you home, Daisy. I'm on fire watch this evening.'

As she stood up he took her into his arms and kissed her. As she twined her arms around his neck and returned his kiss, Steven murmured as he nuzzled her neck. 'It's just as well we have to leave because I want to make love to you again.'

'I would like that too,' she whispered as she felt her body long for his touch.

He picked her up and lay her down on his bed. 'Let's make the time, darling Daisy,' he urged.

She didn't deny him.

On the Monday morning as Daisy was getting dressed she hummed happily to herself. Yesterday had been brilliant! The tour of the *Mauritania* had been an eye-opener for her. Living on board an ocean liner was like being in a different world. An exciting one at that and she could understand why, when members of the crew eventually retired, they found it difficult to settle to a life ashore.

Steven had been so interesting to listen to and as good a lover as she remembered, and as thoughtful. This time when they made love she was more experienced, but she was grateful that he didn't remark on that fact – but she knew she'd been able to give him a lot of pleasure too. It had been a memorable time and she didn't regret it one bit. He had been thoughtful enough to provide a contraceptive so she had no concerns there. But she knew that even if he hadn't, she would still have consented, she longed for him so much.

As she unlocked the door to the shop in East Street, Daisy was still singing to herself. She stopped at the reception desk and looked at the appointment book to check on the clients who would be calling that day to either collect their gowns or come in for a fitting then, taking her coat off, she made her way to the workroom.

Daisy opened the door and screamed! The sewing machines had been smashed, the gowns on the tailors' dummies had been torn to shreds and the place had been turned upside down. Daisy staggered back against the wall as she surveyed the chaos.

'Bloody hell!' Agnes stood in the doorway. The others followed within minutes and lastly, Grace, who looked at the room in disbelief.

'No one touch anything!' she said. 'I'm calling the police.' And she walked out of the room.

Looking around Agnes said, 'Who on earth would do a thing like this?'

'I've no idea,' said Daisy, 'but whoever it was meant to cause absolute havoc. They have put us out of business. There isn't a sewing machine that isn't damaged.'

Grace returned. 'I've called the police and they are on their way. I suggest we all wait in reception until they come. Agnes, be a dear and pop down the road and bring us back a large pot of tea; that's good for shock and I think we all need it.'

East Street that morning was a scene of great excitement for some. News soon spread that the gown shop had been broken into. Members of the public lingered outside. Police milled around and clients called and were sent away. Daisy was despondent. They had worked so hard to get the business off the ground and it was in ruins.

One of the detectives on the scene took her aside for questioning.

'Miss Gilbert, do you know anyone who would have such a grudge against you that they would want to harm your business?'

'I can't imagine,' she said.

'What about clients? Was there one perhaps who wasn't happy with your work?'

'No, they have all been absolutely satisfied.'

'What about your personal life?' he asked.

With a frown she said, 'What ever do you mean?'

'Forgive me, but your past is no secret. Is there anyone from those days who would hold such a grudge?'

Daisy's eyes widened. Of course, how could she have forgotten? 'Yes there is. Bert Croucher. He used to come into the Solent Club. He did approach me recently and offered marriage. I refused of course and he was furious! I'd forgotten all about him.'

'Do you mean Croucher the butcher?'

'Yes, that's him!'

The man looked concerned. 'We've had dealings with him in the past. He's a nasty piece of work. Has he been back to see you since?'

'No, I've not seen him at all.'

'Of course we have no proof as yet but it does give us a suspect. We'll have to search the premises for fingerprints and any kind of evidence that might help us. I'm afraid you will be unable to use the workroom today.'

Grace sent the girls home and she and Daisy waited as the police did their job. Daisy told Grace what she'd told the detective. 'It's got to be Croucher,' she said. 'He's mean enough to do this just because I turned him down. I mean who else would do such a thing?'

'The back entrance was forced,' Grace informed her. 'That's how he or someone got in.'

'What are we going to do, Grace? Several gowns have been ruined beyond repair and will have to be made again, but we have no machines.'

'I'm not an army wife for nothing!' Grace declared. 'I have a battle plan. I've been on the phone to a firm who will let us hire three machines to tide us over. Fortunately I have several rolls of cloth at home, so we do have some material. Cheer up, Daisy, we'll get over this.'

'But at what cost?'

'It will be our loss, unfortunately. We'll all have to work doubly hard to make up the financial loss, but the staff are willing I'm sure.'

'If it is that bastard Croucher, I hope the police can prove it.'

Bert Croucher was working away in his butcher's shop whistling as he cut up the sides of beef ready for the counter. He was wondering how that bitch Daisy Gilbert was feeling this morning? He'd broken into her shop in the early hours and vented his frustration on everything he could get his hands on in the workroom. He'd taken a sledge hammer to the sewing machines, scissors to the gowns he could find and caused as much mayhem as he could in the workroom, keeping clear of the shop front in case he was seen there. It had felt great. Consequently, her business would suffer and she'd be forced to close. Serve her right! He was the wrong man to mess with and what's more, there was no way he could be blamed for it. He'd been very careful to wear gloves and no one had seen him at that hour. The streets had been empty. Now she may think twice about his proposal – with no business, how would she make a living?

The next morning, the staff at the gown shop cleared away the debris. Giles came in with Grace to help move the heavy stuff after she rang and told him what had happened. All broken machine parts had been kept together in boxes, just in case they were repairable. The torn gowns were carefully examined to see if there was anything that could be salvaged for future use and the room cleared. Later in the afternoon, the rented sewing machines arrived and once they were installed, work commenced. All the girls stayed late to try and make up for lost time, but they were having to remake several of the gowns. It was soul destroying for them all.

Giles went to a local cafe and provided sandwiches and tea to keep them going. He handed a cup to Grace. 'You must be exhausted,' he said. 'Drink this, it will do you good.'

She looked tired. 'Oh, Giles, how could anyone be so cruel as to do this?'

Shaking his head he said, 'I can't even begin to understand the mentality of such a person, but, Grace, it does worry me. For anyone to do such a thing, they must have really got it in for you or Daisy. She thinks it is this butcher chap.'

'I know, but what else can we do but carry on as best we can? At least the police are looking into it.'

At that moment the new back door arrived and was fitted and heavily barred to stop another break-in. But the damage had been done. The business had lost a lot of money. They hadn't taken out any insurance to cover the loss as both Daisy and Grace had agreed it could wait. Neither one had envisaged the need and thought it would save money. Now they both realized how foolish they had been.

'It'll take months of work to cover the costs,' Daisy stated wearily.

'Never mind,' Grace told her. 'It just means that we will have to work for a longer time before we make any money.'

'I feel dreadful,' said Daisy. 'You have so much more invested than I do, so you will be the main one to bear the brunt, financially.'

'We're in this together, Daisy. Your money was earned the hard way, mine was an inheritance. In my mind that makes you equal in the loss.'

At that moment, a worried-looking Steven hurried into the shop.

'I read in last night's paper about your break-in,' he told them. 'Are you both all right?'

They told him what had happened and introduced him to Giles who was just leaving.

'Who on earth would do such a thing?'

Grace said nothing but looked at Daisy wondering how much she wanted Steven to know. But Daisy told him about Croucher being a suspect – and why.

'He asked you to marry him?' Steven was incredulous.

'He said he wanted to make an honest woman out of me because no man would want me and he didn't mind about my past.' The words spilled out of her mouth.

'What a damned liberty! Who does he think he is? That man isn't good enough to clean your shoes!'

Daisy burst into tears.

Steven took her into his arms. 'Come on, darling, there's no need to cry.'

'Then stop saying such nice things about me!'

Steven shook his head, smiled at Grace and said, 'I'll never begin to understand women. Now, is there anything I can do?'

'Not really,' said Grace. 'The sewing machines were smashed up and we have some rented ones to tide us over. A few gowns ready for sale are ruined and will have to be made again and that will put us behind with our orders, but we'll get there, eventually.'

Having regained her composure, Daisy said, 'We won't let that bastard finish us.'

'Do the police have any evidence to prove that it was Croucher?' asked Steven.

Daisy shook her head. 'I don't think so. I don't know if they'll question him, but if they do he'll deny it and without evidence what can they do? And of course, it may not be him at all.'

Looking at his watch, Steven said, 'I have to get back to the ship, but I'll call round and see you tomorrow.' He kissed Daisy goodbye. 'Croucher was quite wrong,' he said, then walked out of the shop.

Daisy looked puzzled at his remark. 'What do you think he meant?' she asked her friend Grace.

'I think he was paying you another compliment,' she said smiling. 'He really is a very nice young man.'

'Yes, he is,' Daisy said. 'It would be nice if he stayed around for a while.'

'Why only a while?'

'Don't be silly, Grace. Steven is a good friend and I don't expect anything more from him than that. Come on, let's get on.'

But Grace Portman had her own thoughts on the matter.

Thirty

The detectives in charge of the break-in were sifting through the evidence they'd collected, searching for fingerprints. 'There are masses of prints, guv. We'll have to take all the staff's prints and then compare them, but if whoever did this wore gloves, we won't get anywhere.'

'Keep looking,' said Chief Inspector Riley, 'just in case they got careless. The perpetrator was obviously livid when he did the damage; you can tell, it was like a frenzied attack.' He paused in his work. 'I feel sorry for young Daisy Gilbert. She's been through the mill one way and another – and she managed to pull herself up by her shoe strings – and now this! Doesn't seem fair somehow.'

'When you look at her, guv, it doesn't seem possible that she was one of Flo Cummings' girls. She looks so wholesome.'

'What did you expect, sergeant, all garters and lace?'

The man blushed. 'No, but you've seen some of the brasses. A lot of them are as hard as nails – but not her.'

'Never judge a book by its cover; you should know that better than anyone,' Riley chided.

And the men continued with their work.

Bert Croucher was serving a customer the following morning when DI Riley called. Croucher recognized him immediately. When the customer had left, he glared at the policeman.

'Not here to buy meat I suppose?'

'No I'm not. Where were you in the early hours of Monday morning?'

'In my bed of course, where else would anyone be? And anyway what's it got to do with you?'

Riley just stared at the man. 'Wouldn't have been anywhere in East Street I suppose?'

Shaking his head, Croucher said, 'No, why on earth would I go there?'

'To turn over a business belonging to a young lady, the same young lady who turned down your proposal of marriage? You wouldn't have liked that, Croucher, would you?'

'I don't know what you're talking about.'

'Now you're being stupid. I know you proposed to Daisy Gilbert, there were two witnesses to the fact.'

'What if I did?'

'Piss you off did it, Daisy telling you to sling your hook?'

There was a thunderous expression on the face of the butcher. 'That's none of your business!'

Riley could tell he was getting under the skin of the other man and he pushed him even further. 'You couldn't have her at the club could you? I know that Flo barred you from hiring any of her girls because you have a reputation of beating up your women.'

Croucher didn't answer but his face reddened with anger.

'And Daisy didn't want anything to do with you once she was no longer on the game, so you offered marriage. She'd belong to you then, you could do what you liked to her and as often as you wanted. That's right isn't it?'

'What if it was?' Croucher roared. 'Nothing wrong with that. No other man would want her with her past. She'd have been an honest woman married to me.'

Riley laughed. 'She's far too good for you and I bet she'd rather die than share a bed with you! The whole idea is laughable!'

Croucher grasped the handle of a meat cleaver, but didn't lift it as he leaned against the butcher's block. 'Get out of my shop, Riley. You've asked your questions, now sod off!'

The detective gave a sardonic smile. 'I'll be seeing you in the future, Mr Croucher. You can bank on it.'

When he returned to the police station, Riley arranged for a twenty-four-hour watch to be kept on Daisy Gilbert and another on Croucher. 'I lit a fire under him today and if my instincts are correct he'll find out that Daisy is still in business and he'll not be able to rest there.'

His sergeant looked at him with horror. 'You've set her up as bait!'

Riley didn't change his expression. 'Yes, you could say that, but we have no evidence against him at the moment and after today's visit, I'm certain he's our man. Now we have to watch them both. Croucher isn't a man to cross. The police have had dealings with him in the past. He's been fined before now for causing a public disturbance and there was a rumour that he beat up a prostitute in Canal Walk one night.'

'What do you mean, a rumour?'

'The woman didn't make a complaint and it's believed he paid her to keep her mouth shut. He's a bad bastard.'

'Then Daisy Gilbert could be in great danger?'

'I'm sure she is, with or without our protection. But after today I don't think Croucher will hang around before he makes his move and that puts us in control.'

'Right,' said his colleague, 'I'd best get on with arranging a watch. It'll mean overtime, guv.'

'If it gets that man off the streets, it'll be money well spent. I know he was running some racket with Woods when he was alive, but we couldn't finger either of them.'

Harry the barman was the next caller at the gown shop. He'd been away visiting relatives and had only just heard about Daisy's shop being broken into.

'Any idea who it was?' he asked her as they sat talking at the end of the day.

With a worried look she said, 'I think it was Bert Croucher,' and she explained why.

'Bloody hell, girl! Being married to that nutter would be madness.'

She agreed. 'Can you imagine the shock when he asked me? He came in here with a bunch of flowers would you believe!'

Harry doubled up with laughter. 'Sorry, love, it isn't really funny but the picture I have of that big ugly brute, clutching a bunch of flowers like a lovesick fool, is just too much.'

'He certainly wasn't like any lovesick fool when I turned him down, he was livid. That man scares me to death; he always did when he used to sit and watch me in the club.'

As Harry walked home, he couldn't help but worry about his conversation with Daisy. Bert Croucher was a dangerous bloke and whereas he had been in a position to threaten Woods into leaving Daisy alone, there was nothing he could do about the butcher.

★　　★　　★

During the next few days, the staff in the workroom worked extra hours to try and make up time to enable them to fulfil their orders, although it did make delivery of them later than was planned. Their clients understood their difficulties and the majority of them were very understanding. Only two of their clients complained bitterly at being kept waiting, but Grace dealt with them in a firm but ladylike manner.

'Now, Mrs Frampton,' she said to one who was causing a scene in the waiting room, 'as you are aware, there's absolutely nothing I can do about you having to wait for your gown. However, if it is so very inconvenient, perhaps you'd like to cancel and go elsewhere?'

The woman huffed and puffed but in the end she decided to wait.

Grace smiled sweetly at her. 'I'm sure the wait will be worthwhile, after all, Miss Gilbert does have a waiting list, she's so much in demand.'

As the woman left the shop, Grace chuckled. 'Selfish old trout!' she murmured.

'Who's a selfish old trout?' asked Daisy as she walked into the reception.

'Mrs Frampton. She has nothing to do in this life but spend her husband's money and she was complaining at having to wait. She has absolutely no consideration for others.'

'But she spends a fortune, don't forget,' Daisy chided laughingly. 'We've finished for the day and the girls have just left. Are you ready to lock up?'

'Yes,' said Grace. 'I'm staying with my parents in Southampton for the next few days. The journey to Brockenhurst every night when we're working late is very inconvenient. Besides, mother spoils me and I love it; it's like being a child again.'

They locked up and parted outside, each going in a different direction.

'Are you all right to walk home?' Grace asked.

'Yes, why ever not?'

Grace refrained from voicing her concerns, but in the back of her mind she wondered if they were now free from the vengeance of whoever it was that had trashed the shop. Giles too shared her concerns as he'd told her. She herself was very careful to make sure no one was following her.

Daisy wasn't blind to Grace's concern for her safety and she wouldn't admit to her friend that she was nervous once she'd left the shop, but as each day passed, she began to relax a little.

The plain-clothes policeman who followed her was good at his job as never once was Daisy aware of his presence, and neither did she notice a man keeping watch outside her house.

Bert Croucher, however, cottoned on to the fact that he was under surveillance. He was from the old school of criminals, always aware of a police presence and after the visit to his shop by DI Riley, he'd been very watchful. It amused him. He'd clocked the man watching his shop almost immediately. Did the police think him a fool? Well he could play them at their old game.

Each evening, he went from one pub to another, giving the officer assigned to him the runaround. It became a game. He even stopped one and asked him for a light. The man had been leaning against the wall outside the Lord Roberts waiting for Croucher to come out. He was more than a little startled when Bert stopped in front of him waving an unlit cigarette. The look of amusement in the butcher's eyes made him realize he'd been noticed. The next night a different man took his place. One with more experience.

After a couple of days, Bert Croucher was convinced that the police, realizing he knew they were watching him, had dispensed with their man. He didn't see anyone watching the shop and although when he was out in the evenings, doubling back on his tracks to catch any tail out, he wasn't able to see a police presence, which gave him a false sense of security.

Walking along East Street, he discovered to his dismay that the gown shop was still in business and it infuriated him! That little bitch was still making a living and that didn't fit in with his plans at all. He glanced around but didn't spot the policeman shadowing him. He stormed off in high dudgeon. This was immediately reported to DI Riley.

'We need to be really vigilant now,' he told his men. 'He obviously thinks he's not being followed any more or he wouldn't have gone to East Street. Now he knows that Daisy Gilbert is open for business despite everything, he'll make a move. We must be ready for him.'

They didn't have long to wait.

Thirty-One

The policeman, who was watching Bert Croucher's house, leaned against the wall and took a final drag of his cigarette. It was past ten o'clock at night and all the lights in the house were out and the copper presumed that his quarry was now in bed. Needing the call of nature desperately, the man disappeared up a nearby alleyway to relieve himself and therefore didn't notice Bert leave his house and turn the corner of the street.

The butcher made his way towards the home of Daisy Gilbert, constantly looking over his shoulder to see if there was anybody about. Apart from a few customers at the local pub and the occasional seaman making his way back to the docks, there was no one of note.

Daisy was sitting alone, tired after a long day in the workshop. Her mother, Vera, had long since taken to her bed. Daisy stood up and stretched before taking her cup into the scullery, ready to lock the back door for the night. As she reached up to move the bolt, the door was thrust open, knocking her backwards and she was faced with the towering figure of Bert Croucher. She opened her mouth to scream but the butcher grabbed her and clamped his hand over it to smother any sound.

He leered at her, his face close to hers. 'Took you by surprise didn't I?' He could feel her trembling in his arms. It fired his lust and he removed his hand and covered her lips with his. His mouth moving greedily over hers.

Daisy tried to fight back, twisting her face away from him.

'You make a sound you bitch and it will be the last you'll ever make,' he threatened, as he tore at her blouse to reveal her camisole. He fingered the lace trim. 'How pretty. I like my women to be feminine,' he said as he clasped her breast.

'Let me go you bastard!' she cried.

He held her chin in one hand and squeezed. 'Now then, that's no way to talk to me.' And he held her closer.

She was even more terrified as she felt his erection pressed against her.

He moved from side to side against her. 'Feel that my girl? Well very soon that will be deep inside you. I'm going to have you whether you like it or not.' She started kicking out at him, but he lifted her off her feet and carried her into the living room where he threw her down on the floor, placed a foot on her neck and proceeded to unbutton his flies.

'What I want to know,' he said, 'was did you knock off Kenny Woods before or after he had you? I'd be really pissed off if he got to you before me.'

While her attacker was talking and was therefore distracted, Daisy, now bruised and battered, looked around desperately for something to defend herself with. There was nothing. But she suddenly spied a small stool and thrusting his foot away with all her might, she lunged for the stool and threw it at the window.

The window smashed into smithereens as the stool sailed through it, alarming the policeman on watch who ran to the front door. He couldn't open it and he tried to move it by hurling his shoulder against the wood and then gave it a hefty kick. The door flew open and the man ran into the living room in time to see Croucher astride Daisy – about to sexually assault her.

The man took a flying leap at Croucher sending him spinning. With his trousers around his ankle, the butcher was hampered and before he knew it, the officer had pulled his arms behind his back and handcuffed him.

'You're nicked, Croucher!' Then he read him his rights.

Vera came running into the room, alarmed at the noise. She stood looking aghast at the scene before her. Daisy was on the floor her clothes in disarray, and this large man was face downwards on the floor with a policeman standing over him. She ran to her daughter.

'Daisy, are you all right? Whatever happened?'

Shaken by the ordeal, Daisy told her mother about Bert Croucher appearing suddenly at the scullery door. Then she burst into tears.

The policeman dragged the butcher to his feet, pulled up his trousers and turning to Mrs Gilbert said, 'You take care of your daughter and I'll take this villain to the station. I'll find someone to block in the front door until the morning, when a new one can be fitted.'

Vera looked at him with a puzzled expression.

'I'm afraid I had to kick it in when the window broke.'

'I heard the sound of broken glass,' said Vera, 'and that's what woke me up.'

'Put the kettle on, love. Your daughter could do with a cup of tea to calm her down. I'll be back in the morning for a statement.' He led Bert Croucher out of the doorway. Then the two women heard him blowing his whistle, summoning assistance.

Vera put a small rug around Daisy who was shaking all over with shock. She built up the fire in the stove to warm her and put the kettle on the hob, and then she sat holding Daisy's hands.

'I was terrified, Mum,' she said. 'I thought he was going to kill me at first. It was like Ken Woods all over again! I couldn't get free of him. I threw the stool out of the window in the hope that someone would hear it and come out to see what was going on. Wasn't I lucky that a copper was nearby? He saved me in the nick of time from being raped.'

'Oh, Daisy!' Vera could hardly think of what might have happened.

'I'll make you a nice cup of tea, then you get off to bed. I'll wait until someone comes to fix the door.'

Later when Daisy was asleep and the doorway had been boarded up, Vera sat in the firelight wondering when her daughter's life would be free of traumas. Even when she wasn't looking for it trouble seemed to follow her. And she cursed the day that Daisy had taken the job at the Solent Club. All that had happened to Daisy was through that association and although it afforded Fred a comfortable death, Vera wished Daisy had never gone there in the first place.

Bert Croucher was sitting in a cell, having spent the night there and when DI Riley arrived in his office the following morning and was told about the arrest, he visited the prisoner.

The officer on duty opened the cell door and Riley walked in.

'I told you I'd be seeing you, Croucher,' he said with a slow smile. 'Now I've got you banged to rights. You'll be charged with breaking and entering, assault and attempted rape and that's without the damage you did to Miss Gilbert's shop. You'll go down for quite a spell for that, I can tell you.'

The butcher glowered at him. 'Wipe that satisfied smile off your face or I'll do it for you.'

'Not even you would be that stupid,' snapped the detective. 'I'll see you in court.' And he walked out of the cell. He then summoned the policeman who had been watching Bert's house.

'Where the hell were you when Croucher left his house?' Riley demanded.

'Sorry, Guv. The house was in darkness and I thought he'd gone to bed. I needed a leak badly and I popped up a nearby alleyway. He must have slipped out then.'

'Just thank your lucky stars that Miss Gilbert had the brains to hurl that stool at the window or we could be dealing with a much more serious crime – and you'd be looking for another job! Now get out before I lose my temper.'

When Daisy didn't appear at the shop the following morning, Grace Portman was worried. She saw to the tasks in hand and then she hurried off to the home of her friend to be told of the latest happenings.

'Oh, Daisy, I was always worried that whoever had trashed the shop would come after you and it seems I was right. How are you?'

'A bit shaken if I'm truthful,' Daisy admitted. 'I have to give a statement today and I suppose that means another day in court. Oh, Grace, I'm so sorry to bring all this scandal down on you.'

'Don't be ridiculous. The main thing is that you were rescued in time and I thank God for that.'

'But it will be in all the papers yet again!'

What could Grace say? Ever since the shop in East Street had been opened there had been so much drama, but thankfully business didn't seem to have suffered, thanks to the exceptional talent of her partner . . . but would this be a scandal too far?

When Steven Noaks called at Daisy's early that evening in the hope of taking her out, he was horrified to hear about the intruder.

'Oh my God, Daisy! Are you all right?'

She shrugged and said, 'I'm a bit battered and bruised, but thankfully the policeman arrived in time before things got too serious.'

'She was almost raped!' Vera retorted.

'Mum,' Daisy begged, 'please, no more about it.'

Steven took her into his arms. 'Well once that dreadful man is put away, all your troubles will be over.'

'But will they? You can only push your clients so far. This I think may well be just too much to maintain my credibility.'

To everyone at the shop, the latest headlines in the local paper, once again naming Daisy and bringing up her past, filled them with trepidation. It wasn't good for business and the orders began to dwindle. A few stalwart ladies stuck by her, but those wives whose husbands held positions of importance in the town, had been forbidden to go to the shop again, lest by association their characters were marred. One or two wrote their apologies, the others found another seamstress.

'I don't know what we're going to do,' Daisy said to Grace as they eyed the empty order book. 'We can't go on like this; we are losing too much money.'

'We need a plan of action,' Grace said forcibly.

'Like what?'

'I don't know yet, but I'm going home to think about it.'

As she watched Grace walk down the street, Daisy was filled with despair. All her dreams were in tatters and as far as she could see, the shop would have to be closed. The time she spent at Flo Cummings' place sleeping with men she hated was all for nothing, and the inheritance her friend used to help set her up was down the drain.

She sent the girls home and locked up the shop.

Thirty-Two

Sitting on the train to Brockenhurst, Grace Portman wracked her brains, wondering just what she could do to boost the falling sales, and restore Daisy's reputation as an exceptional seamstress. The majority of their clients came from the upper echelon of Southampton society, where scandal was a dirty word and the final report in the local paper of Daisy's attack was enough, after everything else that had publicly befallen her, to tip the scales against her. Grace, somehow, had to get her, once again, accepted in high society.

When she arrived at the Manor House, she changed into comfortable clothes and shoes and walked around the garden. It looked exceptionally beautiful with the flower beds in full bloom and she suddenly had an idea. Returning to the house, she made several local calls and two to London. Then she sat at her bureau, checked dates on a calendar and started writing.

The next morning, Grace arrived at the shop, cheeks flushed, eyes shining. Her whole being bristled with enthusiasm. Taking Daisy to one side she sat her down.

'I've had a great idea,' she said.

Daisy, seeing the excitement on the face of her friend, waited to hear her news.

'I am going to hold a garden party in aid of our troops fighting abroad, and I'm inviting everyone in Southampton who is of any importance as well as local folk. Garden parties at the Manor House were always an event, but with the war we've not held one.'

'That'll be nice,' Daisy said. But she couldn't hide the disappointment in her voice. She thought Grace had come up with a way to save the business.

Seeing the look on her face, Grace grinned broadly at her. 'We'll have stalls selling all sorts of things. There'll be a tent for refreshments, for a price of course – and during the afternoon we'll have a fashion show.'

Daisy looked puzzled. 'A fashion show?'

'Yes. *Gilbert. Gowns à la Mode* will give a fashion show with half the cost of the gowns going to the troops.'

'But will anybody buy them?' Daisy looked sceptical.

'Oh yes indeed. I have a secret weapon. Believe me, women will be clamouring for your clothes.'

'And what is your secret weapon, may I ask?'

Grace laughed gleefully. 'No, you may not, but trust me, this will pick up the business.'

'When is this garden party?' asked Daisy.

'The first Sunday in September. We must go through the stock we have and then we must make some really spectacular gowns for the show. We need a bridal gown to close with, so the girls need to work hard until then.'

By now, Daisy had become infected with Grace's enthusiasm and she could see that if this worked it could be the saving of their establishment, but she was curious about Grace's secret weapon. What on earth could it be?

'You'd better go and tell the staff your plan. It will be a great lift to them all as they have been really depressed of late.'

The staff warmed to the idea immediately. None of them wanted to lose their jobs if the business failed and the thought of going to the Manor House was an even bigger thrill.

'I can remember reading about the garden parties held at Mrs Portman's place,' said one. 'It was always a very grand affair! Imagine, we'll be part of it, how exciting that'll be.'

When the two women went through the existing stock and made a list of gowns to be made, Daisy was worried.

'Grace, we will have to buy further materials. If they don't sell, we'll be even more out of pocket than we are now.'

'Have faith, Daisy. I promise you, we'll make money even with half the proceeds going to the troops' fund.'

And with that Daisy had to be satisfied.

During the following weeks, the staff worked hard to produce several summer gowns in the most delicate floaty materials, evening dresses in rich colours, blouses in beautiful lace and embroidered jackets in the softest velvet, but the most intricate work was on the bridal gown. Here, Daisy Gilbert excelled. The gown was in the palest ivory voile, over an exquisite fine lace underskirt. The bodice and skirt was embroidered with small flowers in the finest stitches – and small bugle beads enhanced the work. When the finished gown was displayed on the tailor's dummy, the girls gathered round to admire the finished article. It was a work of art.

Grace was enthralled. 'Daisy, that is the finest bridal gown I've ever seen. If the women don't clamour for that, I'll eat my hat!'

Daisy burst out laughing. Grace was well known for her large headgear. 'Oh dear, I hope that doesn't happen!'

The day of the garden party arrived. The weather, thankfully, was fine. Stalls had been set up all over the garden and a large tented gazebo was set out at the far end, where eventually the models would gather to show the fashions, walking down a red carpet rolled out and down the well-manicured lawn.

Balloons festooned the stalls. Bright canopies covered some to help keep the sun off the home-made cakes and jams. Among them, a white elephant stall showed an assortment of china figures. Vegetable stalls were selling produce from the farms on the estate and there was a tent for refreshments. The place was a sight to behold.

Daisy, her girls, and Vera who was also there, were like a bunch of nervous kittens as they waited for the gates to open. Grace had persuaded ladies from her parish to model the dresses and they too were excited about wearing such wonderful creations. Her mother and her friends turned up too, to give their support.

Grace and Giles, who had been roped in to help set up the stalls, stood and gazed at the finished gathering. 'This was an inspired idea,' he said. 'This is like old times; it will certainly cheer people up when they enter the grounds.'

'I do hope so,' Grace said. 'Daisy's future depends on it.'

'And yours as far as the business goes.'

'You're right of course but don't you understand, if the business went belly-up, I would just have lost my inheritance, Daisy will have lost everything and we can't let that happen.'

Photographers from the local press were already in attendance. This was an occasion not to be missed and Mrs Portman had promised them a great surprise which would make good copy for the paper.

The gates opened and the people streamed in.

Daisy and Agnes recognized several of the clients who had

left them. 'Well they certainly will not be buying any of our gowns,' Agnes complained. 'To them we are the evil eye.'

'Not you, Agnes, that's all down to me,' Daisy remarked, but her heart sank when she saw the women. Was Grace wrong? Would they sell the gowns – would anybody buy?

Eventually it was time for the fashion show and chairs had been placed either side of the catwalk for the visitors to watch in comfort. Daisy peered out and was relieved to see that at least there seemed to be a good crowd waiting. But of course they didn't know whose gowns they would be seeing. It hadn't been advertised other than 'A Fashion Show'.

Grace herself, with the aid of a megaphone, opened the show.

'Ladies and gentlemen, thank you so much for being here today. I'm sure you will agree that the garden party is for the best possible cause. Our troops need many things and the money you spend today will help them enormously. Now is the time for our fashion show. The clothes you will see paraded before you are the exquisite designs of *Gilbert. Gowns à la Mode* in East Street, Southampton.'

There was a murmuring in some parts of the audience, but Grace continued.

'These gowns are the design of Daisy Gilbert, a very talented lady as you will see for yourselves. Half the cost of each article will be added to the troops' fund, which I think you'll agree is a very generous gesture.'

There was a ripple of applause.

Grace then announced the first day gown, giving the details of the material and the price. The model walked down the red carpet, turned and walked slowly back, stopping halfway to twirl again, and here she paused.

Grace told her audience the price and there was a silence. Daisy's heart sank.

'Who will be the first person to buy this exquisite gown?'

'I will!' A lady, dressed in what was obviously an expensive after-noon dress and straw hat trimmed with flowers, put up her hand.

'Thank you, Madam. May I have your name?'

'Lady Imogen Wallace.'

There was a gasp from all the women in the audience. The Lady Imogen was always in the society magazines. Her family were wealthy landowners, members of the gentry, friends with the royal family – and she herself was revered as a fashion icon.

'Thank you, Lady Wallace,' smiled Grace.

'So that's her secret weapon!' grinned Daisy, who was well aware of the position the woman held, after following all the fashion magazines.

After that, the sale of the gowns flew. Every woman wanted to buy a garment from the same establishment as the celebrated lady. They could dine out on that fact for weeks afterwards.

When it came to the bridal gown, the audience was enthralled as they listened to the details of the dress and admired the intricate work. Several people put up their hands to buy.

Grace looked around and said, 'I'm afraid there *is* only one of these dresses. It is an exclusive model. The only fair way to decide is to have an auction.'

The bidding was furious. Lady Imogen pushed the price up and up, until one of the ladies from Southampton, who had once been a client of Daisy's, won the bidding. The final bid was sensational! By the end of the show, every garment had been sold. And when Lady Imogen was seen talking to Daisy and Grace, and arranging an appointment, there was soon a queue of women waiting to make appointments of their own.

When the day was over, Grace took all the staff from the shop and the girls who had modelled the gowns, and the two mothers, into her drawing room for sandwiches and champagne. She'd asked Giles to join them but he was expecting a cow to calf and had to get back to the farm.

Holding her glass high, Grace made a toast. 'To *Gilbert. Gowns à la Mode*! We are back in business!'

Everyone began to talk at once about the day and what had happened.

Daisy shushed them all. 'I think we should drink to Grace Portman and her secret weapon!' They all cheered and toasted her.

'That was an inspired idea,' said Daisy to her friend.

Grace laughed. 'Well Hugh always said, faced with overwhelming odds it's time to bring in the big guns, and that's what I did. Imogen is a friend of the family. She likes a good fight.'

'She's an amazing woman,' said Daisy. 'My word, she certainly sent the price for the wedding dress soaring.'

'It was all part of our battle plan,' admitted Grace. 'I knew as soon as the townswomen knew who she was, they would jump on the bandwagon and, anyway, Daisy dear, who could possibly resist that wonderful bridal gown?'

'You'll be pleased to know, our appointment book is full,' said Daisy looking delighted, 'and would you know it, we again have a waiting list. By the way, I did wonder if your mother-in-law would be here today.'

'She was all set to come and lord it over us all and had she known about Imogen, nothing would have kept her away.'

'So why wasn't she here?'

With an apologetic look Grace said, 'I told her we were having a fashion show and your gowns were the ones being shown.'

Daisy grinned broadly. 'Well that put the mockers on it then. She wouldn't want to mix with the likes of me.'

'To be honest it was a relief,' said Grace. 'She would have ruined the whole day. Look, why don't you and Vera stay the night. We can have dinner and go into Southampton together in the morning. I'll get my chauffeur to drive the girls to the station. What do you say?'

'That would be lovely and my mother will get the thrill of her life to spend a night here.'

'Well she deserves it, after all she's part of our success.'

After a delicious meal, followed by coffee with a glass of brandy, Vera and Daisy were shown to a twin-bedded room, overlooking the grounds at the back of the house where the garden party took place. By now it was dark, but the moon shone, silhouetting the trees in the far distance.

'How wonderful it must be,' Vera remarked as she climbed into bed wearing one of Grace's borrowed nightdresses, 'to be able to live such a life of luxury as Grace does.'

'It's not that simple, Mum,' Daisy explained. 'There is a great deal of organization to be done, to enable everything to run well. There are the farms on the estate, the grounds and the house to keep up. That takes time and money.'

'Yes I suppose it does and truth to tell that responsibility would worry me to death. I wouldn't change places with her, I can tell you.'

As she settled for the night in the strange surroundings, Vera

Gilbert thanked God for Grace Portman. Her daughter Daisy was blessed to have such a good friend and now it looked as if everything would work out right, thanks to her.

Eventually of course, Daisy had to appear in court during the trial of Bert Croucher who was sent down for seven years, all written about in the local rag. But this time, it made not a jot of difference to the business in East Street. After all, wasn't that the place that made clothes for Lady Imogen Wallace? If it was good enough for her . . .

Thirty-Three

There was a huge two-page spread of the garden party of the year in the local paper, with photographs showing the various stalls, and several pictures of the fashions being paraded. There was also a big picture of Lady Imogen Wallace, standing beside Daisy Gilbert, who had designed all the gowns, and Mrs Grace Portman, a partner in *Gilbert. Gowns à la Mode* and the owner of the Manor House, where the great occasion had taken place. The amount of money that had been raised was significant and highly praised by the reporter. It was great publicity for the business and moved Daisy and her reputation back into local society.

Grace's mother-in-law read the report and was furious that she had missed the event when she read about Lady Imogen being present. Her mood wasn't improved when she complained to her husband about it.

'It's your own fault my dear. If you hadn't been so against Daisy Gilbert being there, you would have gone. You shouldn't be so judgemental! It seems to me this young lady has done very well and is obviously extremely talented. You don't give the girl any credit.'

His wife was speechless, especially when she read that Lady Imogen had placed several orders.

Steven Noaks had been away when all this had taken place, but on his return he called into the shop and read the report which had been framed and displayed in the reception area.

'Well done, you two,' he said. Putting his arm round Daisy he said, 'I'm really proud of you.'

'I couldn't have done it without Grace,' she reminded him.

'True, but she couldn't have done it without you. You make a great team. I'd like to take you both out to dinner tonight to celebrate.'

'That's really kind of you, Steven,' said Grace, 'but I have made other arrangements, so you'll have to do it without me. I insist,' she said as he suggested another evening.

Grace felt the two of them should be alone. After all, Steven had been away and she would have felt she was intruding. She wanted them to spend as much time together as was possible as Steven would be sailing again in a few days.

Daisy dressed with care that evening, wearing one of her own creations. A gown which was simplicity itself in soft emerald-green velvet. It was exquisitely cut, emphasizing her small waist and the round neckline showing her décolletage to perfection, the skirt just inches above floor level. A necklace of emerald beads with earrings to match completed the outfit. She wore make-up and her hair was dressed off her neck with a few stray ringlets framing her face. She looked sensational.

As they walked into the restaurant, people recognized her and the women stared at her ensemble with envy. The manager stepped forward.

'Miss Gilbert, how nice to see you, please come this way.' He placed them at one of his best tables.

As they were seated, Steven looked at Daisy in admiration and some amusement.

'My goodness, what a welcome. I had no idea you were so famous!'

With a chuckle, Daisy said, 'This time it's for the right reasons. I've been infamous in the past!'

Steven gazed at her and said, 'Thankfully those days are behind you and so they should be after what you've been through. Now you are really established and I'm happy for you.'

At least with Steven she could be totally honest. 'Those days were hard to take, but in truth it was all worth it in the end. Thank God! And how are things with you?'

'I just wish this terrible war would end. The British have broken through the German defences at Loos in Flanders, but the end is nowhere in sight. I hate to see the troops we take out leave the ship, as so many lives are being lost. I long for peace and normality and a return to taking civilian passengers across the Atlantic.'

Daisy looked at the anguish on his face and longed to touch him. To comfort him. To love him.

'Anyway, let's not talk of war, after all we're here to celebrate.' He ordered a bottle of champagne.

At the end of the meal, both of them felt mellow and happy.

Steven took Daisy's hand. 'I want to take you away and make love to you,' he said softly, 'but now you are so well known and respected, I can hardly suggest we book a room in a hotel, can I?'

'No, that wouldn't be advisable,' she laughed, 'after all I've had to fight to achieve my place in society.' She hesitated. 'But we could go home to my place.'

'But what about your mother?'

'By now she'll be in bed.'

He saw the longing in her eyes that matched his. He paid the bill and they left.

Later as they lay in each other's arms, Steven turned Daisy's face to his and said, 'This really isn't good enough.'

Somewhat startled, Daisy asked, 'Whatever do you mean?'

'Snatching these odd moments when I can hold you. I want more than that. I want us to get married.'

Daisy was shocked into silence. She had accepted the fact that marriage was not for her.

'Steven, do you know what you're saying? You of all people know my history. As your wife, what would happen if it was brought up in conversation? Wouldn't it cast a shadow on your career, maybe stop you from getting promotion?'

'Of course not! After all, your past is no secret any more, and now you have your business and have a fine reputation. Even so, you silly goose, I'm madly in love with you and have been from the moment I set eyes on you in the Solent Club. It's time for us to be together.'

Daisy was speechless.

'I'm away a lot of the time, but you have a business to run, so it won't be too lonely for you and imagine every time I come home – it will be like another honeymoon! Of course you may not want to be married to a seaman. It isn't the easiest of lives for a wife.'

Flinging her arms around his neck, Daisy kissed him. 'You ridiculous man, of course I'll marry you.'

The next morning, Vera Gilbert was surprised to see Daisy and Steven sitting down to breakfast. 'Hello, Steven, I didn't know you were home.'

'Good morning, Mrs Gilbert. I docked yesterday early in the morning.'

Daisy poured her mother a cup of tea, then taking Steven's hand she said, 'We have some exciting news to tell you. Steven and I are getting married.'

Vera choked on her tea. When she'd recovered, she was delighted and kissed both of them. 'That's the nicest thing that's happened in a long time. Congratulations!'

'You don't object to me being your son-in-law then?' Steven teased.

'I am absolutely delighted. When is the wedding to be?'

'I have another couple of trips to do, then I have three weeks' leave and that's when we'll tie the knot.'

'Oh my goodness, that doesn't give us much time,' she complained.

'I'm not waiting any longer, Mum. He might change his mind!'

'As if,' Steven said.

Daisy was a little late arriving at the shop, but when she told everyone her news there was great excitement and everybody spoke at once.

'Where are you getting married?'

'When's the wedding?'

'We will have to make your wedding dress!'

'Quiet everybody! I can't hear myself think,' Grace cried and the tumult ceased.

Daisy gave them all the news. She and Steven were going to see the vicar that afternoon to arrange a date, but there would be a rush to make her bridal gown, especially as there were so many orders to attend to.

But the girls said they would work late.

'After all,' said Agnes, 'this will be excellent publicity for the shop.'

There were cries of derision for her remark, but as Grace said, 'That's not being heartless, Agnes is right, and we'll make it a gown that will be the talk of Southampton!'

On a crisp November day at Holy Rood Church in Southampton, Steven and Daisy took their wedding vows. The bride wore a dress of champagne-coloured satin, with an embroidered bodice covered with rhinestones and beads. The skirt with a small train was delicately embroidered to match the bodice. On her head she wore a small lace cap. The bouquet was simple, made with tea-coloured roses and trailing ivy. The groom looked very handsome dressed in his uniform as they walked down the aisle together and stood outside for the photographs, festooned with fluttering confetti.

Apart from the official photographer, the reporter from the local paper was there to record the event and crowds gathered on the pavement to watch.

Steven squeezed Daisy's hand. 'Hello, Mrs Noaks,' he said softly.

Daisy turned to him and smiled. 'I like the sound of that,' she said.

The wedding reception was held at the nearby Dolphin Hotel. It was a reasonably small affair. Steven's parents were there, having met Daisy only a few days before the wedding. Stella came over from the Isle of Wight to stand as the only bridesmaid and Harry was thrilled to give the bride away. All the girls who worked for Daisy and Grace were also in attendance and the wedding breakfast was a happy and joyful occasion.

Vera Gilbert looked on proudly. This was a day she never thought would happen and she was delighted that her Daisy had found such a man with whom to share her life. It had been an arduous journey but like all good things it had a happy ending. Fred, she knew, would be pleased.

Grace Portman looked on and was very happy to have been a part of it all. Becoming a partner in the business had helped her to overcome the death of her husband and given her an interest other than the upkeep of the Manor House and all its responsibilities. And she was delighted to have helped Daisy reach her full potential.

Giles, who had escorted Grace to the wedding, saw the look of pride on her face as she looked at the bride. It was early days, but he hoped that the friendship he had with this wonderful woman would become something more permanent in the future. Like Daisy, Grace, too, deserved to be happy.

In the early evening, the bride and groom retired to their room to get changed ready for the train journey to the West Country where they would spend their honeymoon.

Steven took his wife into his arms and kissed her thoroughly. 'You looked beautiful today, Mrs Noaks, and I was a proud man.'

She laughed and said, 'And so you should be! And don't look at me like that; we haven't the time, we have a train to catch.'

'There, already you're becoming a nagging wife.'

'Oh, Steven, we'll have lots of time ahead of us. A lifetime in fact.'

As they drove away to the station, Daisy looked back at all her friends who had helped to shape her life; then she looked at Steven her husband who would help her shape the future. She leaned forward and kissed him.

'What was that for?'

'For making me the happiest woman in the world.'

And she was.